Miss Gilda's Blues

A Novel

by

Adrienne Lynn Rutherford

Copyright © 2012 Adrienne Lynn Rutherford

All rights reserved. No part of this book may be reproduced in any form or by any means, electronic or mechanical, including photo-copying, recording, or by any information storage and retrieval system, without written permission from the author. This excludes a reviewer who may quote brief passages in a review.

To request permission, please contact Adrienne L. Rutherford at imanidriven@gmail.com.

This novel is a work of fiction. Names, characters, places and incidents either are the product of the author's imagination or are used fictitiously. Any resemblance to actual persons, living or dead, events, or locales, is entirely coincidental.

Cover Design: Brittany J. Jackson

Published by G Publishing, LLC

Library of Congress Control Number: 2012937185

ISBN: 978-0-9849360-5-2

Printed in the United States of America

Prologue

The year was 1926 the time of America's "Great Depression." Many southern blacks just like other Americans across the country were caught in the downward spiral of a decaying economy. Prior to this crisis, Post-Reconstruction policies had forcible destroyed what little progress that the Emancipation Proclamation had promised. These policies would soon be replaced by sanctioned Jim Crow laws that attempted to cripple the black community both politically and economically.

Many americans took a stand and fought on the political front by protesting and developing organizations for the improvement of these conditions.

Nevertheless, the struggle would be slow to progress as the majority of southerners continued to live out their lives as sharecroppers for inhumane wages

However, while these historical events of the day were unfolding another world was unfolding as well. The introduction of Blues and Jazz along with Prohibition and the rising culture of Speak Easy's, all marked the beginning of the largest leading underworld businesses in the country at the time, "Bootlegging."

After the death of her mother Gilda's passion for life gave her the hope of one day getting out of her hometown, Culloden Georgia. Never in a million years did she think Po Fisher's decision to hop a train heading north would be the one event that would soon change her life forever.

Ki'Somma: A word derived from the Algonquin and Blackfoot Indian languages, meaning sun or light.

When we walk to the edge of all the light we have and take that step into the darkness of the unknown.....

We must believe that one of two things will happen...

There will be something solid for us to stand on or we will be taught to fly.....

Author Unknown

Chapter 1

Culloden, Georgia
1926

"Come on girl hurry it ain't no time to waste."

Once again Gilda stopped to go back for Julia, they were running for their lives or so they thought. Many times the two girls would go up to Mr. Paul's place. He was the old one-eyed ornery pirate who stayed in the wooded area down by Wylie River just outside of Colluden Georgia. They would take a risk from time to time to climb his peach tree. Mr. Paul's tree was the oldest and had the sweetest peaches in all Monroe County. He didn't take too kindly to visitors of any kind and as a result he would let his hound dogs out for the chase. The girls fled through the woods holding steadfast to their treasure of goodies.

"Hurry Julia we're almost in the clear."

The girls leaped through the waterway and across to the other side of the creek. They left the old dogs barking on the bank. Julia bent over resting her hands on both knees trying to catch her breath.

"Whew, them ole hound dogs couldn't even catch us." Gilda shook her head, while inspecting the treats she was able to salvage.

"We were lucky that time Julia, why you slow down?"

"Chile I was tired."

The girls tackled the steep hill as they finally reached the old red dirt road that would lead them back to Gilda's house. Julia was Gilda's best friend and they had known one another since they could remember, thanks to the childhood friendship of their grandmothers.

After a long two mile walk in the hot Georgia sun the girls finally made it to Gilda's house. They each pinched little

Bobby who was sitting under the tree waiting for Gilda's mother Beauty to call for water from the pump out back. Gilda dropped the peaches from their adventure in the large flower basket and entered from the rear of the house. The smell of honeysuckle oil and freshly pressed hair filled the air.

Gilda's mother Beauty and her best friend Minnie were a lot more high-spirited than most women that resided in Culloden. At sixteen Beauty, against the will of her mother Fannie left Georgia. She traveled north to Madame C.J. Walkers Cosmetology School in Pittsburgh Pennsylvania. It was here she was trained in the "Walker Method" and received her certificate as a hair culturalist. She returned to Culloden in 1910 when Madame C.J. moved her school to Indianapolis.

Beauty now made her living doing women's hair in a modest wooden attachment built by family friend Uncle Rufus. She had two large porcelain bowls for washing and rinsing hair and a flat top coal stove next to her styling chair she used to warm her iron pressing combs and curlers. Beauty was quite fond of her chair because it was given to her by Madame C.J. Walker herself after she finished at the top of the class. In front of the styling chair hung a large beautiful mirror. On the opposite wall was a portrait of Madame C. J. Walker herself and below the picture was engraved her most famous quote:

> I had to make my own living and my own opportunity
> But I made it
> Don't sit down and wait for opportunities to come
> Get up and make them.

Beauty did just that and she was proud of her accomplishments, especially Gilda. Gilda in many ways was like her mother. She had been trained well in the small family business, which also included producing natural hair and body products. It was also her job to care for the large flower and herb garden started by her Grandmother Fannie on their land of ½ acre. Gilda's mother had done quite well for herself over the years as an entrepreneur supporting both herself and Gilda. Oftentimes when they were alone Beauty would teach Gilda everything she knew about doing hair. She felt it necessary because she wanted her to have other options besides housekeeping or working the fields for a living.

Today was Friday, which marked the beginning of the weekend. Beauty's little shop was filled with ladies waiting patiently to get their hair done. Her clients came prepared to stay all day bringing their lunches, books and quilting materials to keep them busy. Some of the women were getting ready for the weekend nights down at "Ole Rufus' Juke Joint".

The women spent hours at the little shop laughing and talking about the nights to come and the men they enjoyed shuffling the floor with. Meanwhile, the mothers of the church who also needed Beauty's skills for Sunday morning service were also there with Bible in hand. They sat attentively amongst themselves sometimes even occasionally sprinkling holy oil and saying prayers over some of the conversations that went on around them.

It was situations like these that displayed the diversity of souls that flocked to Beauty's little hair shop. Beauty didn't judge either way. She had always been a God fearing woman, but from time to time she was known to stop by Rufus old juke joint. She didn't care what folks thought about her. Beauty had gained her freedom from local attacks long ago after her unmarried pregnancy with Gilda. The juke joint embraced an addictive sweet sounding music that was beginning to capture the hearts and souls of folk all over the world. In Alabama they called it the "Blues" the "Delta Blues" and it traveled along the gulf in both directions going southeast through Georgia and westward down into Louisiana.

As the girls approached her, Beauty looked them over.

"Chile, where on earth have you two been?"

Beauty scolded Gilda and Julia as she continued pulling the pressing comb through Miss Minnie's hair. The girls were happy to see Miss Minnie and interrupted Beauty as they gave her an excited greeting of hugs and kisses. She was Gilda's godmother and also a vessel of wisdom to the young girls.

Beauty and Minnie each possessed an independent spirit that moved them to explore new places and new things. This was a gift that led them down a path of freedom that only few women in the little town would ever acquire.

Miss Minnie was the "Madame Cadenza" of all Monroe County. She used her skills to leave the small town and spent much time traveling all over the country singing the blues with her very own band. She often returned home bringing Gilda and Julia gifts from afar and stories of love, life and laughter. However, the dark secrets that haunted her soul from the little town always seemed too suffocating to her spirit so she never stayed long.

The girls would be amazed at her adventures about far away cities and the rich gentlemen who had been hypnotized by her voice, as well as her beauty. Minnie would share the stories of how they spoiled her with all kinds of lavishing gifts. Many had proposed but she had declined them all, keeping the freedom that she treasured so dearly. Minnie was uninhibited and always felt compelled to relieve these young girls of what she thought were the disadvantages of living in a small detached country town.

"Beauty just look at them girls, they are gorgeous and they growing up to be just fine as they wanna be."

She looked over at Gilda.

"Gillie, you watch yourself with dem hips of yours, you hear."

"You gotta be prepared to deal with dem men folks because they gonna be after you soon and you know what I told you chile." She then turned her attention to Julia.

"Julia you too, them long pretty legs of yours gonna get you in trouble I tell you if you don't keep em closed, yah hear?" Beauty nudged at her life long friend.

"Min, why you telling them girls that?"

"Because I want to give them a little short cut is all."

"After all, that's what we here for isn't it?"

"Come on Beaut, you know what it was like." Turning her hips in the chair as she nodded politely at the mothers of the church.

"Shoot, we both know we had a decent upbringing with the fear of the lord and we also learned repentance."

"But, he also blessed us women with passion for life and the choice to live it the way we seen fit."

"All we have to do is keep a humble heart and don't spend time passing judgement on others for the decisions that they make about their own lives." Minnie turned and looked up at Beauty.

"Now ain't that how we were brought up?"

"Now we just passing it on to these girls is all, they need to know how to deal with this world we living in, staying strong, just like me and you."

"Shoot, we only get one time around you know."

Minnie then smiled at the girls and gave them a wink. Gilda and Julia were more fortunate than a lot of the other young girls in their town because of conversations like these with Minnie and the small talk that came from Beauty's clientele.

Many of these women had come in with testimonies of their personal heartaches and spoke of how the sweet sound of the southern blues had comforted them through the rough times of their lives when they visited Uncle Rufus place. Beauty's attention returned to the girls.

"Look at them clothes, just as filthy!"

"You two get in there and clean yourselves up."

"Ain't no young women got no business walking around like that."

"Gillie you were supposed to clean that room chile."

"How many times do I have to tell you, that room of yours represents you."

"Now go on now, you gonna be asking me for something and I'm gonna have to tell you no because you ain't minding Gillie."

Gilda and Julia left out of the back room and each took their turn in a luke warm bath. After putting on a change of clean clothes the girls relaxed in Gilda's room. The room was small, but large enough to hold a full size bed and a small chifforobe in the corner. There was a mirror that hung on the back of her door and clothes and books everywhere. Julia went up the hall into the living room and turned on the radio. The sounds of the delta blues echoed throughout the front of the house as the breeze from the summer air crept through Gilda's bedroom window. The two girls stood in the mirror and pretended to be blues singers using Beauty's hairbrushes. It was times like these that Gilda would think about her grandmother Fannie. She would always encourage Gilda to listen to the sweet sounds of music and show her a little dancing to go with it.

Gilda could still hear her saying, *"Now that there is music you here! Don't nothing sound like it I tell you."*

Fannie was one of the few colored women in town who had the modern luxuries of the time, such as a pipe with running water, light switches and a large French porcelain bathtub that Gilda deemed her most prized possession. All these luxuries were attributed to grandmother Fannie's employer Miss Ann, whom she worked many years for on Culloden Hill before her death. Miss Ann was an honest lady who suffered from what she called "The Curse", which meant having to live with being the product of a forbidden union. She despised knowing the treatment that her grandfather and his father before him had bestowed on her mother's family and other African decendents during slavery. Miss Ann was one of the few wealthy offspring of plantation owners left in

Culloden. She unlike many refused to sell her land to northern businessmen during the depression. She felt it improper and therefore managed to hold the deed to the land and property her ancestors had toiled many generations before the Emancipation Proclamation. Now the land was used as a garden and grew vegetables for the AME Church of Monroe County for "The Women's Missionary Society".

Miss Ann's mother Honey was a house slave purchased from Savannah, Georgia as a teenage girl by a Frenchmen named of Sir Jacque Baptiste. She bore him two children a son Jacque II and a daughter Ann Marie. These were his only heirs and because he was nothing like his father before him he did the unthinkable at that time. Sir Jacque left his entire estate to his children under the shield of his family in France.

Grandmother Fannie was very dear to Miss Ann and it was because of this long lasting friendship that Ann was able to watch both Beauty and Gilda grow up, giving them a special place in her heart.

After an hour or so of performing, Gilda sat down on her bed.

"I'm so bored."

Julia sitting on the stool in the corner of the room was glancing through some of Gilda's books..

"You suppose to be cleaning your room Gillie." "Aww shoot on this room, my mind just ain't on this right now."

Gilda heard her mother calling her from the distance.

"Gillie, Gillie come here chile."

Gilda got off the bed with a long sigh. She opened the door and there her mother stood peeking over her shoulder in the doorway.

"You haven't did a thing in here chile what's dun got into you?"

Gilda bowed her head in shame while holding on to the edge of the door.

"Mama, imma clean it I-I-I."

Miss Gilda's Blues   13

"I-I-I nothing chile, I need you to run up to the store and get me a couple of cases of soda for my patrons, It's only two left and my appointment book is full."

Gilda looked at her mother, took the money and her and Julia were out again. The girls took the wagon up the old dirt road to Mr. Johnson's market. Once inside the store the ladies greeted Mr. Johnson and proceeded to the back of the store pulling the wagon. There were two young men standing in the aisle and they quietly walked pass them making eye contact with both. The scent of honeysuckle that the young ladies wore made the heads of these young men turn again in their direction.

Gilda and Julia assumed they were visitors, because they had never seen them around town. As the ladies continued to discreetly take peeks at the handsome visitors while shyly whispering to one another other about their unique appearance. The one that appeared to be the tallest of the two wore a long dark braid down his back. The other had two similar braids and wore an old dingy hat atop his head. Their skin reminded Gilda of a beautiful dark mahogany wood and right away Gilda knew they were of African and Native American heritage. It was obvious that they were both young working men. They were dressed in overalls with a huge pair of old gloves in their back pockets and large old dusty boots on their feet, much like the ones they saw on the men that worked up at the lumber yards.

The ladies did not stare; they had learned that much about men from Beauty and continued with their business. The younger of the two gentlemen could not keep his eyes off of Julia and he watched her the entire time they browsed through the store. Gilda nudged Julia.

"I think that fella has an eye for you, chile." Julia then turned around and gave him a smile. Without hesitation he took that as an invitation and walked right up to her and introduced himself.

"Hello ladies, my name is Joshua."

"I couldn't help but notice that beautiful scent that you're wearing."

"What is it may I ask?" Julia, in a very shy demeanor explained. "I'm sorry sir but it isn't proper for a young lady to reveal her beauty secrets to a stranger."

Joshua could not keep his eyes off of Julia.

"I don't plan to be a stranger much longer ma'am."

Julia began to blush and Joshua continued.

"I'm sorry but I hope you won't find it improper if I tell you that you are a very beautiful young lady." He then looked at Gilda.

"I mean both of you are…."

But before he could finish Gilda politely interrupted.

"Chile, there is no need to apologize."

"We've been watching you watch her from over there."

"I'm Gillie and this here is Julia, you ain't from around here are you?"

"No, we moved up this way about a week ago."

Soon the other youngman walked over to the huddle.

"Joshua we best be going." Gilda looked him over. Elijah in his coarseness made a quick affirmative observation of Gilda, but never spoke a word. Gilda had no problem reading that kind of language either.

"Joshua, we want to finish up before sundown and I am sure these ladies have something they have to do as well."

Gilda stepped up, her stature short compared to his large muscular frame. "Well aren't you going to introduce yourself?"

"Your manners are nothing like your brothers."

"This is your brother isn't it?"

"Yes he is."

"And let's see, you must be the oldest, because you seem to be the most protective." She looked over at Julia, but Julia was not the least bit interested in the conversation that Gilda had begun with the gentleman. She had eyes for Joshua and he had eyes for her. Gilda continued trying to get a rise out of the handsome young man. "What did you say your name was?"

"I didn't." He shot back at her.

Joshua then turned around to his brother while shaking his head.

"Come on brother, lighten up the lady is just messing with ya."

"Why don't you be nice to the ladies Elijah?"

Joshua patted his brother on the shoulder.

"You have to excuse him, he gets that way sometimes."

"Oh does he?"

Gilda commented as she looked him over once more. She then made a trip around his entire frame and placed herself directly in front of him again and waited for a response for the behavior that she had displayed. Finally, Elijah let his guard down. He had an attraction to this young woman so full of passion, but he would not let on to that. This was not the way Elijah was use to dealing with the opposite sex in his 19 years. He was quite familiar with the games of courting women both young and old and would not attempt to expose himself.

"The name is Elijah, Elijah Mason and you are?"
Gilda extended her hand.

"Gilda, Gilda Harris, but my friends call me Gillie."

Gilda looked up in the dark eyes of this man.

"Well Miss Gilda what should it be Gilda or Gillie?" Gilda paused for a moment; she had not felt these feeling before. It was a strange electric current that moved through her. She soon regained her composure and responded.

"I guess Gillie will be fine."

Elijah gave her a bright smile and she returned the gesture. "Could we give you young ladies a lift?"

"We don't stay far just up the road, thank you kindly though." After paying Mr. Johnson for the soda the ladies made their way toward the door. Joshua, on the other hand had other plans of his own after helping them load the soda into the wagon.

"Julia, ummm look I know you don't know me in all, but I would like to see you again." Joshua stood there in the doorway patiently waiting for some type of reply from Julia. "Well about two miles out, there's Wylie River."

"Me and Gillie will be fishing there after church on Sunday."

"The two of you can join us if you like."
Relieved, Joshua grabbed his hat tight in his hands and smiled.

"Well I guess I will see you then." Julia returned the smile as she and Gilda walked out of the door. "Don't forget to bring your fishing rods fella's." The young men hopped in the old dusty pick-up truck and drove down the road.

Chapter 2

After church on Sunday the ladies couldn't wait to get home. Beauty and Julia's mother Grace were wondering what had gotten into them. The two of them rushed to Julia's pulled their hair back in a pony tail and put on their blue jean overalls, boots and white t-shirts and were out the door. The ladies made their way down the dirt road holding their fishing rods and the pail of worms they spent the majority of the night digging up. Their conversation about their lives were now beginning to change since their new found interest. They talked of love, life and even children, things that they hadn't thought about a week ago. Soon the girls ran into James Fisher, also known as Po Fisher.

Po Fisher had a reputation of being messy. He was known as the town nuisance because he was always fighting and keeping up havoc. The sheriff had threatened him on plenty occasions but that didn't stop Po Fisher. Gilda and Julia were never concerned with the rumors and degrading remarks that left scars so deeply embedded in him. Both knew Po Fisher, a very kind hearted young man whose bad luck and many difficulties in his life sometimes made him unbearable to those who didn't quite understand him.

"You wanna go fishing Po?"

"Naw kind of got things to do today."

"How yo Papa?"

"He good Gillie, I just can't get him off that dang on corn likker."

"He stays drunk all the time and that just doubles my work over at the farm."

"I believe that old Mr. Crawford is cheating us on the harvest, this is the third year in a row he's done that."

"Shoot, I'm sick and tired of it too!"

"I been thinking about going up North, up there I can make a lot of money you know."

"Then I can come back and take pops far away from this here place."

Both girls had heard that story from Po Fisher plenty of times, about going up North and making it big. Most black folks during the late twenties were traveling either North or West because it brought hopes of a better life, free from racial hatred and the despair they experienced daily in the South.

"I'm going far away then I ain't gotta look at the likes of these folks around here teasing me because my pops likes that corn likker or that my colored skin at times don't suit their mood."

Gilda always had a way of making Po Fisher feel more important than he believed, like he was somebody.

"Fisher, now that ain't got anything to do with you, what folks think about your papa."

"He your papa but he ain't you and ain't no body studding them white folks anyhow."

"My mama tells me in these days and times they got it just as bad as we do." Fisher gave Gilda a wide smile. He'd always had a crush on her, ever since they were children in the schoolhouse. However, at the age of eight years old Fisher left school to work in the fields, like so many of the other young men in the area. Fisher wasn't able to spend a lot of time with his friends and when he was old enough he quit school all together.

The need to work the fields didn't stop James Fisher and from time to time he would visit Gilda and receive tutoring lessons in his reading, writing and arithmetic.

"Po, whatcha got covered up there in the wagon?"

"Oh just some fliers."

"Uncle Rufus want me to put them up all around the village."

Gilda was curious. "Hey let me take a look."

Shimmering Shirley is back
One Night Only
Rufus' Place Next Saturday Nite 8pm sharp.

The girls looked at the flier with the beautiful woman and then back at Po Fisher.

"What's this all about?" Po Fisher stuck his chest out and pulled on his suspenders. He was always proud to be the one to explain what was going on in a situation.

"Aw shoot, you don't know anything do you?"

"That there is Shimmering Shirley she's a shake dancer."

"She come around to the juke joint ever so often and shakes her stuff." The girls looked at each other. "Shake her stuff, whatcha mean?"

"Like this."

Fisher demonstrated to the girls, he began moving his hips around and around and they began to laugh. Gilda put her hands on her hips and looked at Fisher.

"That is not how you shake your stuff."

Gilda sat her rod against the fence and her pail on the ground. As the sounds of Bessie Smith floated through her head she began moving and swaying her hips, then looked at Fisher.

"This is how you shake your stuff, chile." Fisher stunned, jumped back and took another look at Gilda in motion.

"Lord girl where you learn to move like that?"

"Grandma Fannie taught me."

Fisher shook his head.

"Now that is how you shake your stuff."

"You ever thought about shake dancing Gillie?"

"Shake dance, In front of people?"

"Yeah women doing it all up and down the delta."

"You do lots of traveling too, down the Bayou and the Mississippi River they even go as far down as Louisiana."

"Is that right?"

"Yep that's right."

"That sounds exciting." Julia shook her head and looked over at Fisher.

"Po, how you know so much about shake dancing?" "You saw one before?" Fisher waved his hand at Julia.

"Oh sure, plenty of times."

This was the point that Fisher would begin his famous talent for exaggerating. Julia stood with her arms folded not so convienced, waited for a response. "Well! What was it like Po?" Fisher began his story.

"Well the men folk they were going mad and Shirley, she was moving to the music shaking her stuff all around the tables and even her belly just like this."

Fisher lifted his shirt up and both girls covered their mouths and began to laugh. "Po you sho is crazy."

"It was something I tell you, and then they started throwing money at her and she would walk up to them and shake her stuff some more."

"That Shimmering Shirley was stuffing that money down in her costume as fast as they gave it to her."

"I tell you if I was born a woman I would be a shake dancer."

"Costume?"

"Yeah Gillie costume, you didn't think they wore regular clothes did you?"

"They make costumes for them to dance in, you know skimpy shiny like stuff, look at the picture."

"That is why they call her Shimmering Shirley because of her costume and how it shimmers when she dances."

Fisher looked on and just as he intended, had finally caught the curiosity of the girls. Gilda put on her hands on her hips looking at Fisher with a suspicious look on her face.

"Well are you going by there Saturday night?" Fisher cleared his throat, he didn't expect to hear that coming, but he continued with his charade.

"Sure uhh sure I am, me and Big Ted."

Big Ted was Po Fisher's best friend. He was the only guy in town who would put up with Fisher. Ted stood well over 6 feet tall. Fisher felt comfortable around Ted because he trusted him. Both grew up together on the same sharecropping farm.

"Well Ladies, I got business to tend to, imma have to see you later." Gilda thought for a minute as she watched Fisher stroll down the open road.

"Hey Fisher, we wanna come Saturday night."

"Okay, meet us behind the joint by dusk." Gilda picked up her rod and pail, and she and Julia continued their journey.

"Gillie, what you thinking about chile?" Julia knew Gilda almost too well.

Gilda turned and smiled at Julia. "Nothing!"

"Don't you dare say nothing Gilda Jean Harris, I know that look."

"What look?"

"That look, Gillie if you thinking about shake dancing you might as well get that thought out your head chile."

"We only sixteen years old and any way your mama would kill you if she knew you were in a juke joint shaking your stuff."

"Dancing at home in the living room is one thing, but in front of the men folk for money, Ms. Beauty would have your hide and mine too, for going along with you."

Gilda said nothing, she didn't want to give Julia anything to feed on. She was known for talking too much about things with Ms. Beauty because she had such a difficult time talking to her own mother.

"Aw Julia, I ain't crazy, I'm just thinking about grandma and how we use to be in the living room listening to that good ole Blues and she would have us up there dancing with her, remember that?"

"Yeah I remember." Julia's face lit up.

"I show do miss, Ms. Fannie."

"So do I Julia, so do I."

The girls finally made it to Wylie River. They were there long enough to bait their hooks when the Mason men rode up. Gilda and Julia looked at the pickup truck as it stopped in front of the old shed. Elijah and Joshua got out of the truck and Joshua waved at Julia. Both reached in the bed of the truck and pulled out their fishing gear. Julia couldn't stop blushing while Gilda looked at her and shook her head.

"Hello ladies." Elijah spoke out in his deep voice. Gilda responded.

"Good Afternoon Mr. Mason."

"No need to be so formal you can call me Elijah, like I said before." Gilda looked up and he was staring right down into her eyes. She couldn't give in, if she turned away that would surly be a sign of weakness so she doubled his glance and he graced her with a smile.

"Lord have mercy." She thought to her herself. *"What a handsome man."* She had not looked at Elijah so closely when they first met at the store. But right now to Gilda, he appeared to resemble a Moroccan prince she once read about in Miss Ann's library. *"Could he be my prince?"* She thought to herself.

"May I join you?"

"Sure you can join me."

Before Gilda realized it, Joshua and Julia made their way further down the river's edge with their fishing rods. Gilda baited her hook, tossed her line into the water and placed the fishing pole deep between two rocks. She then sat down on the rocky bank and enjoyed the breeze from the river while she washed her hands in the cool water. The sounds of the running water and the birds overhead were soothing to her ears. It was a sound of peace something that she had treasured since a child. She then turned her attention to Elijah attempting to encourage conversation.

"So, where you from?"

"We're from South Carolina near the coast."

"Ohh, what made you come all this way to a small town like, Culloden."

"Well, rumor has it this part of Georgia has some really good peaches." Gilda smiled.

"Are you serious?" Elijah laughed to hide the hurt he still felt, he didn't really want to get into why he and his brother had left their home.

"No, I was just kidding with you, but the peaches are the best I've ever tasted."

"We came here to Colluden because of the work opportunities."

"I'm a master carpenter."

"You look too young to be a master carpenter."

"Well, my father started us out pretty young and it's been with me ever since."

"Where you planning to staying a spell here in Culloden or you just passing through."

"So far we've considered staying a spell."

"Well I want to welcome you to Culloden where we dare to dream."

"Why thank you Miss Gillie."

"We been prospecting the land just up the road there near the Payton's"

"Do you know Mr. and Mrs. Payton?"

"Oh sure all my life, Mrs. Payton is the midwife around these parts."

"Her and my grandmother use to be really good friends, she helped bring me into this world."

"My grandmother passed away a few years back though."

"I'm sorry to hear that, I know how important grandparents are they bring wisdom far beyond our years."

"That is very true Elijah; my grandmother was a very wise and very spirited woman."

Elijah listened to Gilda attentively and watched how she used her hands to express her self when she spoke. To him it was quite pleasant to listen to her and even more pleasant to watch her. His thoughts transformed into words as he unintentionally took Gilda off guard.

"I hope I'm not being offensive, because it's not my intention, but you have the most beautiful smile I've ever seen."

Unable to resist, she finally did look away. Gilda did not expect such sincerity to come from a man who seemed so abrasive a few days ago. After quickly regaining her composure she turned back, facing Elijah. "Well grandma Fannie always said you can take a compliment just as long as it is a decent one."

"You read and write Elijah?" Elijah began to smile.

"Of course I read and write, why you ask?"

"Well, I was just curious is all, because some of the men around here, both black and white don't read and write."

"Most left school to help out their families in the fields." Elijah nodded his head.

"Oh I see."

"Well me and my brother were fortunate enough to get our certificate."

"There was this lady who came all the way from England. She was the wife of a wealthy businessman who settled in our town for a spell.. Her name was Mrs. Ivy and while they were there she opened up a school in our area. She was quite a lady and very strict about writing and pronouncing what she called the queen's English." Elijah shook his head as he remembered her scolding and correcting the children about speaking proper English when they spoke in her class.

"I read and write rather well if I should say so myself." Gilda was delighted.

"I do too, my grandmother and Miss Ann encouraged me to get my education. I liked school a lot coming up and I would like to one day teach children to read and write."

"Who is Miss Ann?"

"Oh, Miss Ann, she's like family she stays on the hill near Mr. Johnson's store."

"My grandmother use to work for her before she passed away."

"I still go to visit Miss Ann and just sit in the library and read as much as I like."

"She has books with stories from all over the world."

"She's also very dedicated to providing for those who are in need."

"I help her with that from time to time too."

"My grandmother, well she always said it was different working for Miss Ann."

"You speak very highly of your grandmother."

"Yeah that was my best girlfriend."

"Enough about me, what about you Elijah." Elijah hunched his shoulders as he checked the fishing rods.

"Well there's nothing to me, I lost my mom when I was a child, she died of scarlet fever."

I was very young but I do remember her beautiful jet black hair and her skin was so smooth, very dark and beautiful."

Her smile was bright, I remember her being very gentle with us, just a beautiful spirit."

My father is an ex-slave, he and my mother's father raised us."

"My Mother and grandfather Black Eagle were Blackfoot Indian."

He taught me to respect the natural origin of all things and to respect life and nature."

"My dad, well is my dad and he had a very rough life."

"He drinks a lot from time to time but he's a good man."

"My mom, I remember she could always bring that tender side out of him."

"He's not a religious man but he's spirited and taught us how to be men."

"He taught us how important reading and writing would be to our lives." "He felt it was very important that we could tell our own story and demonstrate the dignity of who we are as black men."

"Well, what about your father Gillie?"

"I never knew him, so I never missed having him around."

"My mother's name is Beauty, she is something else too!"

"She has her own business dressing hair at our home for a living."

"I'm gonna introduce the two of you one of these days."

"Elijah, do you like the blues?"

"Sure I do, why do you ask?"

"Oh because I love it very much, it's the one thing that keeps me close to the people that I love that are no longer here, like my grandma Fannie."

"I listen to it on the radio broadcast all the time, and I got vinyl that I play."

"I just love it."

Elijah went into his shirt pocket and pulled out his harmonica. Gilda's face lit up as he begin to play. His hand vibrated continuously over the instrument with ease as the southern sounds echoed along the river bank.

"Oh that was beautiful."

"How long have you been playing?"

"My pops brought it for me when I was just a boy."

Suddenly the two were distracted by Julia's voice as she and Joshua tasseled with her fishing rod.

"I got one, I got a big one!"

After a few minutes of struggling Joshua finally pulled the large catfish onto the bank. "Way to go Josh!" Elijah yelled out. Joshua then strung it up and held it up to for them to see. Gilda looked over at Elijah and smiled.

"Those two seem to be hitting it off quite well."

After a few more hours of discussion, both girls agreed at their bathroom break that it was the appropriate time to leave. They packed their things away and the fish they'd caught.

"I had such a nice time with you Elijah."

"Yes me too."

"When can I see you again Gillie?"

"I don't know, maybe you can come by the house meet my mom and have some peach cobbler."

"She makes the best peach cobbler."

Elijah nodded his head in confirmation.

"I think I would like that very much."

"Okay then, let's see maybe next Sunday after church."

"More than likely Julia will be there, so both you and Joshua are invited."

All agreed on next Sunday. The girls bid the young men farewell and started their two mile trek home.

****

That following Saturday evening, Gilda and Julia met Po Fisher and Big Ted in the woods behind Rufus' juke joint. Beauty was still doing her last client and the girls each gave her a kiss and left to meet up with Fisher.

When the girls arrived, the people were pouring in. Gilda covered her mouth in surprise as she recognized a few of the women from her mothers shop. Fisher, in the excitement of it all unknowingly blew his cover.

"Wow, that show is a lot of people going in there." Gilda pushed Fisher. " Hey whatcha, doing Gillie?"

"I knew it, I knew it, you ain't hung out in Uncle Rufus' place, because he won't let you."

"Shush be quiet Gillie."

"Don't be shushing me Po, I know he don't let no young folks in there til your 18th birthday."

"You know how I know?"

"My mama told me he had to chase you and Ted from out back spying in a plenty times too."

"You and Ted were sneaking just like we doing now."

"Shhh, okay okay, but would you please be quiet Gillie." Fisher was embarrassed by the only woman he had truly loved besides his mother.

Soon the dusk became the dark of night. They all stooped low in the brush behind the wooden shack as they heard the constant beat of music from the piano. There were well known tunes played by famous composer Scott Joplin and Blues singer Jelly Roll Morton. Gilda was humming quietly and Julia was quietly patting her feet and snapping her fingers. The guys were waiting patiently to get their big peek. Big Ted became ambitious and got up.

"I'm going in a little closer y'all."

He moved in and they all followed him as he stooped down lower with his eyes looking in through the wide spaces of the weather warped wood. Once in the light, Gilda could not believe her eyes. There was Shimmering Shirley just like Fisher had said and she was sure enough shaking her stuff. She had a large blue feather in her hair and a pair of satin panties with a brassiere lined in feathers to match. Gilda looked down at her shoes and to here surprise they were high heeled and shined like a brand new nickel. She and Julia looked at each other and at that moment Gilda got an epiphany.

Julia tapped Gilda on the shoulder and pointed at Fisher and Big Ted. They were stooped down not far from them with their mouths hanging wide open. Gilda shook her head, because she knew it was possible that neither of the two had gotten a good look like this one before. Suddenly, out of nowhere came a most disturbing voice.

"What y'all doing?"

It was Sheriff Bradford; he didn't take to kindly to the young black men around the area especially Ted and Fisher. The sheriff was also known to harass and even terrorize many black families in the area. He and his deputies were the unspoken leaders of the Ku Klux Klan and the black community knew they had contributed excessively to the racially targeted crimes that went on in most Monroe County.

"Get outta here, before I put all of ya in jail." The four of them quickly scattered and ran away into the night. Gilda and Julia went their way and Fisher and Ted went another. Then Sheriff Bradford got into in his car and sped off down the road in Fisher and Ted's direction. He fired two shots in the air and both stopped in their tracks. The sheriff pulled up on the two young men with his high beams shining directly in their faces and got out of the car. He then took his gun and stuck it in Fisher's face.

"You see this here gun boy, next time I catch you alone out here in the dark of the night I'm gonna blow your head clean off."

Ted stood with both fist balled tight and standing almost a whole three feet above the sheriff. It took everything in him not to respond to the threats that he'd made to Fisher. Ted knew the consequences of a young black man speaking out against the law in Monroe County. He knew he would never have any peace from that night forward if he did the unthinkable. Fisher looked the sheriff in the eyes as he pulled the revolver back, but this time he didn't flinch. Sheriff Bradford, seeing no evidence of fear in Fisher's eyes finally released the trigger on the gun. He then put it in his holster and let out a loud burly laugh.

"Now you two no good niggers get." Without hesitation the boys took off again.

By the time the girls reached Gilda's house they were laughing at how both Ted and Fisher looked when the got a look at Shimmering Shirley. The Girls leaped onto the porch laughing as they made their way into the house. Gilda called out to her mother, but she did not respond. Both girls went to the back of the house toward the beauty shop. Gilda screamed as she saw here mother stretched out on the shop floor. The girls went into a moment of shock. Gilda kneeled down next to her mother and tried to get her to talk but nothing came out. She then began shaking her hysterically.

"Mama wake up, mama please wake up."

While Beauty's body lay limb in Gilda's arms, Julia went to Miss Ann's for help. It took both doctor Norman and Miss Ann to remove Gilda from her mother's side. After examining Beauty's body, doctor Norman diagnosed that she suffered a stroke. Mrs. Payton offered to take Gilda to her house, but Gilda refused. That night Miss Ann and Julia stayed with Gilda. She sat up all night crying to herself in the corner listening to the radio in her grandmother's favorite chair until she rocked herself to sleep.

Minnie arrived the night before the funeral. She saw a light burning in the back of the house and came through the entrance of the shop where she found Gilda sitting in her mother's client chair. She looked at Gilda and could see the hurt on her face. Minnie put her luggage down and Gilda jumped up and gave her a hug. She was so very happy to see her mother's long time friend and she held her tight.

"Oh Minnie, It hurt's so bad inside."

"It's like an ache deep down in my soul."

"I don't know how I'm gonna get on without my mama and grandma both gone from me." Gilda begin crying once again as Minnie held her even tighter while she also began to shed tears for her dear friend. Then she begin quietly singing to Gilda;

> *"Hmmm, hmmm, hmmmm hmmmm, them that's got shall have them that's not shall lose so the Bible says and it's still is news, mama may have and papa may have, but God bless the child suga, that's got his own, that's got his own."*

"Gillie baby don't you worry bout nothing, you'll always have me."

"Now, I know I ain't your mama but I am a mama to you, hear what I say?"

"I ain't left this world yet and as long as I'm here, you won't be without a mama."

"I was thinking about you probably come traveling with me some."

"Now Gillie, I know It ain't a stable life and all, but I would love to have you Gillie." She thought it was very kind of Minnie to offer such a huge sacrifice, but Minnie lived spontaneously and that was not the life she wanted for herself right now. Gilda was eager to get out of Culloden, but not like this.

"Miss Minnie I love you and you've been such a gift to my mama and me."

"You were always there for her."

"I appreciate you wanting to take me with you and all, but I think I wanna hang around for a spell."

"Please understand, I just wanna to see what the lord got planned for me is all."

Minnie grabbed and hugged Gilda.

"Oh you gone be just fine chile, you so strong and you talk just like yo mama."

Minnie wiped her eyes and then grabbed Gilda by the hand.

"Oh shoot, come on here chile and fix my hair up for tomorrow."

"Your mama would have killed me if I came to her funeral without my hair done."

That morning Gilda awoke still, with a heavy heart and mind. She proceeded to her mother's funeral accompanied by Ann, Minnie, Julia and her mother Grace. Big Ted was there, but not Fisher. Ted explained to Julia that on the same night they saw Sheriff Bradford, Po Fisher was so angry he hit the tracks and hopped a train up North.

The turnout at Beauty's funeral made it evident that she was loved and admired by many. Julia feeling inspirational sang Beauty's favorite Hymn: "Amazing Grace". Elijah and Joshua had also come to pay their respects. Miss Ann made sure Beauty received the best of everything. She had a mortician brought up all the way from Atlanta to tend to the body. She laid her to rest in the most beautiful casket and gown that anyone had ever seen in those parts. She was buried next to her mother Fannie. Gilda thought she looked like an angel. Julia looked over at her friend as she laid her head on Miss Ann's shoulder. It had been a hard blow to her, and Julia knew it. Gilda was her sister and therefore Julia's concerns lingered. No one was closer to Gilda than she. Up until now, Gilda had been agile about the misfortunes of her life. *"Would she ever recover from this?"* Julia thought to herself.

Before returning to the house Minnie gave her goddaughter a big hug. She passed Gilda a piece of paper and closed it tightly in her fist.

"Chile, you hold on to this, this here is where I will be."

"I wanted to tell you and your mama in a better way than this, but since my sister friend has passed on I'll leave it with you."

"I was offered an opportunity to go over seas to sing."

"I wasn't gonna look more into it because I wanted to make sure I was here for you."

"I wanted to take you home with me."

Minnie then pulled out her handkerchief and wiped her tears.

"I would sacrifice it all for you Gillie."

"But after talking with you last night it let me know that you gone be just fine."

"I admire that in you chile."

Gilda knew that Minnie meant well for her, but she also knew that she carried a secret pain of her past that kept her always running from Culloden. Gilda didn't feel abandoned at all by Minnie, because she knew her heart and they'd shared their special time in mourning together.

"Miss Minnie I'll be fine, really!"

"Don't worry about me, you just make sure you keep in touch." Minnie grabbed Gilda gently by the chin.

"Gilda you know me, I can't stay in this place too long."

"I get to thinking about my own past life, I got to stay ahead of myself so I don't lose myself, you understand?"

Gilda nodded her head and gave Minnie a big hug and stood at the edge of the road as she drove off. The dust lifting behind her departure reminded Gilda of her own desires to one day find her own destiny outside of Culloden Village.

Gilda, Julia, Grace and Ann, along with other close friends went back to Gilda's house. Mr. and Mrs. Payton, Uncle Rufus along with Mr. Walker, the fine gentleman Beauty had courted until her death had all set out the food and refreshments for the guests. It's going to be a long night Gilda thought as she went into her room and shut the door.

Suddenly, Ann knocked on the door.

"Gillie, sweetheart, it's me Miss Ann may I come in?" Gilda's voice was sullen and her eyes were still deep red from crying.

"Yes ma'am."

She slowly opened the door and entered.

"There is a very handsome gentleman out here to see you by the name of Elijah."

"He appears to be very nice and he is concerned about you Gillie."

Gilda begin wiping her eyes and checking herself in the mirror. "I don't think I wanna see him now Miss Ann."

"Look at me, I look a mess."

Miss Ann sat on the bed with Gilda and lifted her head "Baby, let me tell you something."

"It was a terrible thing that happened to your mama, she was so very young."

"I know it hurts awfully bad, but she would want you to be strong now more than ever, yah hear."

"No one's expecting no particular behavior from you right away chile."

"I'm gonna tell you this, you come from a breed of very high spirited, strong and gifted women and that same blood runs through your veins don't you ever forget that."

Miss Ann grabbed Gilda's hand and squeezed it tightly, she then gave her a big hug and proceeded to the door. "Shall I let the gentleman in?" Gilda nodded and soon after Elijah came into the room. He saw Gilda in the mirror and didn't say a word. He just sat in the corner on the stool and watched her. He wanted to be there for her. Elijah knew that there were no words of comfort, because he too had experienced losing his mother.

"I look a mess."

"No Gillie, you are beautiful." Gilda then went into the drawer and pulled out a pair of scissors and after a few minutes of cutting her beautiful head of hair, the pile lay on the floor. Elijah walked over to her and looked into her grieving eyes. His heart was heavy for her and It hurt him to see her grieve, but still he didn't say a word. Elijah slowly took the scissors out of her hand, looked into the mirror and begin to work at his long thick braid as well. Soon it fell with the rest of the hair that lay on the floor. He kissed her on the cheek and walked out of the door. Gilda continued to trim her hair until it was even all over her head, to her it relieved some of the pain she felt.

Chapter 3

Culloden Georgia
1931

Five years later, Gilda sat in her grandmother's large rocking chair thinking about all that had come to pass since her mother's death. Miss Minnie had finally made her way to Paris, France and forwarded her address to Gilda. She had found the love of her life and would not be returning to America. Over time she made many attempts to encourage Gilda to join her, but each time Gilda declined the offer. Miss Ann continued to come and check on Gilda from time to time and made sure that she was okay being home alone. She even brought her a dog and Gilda named him Battle.

Gilda spent most of her time at home doing hair, just as her mother before her. However, with the economy getting worse as the years went by and as a result her clientele dwindled because many of the women in the area had cut back on getting their hair professionally treated. Gilda begin to snap her fingers as she listened to the tunes on the gramophone. Miss Ann had given it to her along with a few vinyl recordings of her favorite singers to cheer her up after the death of her mother. She had acquired the sounds of folks like Billie Holiday, Louis Armstrong and Jelly Roll Morton and the great composer Scott Joplin. She played them over and over again because it had given her some peace of mind. She sat back with a glass of cool lemonade and closed her eyes. It was now 1931 and she was now thinking it was time to make some type of plans for her life.

Gilda begin to smile to herself as she thought about Julia and how she had gotten pregnant the same year Beauty passed away.

Julia's mother was so sad, she had wanted so much more for her daughter. She scolded her and put her out of her house. Julia came to Gilda crying her eyes out. Gilda remembered how she borrowed Ole Rufus's truck grabbed her shotgun and she along with Julia headed up the road. Gilda had been seeing Elijah off and on. However, after her mother's passing she was unable to share with him the tenderness that they had once had at the river that day. To her that seemed such a long time ago.

Every now and then she would still hear the women at church carrying on about Elijah, how handsome and single he was. This didn't bother Gilda one way or the other. She knew one thing for sure and that was that Joshua would do the right thing by Julia, even if it meant her taking a shotgun to him.

Once at the Mason home Gilda walked up to the porch with her shotgun and took a look around the house and the land. Joshua and Elijah had worked awfully hard fixing up the old run down shack. They had cut most of the trees down and turned the land in to a very comfortable farm. The brothers were doing well and managed to acquire a couple of horses, and build a chicken shack with a few chickens and a rooster and a barn out back. They had a small vegetable garden lined with collard greens, carrots, and tomatoes, and a peach tree that was still maturing that Joshua had planted. The tree was growing at a steady pace and would one day promise to produce peaches just as juicy if not juicer as those she remembered at old man Paul's place. Gilda looked over at Julia.

"You spoke with Joshua?"

"No."

"What, cha mean?"

"You haven't told him anything Julia?"

"I just found out myself, I missed my monthly twice."

" I told my mama and right away she assumed I was pregnant."

"Have you been sick?"

"A little off and on, but only in the morning, but I feel better in the afternoon."

The girls stepped up onto the porch. By this time Elijah had come out the house. Seeing Gilda always made him smile inside. He would frequently reminisce about the times they'd spent together. No woman had ever made him feel like she did. He looked down and saw that she had a shot gun on her side. Gilda noticed his observation and slightly hid it behind her dress. Elijah had never felt the way that he felt when he was around Gilda, even back home as a younger man the older women would approach him and show him favors of lustful pleasures. In his experiences however, no one had displayed a passion for life like Gilda.

"Good afternoon ladies." Elijah waited patiently to find out what this was all about and thought it quit humorous that Gilda was carrying a shotgun.

"Afternoon." They said in unison.

Joshua came out of the door once he heard Julia's voice; he had not seen her in a few days. Gilda looked over at Joshua with a threatening eye.

"I think you two need to talk." Elijah looked over at his brother and Joshua looked at Gilda noticing the shotgun that she had tucked behind her dress. Joshua without argument took Julia by the hand and went for a walk.

"Hello Gillie."

"Hello Elijah."

Elijah was still amused by the fact that she was toting a shotgun. "How are things going for you in town?"

"They're pretty fair, thank you very much sir."

"What about yourself?"

"Well I can't complain."

We keeping busy with the jobs in and out of town, so work is steady now."

Both had missed the others touch, but neither dare not say it. They both carried the burden of being stubborn as a mule and refused to admit it. Elijah had taking Gilda's virginity a couple of years after her mothers passing. She could remember the love song that he played on his harmonica as he explained it to be part of his Blackfoot and Algonquian heritage. She could remember the sensual words of love that he also passionately whispered in her ear. He had been there for her and supported her when most thought she had lost her mind for cutting off all her hair. Elijah loved the short hair on Gilda. He thought that their daring new look suited them both just fine.

To Gilda, Elijah was the most magnificent man she had ever met. His eyes were black as coal and always left her speechless, but today she had to be strong she thought. "What is that all about?"

"Well Mr. Mason."

Gilda stated as she took the shotgun and sat it up against the porch and sat down on the step.

"It looks like you gonna be an uncle." Elijah's eyes got wide.

"You are kidding right?"

By that time Julia and Joshua had made their way back to the porch.

"Elijah bro, I'm gonna be a daddy and me and Julia gonna get married!"

Gilda looked at Julia and winked her eye. She had refused to see any child of theirs grow up without a father like they had. Elijah tried to talk him out of it. He was quite amused at the whole thing but had his reasons.

"Where will the two of you stay?"

"There is no room here for three adults and a baby in this here little shack of a house."

Gilda wouldn't back down.

"What do you mean?"

"It wasn't so small when all of us were courting up in there!" Elijah scratched his head and gave her a mischievous grin and then put his hands atop his head. He carried a strong domineering character that Gilda seemed to have the gift to always penetrate.

Just like the man that Gilda knew he was, Elijah started building on that old shack. He even added an upstairs giving the excuse that he wouldn't have to hear the baby crying. He also helped Joshua build an oak wood baby bed and chest along with a rocking chair to match for his new sister-in-law.

They worked through the winter and part of the following spring fixing on that house. When summer came the house was completed and the baby was born. Julia had a little girl and named her Josephine, after her proud father.

Gilda called her Josie for short and it stuck with the baby girl.

Gilda's thoughts were interrupted as Battle began barking at a loud knocking on the door. It was Li'l Bobby

"Miss Gillie, Miss Gillie."

"What's wrong chile?"

"Nothing, gotta message for ya, and I promised I'd deliver it to ya, is all."

"Well Li'l Bobby you gone tell me what it is?"

"Yes ma'am, Fisher back in town and he up at Big Ted's place." Gilda put her hands on her hips and looked in awe.

"You shooten me boy?"

"Who told you that?"

"I promised that I wouldn't say, but to just give ya the message, I gotta go."

Li'l Bobby jumped off the porch and headed steadfast up the road toward Mr. Johnson's Market. Gilda grabbed her slippers and made her way toward Big Ted's. She passed by Mr. Johnson's and he was out front sweeping the dust off the market porch.

"Mr. Johnson, you hear anything about Fisher coming back home?"

"Yeah, they say he got in last night."

"Say he was up at Old Man Rufus place bright and early this morning and it's a rumor that he trying to buy him out and take over the juke joint."

"Is that so?"

"Well I'm gonna see for myself about all this commotion." Gilda said her goodbyes to Mr. Johnson and made her way to big Ted's house. Po Fisher's father had passed on early that spring and Gilda had assumed that he had finally returned so that he could settle his business. As Gilda got closer to Ted's she could hear laughter coming from Fisher's old run down shack next door. Gilda peeked into the screen door and two her surprise there was Po Fisher in the flesh. However, Fisher sure didn't look like he did when he'd left. Fisher was dressed like a city slicker. He had on a dark brown suit with a hat to match and fine shoes. Big Ted just sat there grinning as he listened to Fisher tell him about his adventure up north. The men distracted by a sweet scent that suddenly filled the room with the breeze turned their heads to the door.

"Gillie, oh come on in here girl." Fisher grinned.

"I guess L'il Bobby did his job."

"I gave him a couple of ace-notes to do it."

Even with Fisher gone, he still had his picks and Gilda was at the top of the list. Fisher got up gave her a hug and took her hand and gently placed a kiss upon it.

"I apologize for not being here for you when Miss Beauty passed away."

"It's okay I made out fine."

"Big Ted was just here telling me what happened." Fisher carefully looked her over.

"You cut your beautiful hair."

"Yeah I did."

Gilda rubbed her hand across her short curly natural.

"This is better for me, it's manageable and all I have to do is get up wet it and comb it out."

"I'm letting it grow back though."

Po Fisher then he walked around Gilda.

"My, My Gillie sho have filled out woman."

"She look good don't she Ted?"

"Yep I tell her all the time, don't I Gillie?" Gilda smiled.

"Ted I haven't seen you and you know it."

She shook her finger at Ted.

"And you haven't been to church either."

"Aww shoot Gillie, I've been out here working this dang on farm."

"You know I gotta eat."

"Ain't many sharecroppers left around these parts, most have moved closer to Macon and Barnesville."

Fisher stood up and pulled on his suspenders in a proud confident manner.

"Well you ain't gonna be working for them much longer because you coming to work for me."

"Ain't gonna be no more sharecropping for us around here, yah hear what I say?" Gilda and Ted's eyes widened, as Fisher pulled a roll of money out of his pocket. He gave a twenty dollar note to both Gilda and Big Ted.

"I just bought old Rufus Juke Joint, I'm gonna tear that old shack down and build a nice speak easy along side that creek."

"I got plans, lots of plans."

"It's gonna look just as good if not better than those fancy clubs up in the big city."

"But it's gonna have that there down home true blues sound, know what I mean?"

"And ya know what, I ain't gonna be like dem white folks down here, no suh, everybody's green is welcome at my place."

"Yes suh, they can all come shoot the jive at Po Fisher's Place."

Ted and Gilda sat watching Fisher in astonishment; neither said a word.

"I'm what you call an Entre-pre-newer."

The two of them looked at one another and begin to laugh and Fisher got upset.

"Oh you guys ain't taking me seriously, you will see yes suh you will see." Gilda shook her head at her dear friend.

"No Fisher, we do take you seriously, its just we haven't seen you in a long time and you look good, and talking good, bout doing positive things."

"I myself, I'm just proud to watch you get what you always wanted and I'm sure Ted here does too."

Ted nodded in agreement.

"Come here yall." Gilda and Ted followed Fisher out to the back of the house. He then unlocked the underground cellar door.

"Looka here."

Fisher dug into a crate and pulled out a bottle.

"What is that?" Big Ted asked.

"Oh that there is what you call pure distilled imported whiskey."

"That comes straight from Canada by way of the Detroit River." Fisher passed the bottle to Ted.

"Try some Big Ted." Ted took a large sip out of the bottle and then hit his chest.

"Take yo time Ted man."

"That ain't no corn likker you gotta sip on that there stuff or it will kill you." Ted cleared his throat and gained his composure.

"That there is some good stuff Fisher."

Fisher laughed. "Yeah, I know and that there is one of the many refreshing drinks I will be serving at my speak easy."

"I can get it cheap, and I will sell it cheap too."

"I'm gonna to blow dem other speak easy's off the map."

"It's a lot of work that need to be done to Rufus ole place."

"He says it's been kinda rough for him to keep it up."

"Did you guys know the bridge from the main road had completely fallen apart?"

"I told him I would take it off of his hands and he was very obliged to what I had given him for it."

"What did cha give him for the juke joint Fisher?" Fisher started pulling on his suspenders again.

"Ted, let's just say it was enough for him to move outta here and up to Atlanta."

"He and his lady friend will be just fine yes suh."

Fisher continued as he paced the yard.

"I got to get to working on that their place as soon as possible."

"Well I know a couple of fellas that would be willing to do the job and I could help too." Fisher looked over at Ted.

"Oh yeah, who?"

"Elijah and Joshua."

"Whose Elijah and Joshua?"

"Oh, two brothers come here over from South Carolina."

"They come around just after you left."

"They're master carpenters and they do really good work."

Fisher looked over at Gilda.

"You know these fella's Gillie?"

Gilda couldn't help but to blush and it was at that very moment Fisher knew she had known the newcomers far better than she was letting on.

"Okay Ted set up a meeting with these fella's, I wanna meet em and see what they about."

Fisher couldn't help it, but he was slightly jealous. He had loved Gilda all his life.

"You acquainted with these fella's Gillie?"

"Julia has a baby by the youngest one named Joshua."

"Their anniversary is Sunday, so you can have your say with the Mason's then."

"Sho nuff Gillie?"

"Wow a lot has happened since I been gone, but guess what I'm back and we gonna have a real good time, you'll see."

That Sunday Julia and Joshua had their anniversary gathering after church. Gilda introduced Fisher to Joshua and Elijah. Afterward he took them over to the run down building to discuss what could be done to the place in order for it to be the success that Fisher was hoping for. He explained to them that he was expecting a shipment from up North and he really needed to get started as soon as possible. Elijah and Joshua both agreed to take on the job.

Fisher would stop by Gilda's quite often since he'd returned home, and more than a few times Elijah was already there visiting. Fisher was unsuccessful in hiding his jealousy of the relationship that Gilda and Elijah had established while he was away. One evening after Fisher had stopped by, Elijah had inquired about her and Fisher's relationship.

"Was there anything between the two of you before Fisher left Culloden?"

"No, we just grew up together is all; me and Fisher have a different kind of relationship, more like kindred spirits."

"Why do you ask?"

"It's a man thing, I notice when he come by here and we're here together, he gets a little uncomfortable."

"Gillie I do believe Fisher is in love with you."

"You gotta be kidding." Gilda looked at Elijah.

"Maybe it's just you is all."

"Gillie you not a man, I know what I am talking about."

"We get along fine when working on his place."

"I will tell you Gillie that Fisher got some serious cash behind him."

"He has us using some pretty expensive wood, cherry and Oak."

"He even had some redwood shipped all the way from California for the tables and chairs."

"Joshua's been building the bar and the stools with it too."

Gilda was hearing Elijah, but her thoughts were elsewhere. *"Fisher in love with me?"*

Elijah had to be misreading things, or maybe he was saying things about Fisher that he felt himself.

"Gillie, you alright?"

Gilda focused her attention back on Elijah. Deep down it had killed Elijah to say that she was all he had thought about since he moved to Culloden. He dare not tell her that, not yet. He knew one day he would have her for his wife. He watched Julia and Joshua at home and also found himself more often reminiscing on the first time he laid eyes on Gilda.

"You wanna listen to some music Elijah?"

Elijah nodded in agreement. Gilda turned on the gramophone and pulled out her Bessie Smith vinyl. She then pulled Elijah up off the couch and grabbed a hold of him. They began to move to the rhythm of the music.

"Ahh this is nice, this is why I love this woman, so full of passion."

"Will she one day allow me to cherish her like she deserves?"

Gilda had many mood swings since the passing of her mother. At times she would receive Elijah with open arms and other times she would shut him out along with everyone else. Elijah had gotten irritated and very impatient with her spells. He knew she had been through some very traumatic experiences in her life time. She was a very young woman having to cope with so much tragedy alone. Nevertheless, his frustration of the off again on again relationship sent his mind swimming in a state of confusion.

After a night of dancing, dinner and talking Elijah called it a night.

"I guess I will see you another time."

He kissed Gilda on her forehead and she escorted him out onto the front porch. Gilda stepped out into the moonlight behind him and stood as he reared up his pick-up truck. The smell of freshly bloomed Roses filled the air. Suddenly Elijah jumped out of the running truck and walked back up to Gilda, he grabbed her close to him and passionately gave her a kiss for what seemed like an eternity. Gilda gave in not realizing until that moment how much she missed his touch.

"Gillie I want you to know that you will always be my Ki'Somma." Silently Gilda put her finger over his lips.

"Shh, I know dear heart, I know."

****

For the next few days Gilda got up in the mornings with a heavy head. Culloden was home, and as much as she loved Elijah, she begin to grow out of the notion of even staying. Gilda wanted to take a chance like Fisher and possibly see the big cities like Chicago and Detroit or even travel to Europe to visit Miss Minnie.

Gilda's thoughts were interrupted by a knock on the door.

"Who is it?"

"Elijah."

His deep voice always put a smile on her face. Elijah swung the door open.

"I'm back here Elijah, in the kitchen."

"Hello my Ki'Somma."

"Well good morning to you to Mr. Mason, what brings you into town so early this morning?"

"Well gotta a few things to do, figure I would get on up early before the sun gets too hot."

"I thought I would stop by and say hello to the most beautiful woman in the world." Elijah was dressed in a white pull over shirt that showed off his athletic physique and a pair of worn denim jeans and work boots. Gilda looked him over, but candidly changed the subject.

"Nice weather we having isn't it?"

Elijah gave Gilda a grin.

"As a matter of fact the weather has been nice."

Resisting Elijah had become a difficult job for Gilda. As a young girl it was easy to resist the temptation of his touch, but as Gilda blossomed into a woman, the urge to control the deep passion she had for this man had truly became a chore.

"Elijah you just work work work, you need to relax sometimes." Elijah sat down and grabbed Gilda onto his lap.

"Ki'Somma, I've been working all my life, but one thing for is for sure, I've have always worked for myself."

Gilda gave him a great big smile. She loved his entrepreneurial spirit and his inner strength. Gilda knew after spending the years courting Elijah that she wouldn't want to be with any other man. It was not the time that they spent more so than the type of man that he was. He was a rare breed because he was always looking to the future always looking for something better.

"Well Mr. Mason I do think you will be quit the success in your old age, if I would say so myself." After a couple hours of cool herbal mint tea, laughter and conversation Elijah soon departed for his job and Gilda prepared for her clients.

****

After three months of sawing, cutting and hammering, Po Fisher's Speak Easy was finally completed. Fisher, Big Ted, Elijah, and Joshua each had a bottle of Canada's finest. The men were laughing and talking amongst themselves. Over time and through the hard work, they became good friends. Fisher was full from several stiff shots and he stepped to Elijah.

"Man, are you in love with Gillie?" stunned from the question Elijah attempted to get his composure and stood up over Fisher. Joshua sat back amused, he was confident in his brother being able to handle the situation and he also waited anxiously for the reply they all had been trying to tear out of his brother for the last five and a half years.

"Well let me tell you this man, I must say, I enjoy her company in my life." Joshua rolled his eyes to the ceiling and shook his head.

"Man what kinda jive talk is that?"

"Who jive talking man?"

"I just don't think right now, she seriously wants a man in her life, you know around her all the time."

"She very much keeps to herself."

"When she let's me in her life, I step in and when she shuts me out I leave her alone."

Fisher began to scratch his head. The whiskey was obviously working on him because he had no idea what Elijah was talking about.

"Man that ain't what I asked you?"

"Do you love her or don't you?" Elijah never replied, so Fisher stood back.

"Well if you won't tell me then I will tell you, I love her." Elijah couldn't hide the irritation that he felt from Fisher's comment.

"I knew that already." Joshua knew his brother, and now it was a very unpredictable outcome about to take place. Big Ted stayed seated, but he would not allow the two of them to destroy the place that they all had worked so hard to finish. When it was time he would do what needed to be done.

"What do you mean you already knew?"

"Hell I see it all over you when you come by the house and you not expecting to see me there man."

"You would look at me like I was a fox in the chicken coop man."

Big Ted could not hold it in any longer he leaned backward in his chair laughing aloud, but was able to catch himself before hitting the floor. It was obvious that Elijah was also feeling the affects of Canada's best. Joshua shook his head

"Look at you two."

"Gillie, she doesn't want the likes of either one of yah."

"Did ya'll know she planning on leaving Culloden?"

Both Elijah and Fisher looked over at Joshua.

"I heard her and Julia talking on the front porch the other day, said she wanna do some traveling try that thing they call shake dancing."

"Elijah cleared his throat, and quickly sobered up from the all the shots of whiskey he'd indulged in the past few hours. "Shake dancing?"

"Gillie, she don't know anything about no shake dancing?"

Elijah's comment was more of a question than a statement to the fact. Fisher interrupted, while grinning and shaking his head.

"Well suh, I hate to be the one to tell you, but that girl does know how to shake her stuff."

Elijah got up and started pacing the floor and Joshua knew his brother was angry and thought to himself humorously. *Oh shoot he's about to blow.*

Elijah burst out the door, jumped in his pick up truck and sped down the road. Fisher looked over at Joshua laughing out loud.

"What's wrong with that crazy fool?"

"I was just jugging at him, but I do love her doe."

Joshua shook his head.

"My brother is in love with Gillie is all and he won't admit it."

"Strange though, he always shows it with crazy episodes like that."

"He's a little hot now and just need to cool off."

Fisher poured him and Joshua another shot.

"Is being in love really all that hard man?"

"I mean shoot, If you love her just tell her."

"I know what you mean Fisher, when I saw Julia, right then and there I was in love with that woman and I told her."

"I snatched my baby right up, yes I did."

"But my brother, well that's another story."

"He so use to the women putting in all the work, they spoiled him back home."

"This the first time in his life he had to express himself."

"I think he warming up though, yeah I do believe Miss Gilda den reeled the big Carolina catch in."

Big Ted also poured him a shot and turned it up quick. "Joshua, you may be right about Elijah's story, but you a bit off about your own."

"Fisher this cat had a shot gun wedding thanks to Gillie; he was a nervous wreck about Julia." Fisher let out a hearty laugh and they joined in.

Joshua then turned up his last shot and wiped his mouth with his sleeve.

"Hey, one of you fellas has got to get me home."

All that night Fisher thought about what Joshua said about Gilda. This would be a good opportunity to open the business in style.

"Maybe I could offer her a job shake dancing, paying her enough to entice her to stay right her in Colluden." That night Fisher made his plans to go by Gillie's in the morning to discuss his ideas for his grand opening.

Chapter 4

Fisher got up the following morning and made his way to Gilda's place. The rumor had spread around the town about Fisher's new found business. Right now his mind was on his entertainment and he had already begin lining up blues singers and musicians. Fisher knew he would need something else, something that would shoot his grand opening through the roof.

Fisher arrived at Gilda's place a little after ten o'clock in the morning. He stepped on the porch and smiled delightfully as he smelled the aroma of homemade biscuits and fried chicken. He knocked and Battle came to the screen door barking. Startled, Fisher jumped back and pulled his handkerchief out of his back pocket and wiped the sweat off his brow. The sun was a scorcher today and he thought he would die if he didn't quench his thirst. "Who's that?"

"It's me Fisher."

Gilda called for Battle and he ran to the back of the house. "Okay Fisher, you can come on in."

"I put him out in the backyard; I'm out back in the shop."

Gilda was doing a new client from Louisiana whose name was Dot Manchester. Gilda had known her for a while because she had been living in the area the past six months helping her older sister Clara take care of their sick aunt.

"Good morning ladies." Fisher wiped his brow again.

That's some dog you got there Gillie."

"Yeah he looks out for me."

"How you Fisher?"

"What brings you around here this bright and early?"

"You look awfully thirsty, it's some fresh lemonade over in the ice pantry."

Fisher continued his conversation with Gilda as he poured his lemonade into a glass and grabbed a biscuit and a piece of chicken off the kitchen stove. "I wanted to talk to you."

"Oh excuse my manners."

"Dot this here is Fisher and Fisher this here is Dot."

Both gave their salutations and Fisher continued his quest while Gilda tended to Dot's hair.

"We finished the Juke Joint"

"Oh yeah, Julia told me."

"She said it look real classy up in there too."

"She said you guys did a good job."

"I'll see it when you open up, shoot it ain't no use of me going down there to that fancy speak easy if it ain't popping."

Gilda snapped her fingers and Fisher begin to laugh. "Yeah I know what you mean, Yes suh Gillie, soon enough, soon enough." Fisher sat down for a minute while he finished his snack.

"This chicken sho is good Gillie, I must've forgotten how good you can cook."

Fisher was not good with small talk, but he began discussing the weather and the latest town gossip.

Soon the conversation came up about the Jim Crow laws.

"You know I was getting awfully sick and tired of riding the train when I traveled."

"I start out in the passenger cars up North and once I would cross that Mason Dixie line, I was forced to move to the baggage cars like some kind of animal and in my good suit too."

"It just doesn't make know sense."

"I tell you it ain't right how they treat black folks."

"You know on the way home, I got so mad at that train conductor."

"He threatened to kick me right off the train if I didn't respect dem segregation laws." Fisher started to laugh.

Miss Gilda's Blues 53

"Hell, what kind of stupid lop-sided law is that?"

"Laws are supposed to help people live in peace not war."

"Hey, if I wouldn't have had all this money in my pocket, I'd probably be in jail right now."

Gilda shook her head at her friend while she pulled the pressing comb through Dot's long red hair. She knew Fisher, and also knew that he was beating around the bush. Fisher hadn't come by just to talk about Jim Crow laws or the weather. Fisher was much to busy of a man these days to just be casually stopping by so early in the day. He had other things on his mind and Gilda decided she would be patient and allow him to get around to it when he was ready. Dot waved her hand at Fisher to get his attention.

"Honey I agree with you, I stopped riding the railroad long ago."

"I figure you better off driving where you need to go or have somebody drive for you." Fisher ignored Dot's advances and continued his conversation with Gilda.

"I stopped by Julia's and Joshua's this morning too."

"Joshua told me that Elijah was up in Barnsville with his crew."

"He say they been getting plenty of work since they built my place."

"Really?"

"That's good for him."

Gilda hadn't seen Elijah as much as she would have liked over the past month anyway and was now showing some resentment because of it. Fisher changed the subject because he didn't want to get Gilda in a bad mood. That wasn't his intentions for stopping by.

"You know Gillie, I was wondering something."

"Here it comes." Gilda thought to herself.

She looked up from Dot's head with the pressing comb still in hand and sat it on her damp towel. She then got up and went into the kitchen and refilled their glasses.

Dot looked over at Fisher.

"Wait a minute you Po Fisher."

Dot had remembered hearing about him around town.

"You the guy hit it big up North?"

"When you gonna open up that place?"

"We need something down hear to do on Saturday nights." Gilda went back to her stool and sat down behind Dot. Fisher smiled and was feeling good that folks were finally saying good things about him for a change.

"Yes Ma'am that would be me." Gilda placed another part in Dots hair and began curling with the hot iron curlers.

"Well it's a pleasure to meet you Fisher."

"Ouch Gillie!"

"Well, you gone have to be still chile."

Dot rolled her eyes, but continued her conversation more carefully with Fisher.

"I guess folks won't be calling you Po much longer huh?"

"Shoot I haven't had a good party since I came here from Louisiana."

"That's were you from girl?"

"I got a lot good folk around that way?"

"Yes I am, born and raised deep down in the Delta baby."

Fisher shook his head

"Man I must admit, I've had some good times in New Orleans."

"Yes, and don't forget good eating too Mr. Fisher." After a while, Gilda finished Dot's hair and passed her the hand held mirror.

"Gilda you really know how to make a woman look good." Gilda had spiral curled her hair all over with the hot curlers. Dot had thick unmanageable red hair, but after the pressing comb and the curlers she looked like a new woman.

"Now don't you go and get that wet you hear and stay outta the sun so you don't sweat so much." Gilda pulled the cape from around her neck.

"Okay chile you ready to go?"

Dot jumped out of the seat and paid Gilda for her services.

"Come on y'all lets go up front were it's a little cooler."

They both followed Gilda to the front of the house. Gilda turned on the radio and started snapping her fingers to the Big Band Jazz sounds that filled the front room.

"Yes, now that's what I am talking about."

Dot joined in as Fisher sat back in the large couch and watched the two young women move to the rhythms of the beat.

"Hey girls how would you like to dance at my joint?"

Dot turned her attention to Fisher.

"You mean Shake dance?"

"Yeah."

"Really?"

"Sure."

Excited by the offer Dot continued.

"I always wanted to shake dance."

"I use to see them women going down to the Red Light district in New Orleans."

"Gilda you should've seen them, they had the fanciest clothes and the hats, they were to die for chile and they got good money for it too."

"If you offering Mr. Fisher then I'm gonna have to accept."

"When can I start?" Fisher was happy for such a response from Dot.

"Soon as my spot opens."

"What about you Gllie?"

"Here in town? I don't know Fisher."

"Oh it would be great Gillie."

Fisher was excited the conversation had finally come up.

"The two of you would be perfect, I tell you."

"They will come from miles around just to see you two beautiful ladies."

Meanwhile Dot had already agreed and she didn't hesitate to discuss her pay. "Fisher, you the boss and you and me both know it's all about the money so how much?"

"I don't know."

"Maybe five dollar notes a night until things get going."

"What?"

"You can't get me to shake dance for no five dollar notes a night."

Dot appeared irritated by the offer. Fisher could sense the greed and stopped her in her tracks. He was use to dealing with many people like Dot while on his travels. On the outside they appeared to be very friendly and kind people, but when it came to money they could turn ugly very quickly. He despised doing business with people like that.

"Whatcha mean woman?"

"That's a lot of money and your gonna be getting tips too."

"Folks is starving out here and besides, where else you gonna get money like that around here?"

"Unless you plan on bartering your goodies."

"I ain't that type of cat to be cheating nobody, especially my employees." Dot wasn't convinced.

"Well the girls I know back home they getting at least seven dollar notes or eight dollar notes a night"

"You know what Dot?"

"They probably doing a little more for their boss than shaking dancing too."

"It's your call and the offer is there if you want it."

"Think about it and get back to me." Dot folded her arms and fell back into the couch. Fisher turned his attention back to Gilda.

"Gillie what about you? All you gonna be doing is sitting around this house in the evenings."

"You said you were gonna come by my place to have a little fun, so you might as well get paid doing it."

Fisher noticed he had finally said something to Gilda that made sense to her. He also knew as long as Gilda was thinking, she usually could do almost anything she her mind to do.

"Okay Gillie, you tell me how many jobs gonna pay you that much plus tips woman?" Gilda sat quietly in her thoughts, she had been listening to Dot and Fisher quite attentively.

On one hand Dot made a lot of sense five dollar notes were not enough, she made just a little less than that doing hair. On the other hand Fisher made a lot of sense also, because the tips would off set the wages if they were equal or better a night. The economy was starting to affect her business anyway. Her customers had dwindled to only a few women in the area. Also, with Elijah in and out of town she hadn't much of a social life either.

Gilda thought Fisher was confident in his business and she knew that he would be a success.

"Okay ladies y'all doing too much thinking."

"I just wanna say one more thing, who else in these here parts got pure genuine distilled Canadian Whiskey?"

"My next shipment will be here in about two weeks time, along with the muscle to keep the sheriff and his cronies off my back."

"I tell you this is a win, win for us."

Dot was no fool she knew that Canadian liquor was hard to get and only the most prestigious brothels and speak easy's carried it down in Louisiana.

"Come on ladies."

"Okay, I'll throw in the costumes, how about dat?"

Dot could smell money and she knew Fisher had it. Unlike Gilda she had already made her decision. Her mission now was to get as much as she could out of the little town.

"Okay I'm in Fisher."

"What about you Gillie, you gonna take his offer?"

"I don't know Fisher."

"Aw shoot, that don't sound like the Gillie I know."

"Okay how about this, I need a Barmaid to serve drinks at the bar and keep the inventory."

"You can start out there and if you change your mind, you can always go out on the floor."

"How is that?"

" C'mon woman what you got to lose?"

"Alright, alright I'll try that, but if I don't like it I'm quitting you hear?"

"Yeah, Yeah I hear you, but when that money starts rolling in and you hear that good ole Blues and Jazz playing you ain't gonna want to quit nothing."

"You'll see."

For a little more encouragement Fisher dug in his pocket and pulled out two twenty dollar notes.

"Here, this should be all you two ladies need to get started plus any extras."

"I will be opening my doors in three weeks."

"Dot, you have to think up a stage name."

"Gilda you get ready to mix some drinks you hear?" Gilda looked over at Fisher, he was ecstatic about the entire thing and now she knew why he had stopped by the house this morning. Gilda also knew another thing for sure, Dot would be a problem. Dot had a love for money, and Beauty always told her to be very careful around folks like that. Time would tell she thought to herself.

The following morning Gilda got up bright and early for a visit to Julia's. She hitched a ride halfway with Big Ted and insisted on walking the rest of the way. Gilda enjoyed walking the red dirt roads of Culloden because they always reminded her of the walks she shared with both her mother and grandmother. It was on those walks her mother encouraged her to ask questions about all the aspects of love and life. Gilda always enjoyed those special times with Beauty and she treasured them, but times were changing and Gilda could see it first hand. People were setting up small camps along much of the back roads. It was getting harder for the young as well as the old. People were sitting around small campfires conversing while others had huge tubs of boiling water washing and rinsing clothing. One of the children ran up to Gilda and asked her for a penny. Gilda reached in her pocket and pulled out two single notes and gave them to the child. He quickly ran back over to his mother and gave it to her. She shouted out to the road.

"Thank you and god bless you chile, this will help feed us for the next month."

These small camps in the area were known as Hoovervilles.

They were named after the thirty-first President Herbert Hoover, whom during his post-reconstruction term in office had the worst economic downfall ever to befall on the United States of America. People were starving all over the country while struggling to take care of their families. Many of these families in the South were forced out of their homes because they were unable to keep up their payments to the bank. Many roamed the countryside finding anyplace that was suitable to set up camp and shelter. Meanwhile, in the North they were lumped into Ghettos where thousands and thousands of people would live in one small corner of a large city.

"Why did the government punish the poor?" Gilda thought to herself as she walked past the small tent village setup along the road. She wondered how the president and those in office would feel if their families had to endure such inhumane conditions as a means of survival. Gilda continued her journey while deeply inhaling the Monroe County Peach

Farm that sat in the bend of the road. There were rows and rows of peach trees that seemed to go on for miles. In each row she could see the hired hands picking the harvest beyond the barbwire fence.

Each morning was first come first serve and the today the farm was full. The more pounds you picked the more coin you would receive.

Gilda reminisced about the time her and Julia wanted to purchase two baby dolls from Sears and Roebucks Catalog at Mr. Johnson's store. The two wanted those dolls so badly they asked permission from their mother's to work on the peach farm for a days pay. This was not an unusual request because many of the children worked during the summer months.

Miss Ann volunteered to purchase the dolls for the girls, but Beauty had other thoughts. She thought it would do them some good to see what it was like to work hard, be independent, and know the value of a note. Gilda laughed to herself as she remembered her and Julia trying to pull those sacks filled with sweet Georgia peaches across the field. The girls had picked plenty, but hadn't realized they were also responsible for delivering them to the weigh station at the end of the day. A young gentleman by the name of B.J. observed the girls struggling with their earnings for the day. He felt sorry for them and helped them take their sacks over.

The girls had come home with just under enough money to purchase their baby dolls, so Beauty put up the rest. Both of the girls complained of being sore to their bones and vowed they would never work in the fields again.

Gilda shook her head at the thought as she walked over the hill toward the the road that began the pathway to Julia's house. Julia came outside with her hand above her brow, blocking the sun out of her eyes.

"Gilda Jean is that you?" .

"Chile where you been?" Gilda had a huge smile on her face as she came on the porch and sat down.

"Julia chile, what's going on?"

"Not a lot."

"How you Gillie?"

"Girl I'm good."

"How's Joshua?"

"Oh he just fine chile, been working hard though after folks saw the work down at Fisher's place."

"A few businesses have been coming around inquiring."

"That's really good Julia."

" Yeah, they deserve it because they're very good at what they do."

"Gillie c'mon out back with me while I finish hanging these clothes on the line."

Gilda followed her through the kitchen and out into the back. Julia went right to work wringing her sheets and Gilda helped her hang them on the line. Julia knew Gilda wanted to know about Elijah. She also knew Gilda was too head strong to ask. "Elijah has been doing just fine too." Gilda gave her an unconcerned look.

"I don't recall asking you about Elijah Miss Julia."

"I know, but I thought I would just tell you any ole way."

"Chile I am so sick of them women coming around here trying to catch up with that man."

"Especially that Colleen."

"She's always bringing by her fancy fruit preserves and dinners on Sunday."

"I just shake my head and I had to tell her; look here Colleen I'm the cook around this here place."

"If you want to cook for Elijah, get him over to your house."

"I wish you just go head on and snatch that man up out of his misery."

"You know he crazy about you."

"Julia, I ain't got no time for that right now, that's what I come out here to talk to you about."

Julia could only imagine what was on Gilda's mind this time.

"Julia I am thinking about making some big money."

"Lord, I'm scared to ask, but I will."

"Whatcha gonna do Gillie?"

"Po Fisher came by the house yesterday morning while I was doing Dot Manchester's hair."

Julia didn't like Dot and she told Gilda the first time that she met her. Julia always had a good sense for judging folk and Gilda never doubted her.

"Fisher asked me to work for him."

"Oh yeah, doing what?" Julia stopped hanging the sheets on the line and sat on the tree stump, but Gilda hesitated.

"Awww Gillie come on don't stop now." Gilda had to build up her nerve, because she couldn't believe it herself.

"I'm gonna be a barmaid at Fishers place." Julia sat there for a few minutes.

"Well aren't you gonna say anything Julia?"

"Well, what do you want me to say Gillie?" Julia knew that Gilda always had a free spirit and would not dare criticize her for her ambitions. At times she wished she had that same kind of spirit about herself. However, she had more pleasure in playing devil's advocate to Gilda when she came up with her outrageous ideas.

"Gillie, I knew it was something."

Both women began to laugh.

"You think you can pull that off?"

"I don't know Fisher sounded real convincing and even Dot's in on it."

Julia put her hands on her hips

"You gotta be kidding me?"

"Nope, she was right there when he made the offer.

"She gonna be shake dancing though."

Julia laughed.

" Hmm sounds like something she would like to do."

"Chile I watched her do some heavy negotiating with Fisher, she know her stuff now Julia."

"I'm sure she does, you know that girl been around the block a couple of times Gilda, she just too slick for me."

"Well considering his popularity these days Gillie, I don't think you will have a problem making no cash over there."

"On the other hand they'll be gossiping around town you know." Gilda looked over at Julia.

"What about it?"

"Aw Gillie come on now, you know just like with ole man Rufus juke joint."

"Fisher's speak easy is going to be the new hot gossip along the Culloden Hillside."

"Yeah I know, I know, but who care what they think."

"My mama never cared; she always did her own thing and didn't worry about what these folks had to say about her."

"She always told me to let the lord do the judging."

"She also said everybody got their on race to run, so I'm just running mine."

Julia stood up and stretched her legs.

"Gillie, you know you always coming up with some stuff I tell you."

"My mind and prayers never rest about you."

Gilda thought about all the gossip and how cruel the folks in town could be.

"I don't care one way or the other what folks think."

"Somebody is gonna always have something to say about something around here, It's just how they are."

"You thirsty Gillie?"

"I got some cool lemonade in the ice pantry."

"Let's go on up."

The two sat on the porch for hours talking about old times and Gilda's new adventure.

"I think it will be exciting meeting all those different kinds of folk from all over."

"Don't you Julia?"

"Sure I do!"

"You know Gillie, I was just trying to get under your skin out back."

"I figured I would prepare you for these uptight folk around here, especially Colleen and her mother."

"You know, she hate you because Elijah in love with you."

"All shoot that girl hate the world and she hate herself as a matter of fact."

" I ain't thinking bout Colleen!"

"You know what I think burns her up the most about it all Gillie."

"What?"

"That you're unconcerned about the fact that Elijah is in love with you."

"Do you think I'm unconcerned about Elijah's feelings for me Julia?"

"I don't know what to think about you two sometimes."

"I just think that you have been through a lot and you are more concerned with what you need to do to make yourself happy is all."

"Gillie don't misunderstand me, there is nothing wrong with that."

"It's just that it can be more complicated when there is someone around that cares about you like Elijah does."

Soon Elijah's pickup truck made its way toward the house and Julia sat up in her seat.

"Chile we spoke him on up."

"Elijah gonna be happy to see you!"

Joshua and Elijah made it to the barn and began unloading their supplies from the work day. Josephine came out the side door of the house.

"Daddy's home, hey Auntie Gillie."

"Oh well look a there, I haven't seen Josie since I been here, where she come from?"

"Chile napping and as you can see I'm just the mama."

"She will turn on me in a minute, that chile loves her daddy and he spoils her rotten."

Gilda turned her attention back to Josephine and smiled as Joshua lifted his daughter up and gave her a big hug. Elijah continued lifting the heavy equipment from the truck. His strength was evident as Gilda observed the muscular frame that sent chills down her spine each time he was in her presence Elijah hadn't allowed his hair to grow any longer since he had cut it with Gilda several years ago. That silent statement in her room that day was one Gilda would never forget as long as she would live. As Elijah stepped onto the porch, Gilda could not understand how this man could make her feel as though she just met him every time she laid eyes on him. Elijah greeted them both and appeared more distant than usual toward Gilda. Joshua grabbed Josephine again.

"Go look in the truck Josie, daddy brought you something." Ecstatic about what the surprise could be she ran up to the truck.

"Good evening Joshua."

"Evening Gillie, It's good seeing you around these parts."

"Why thank you sir."

Gilda was listening to Joshua but had most of her attention on Elijah. He hadn't said two words as he leaned up against the truck with his arms folded watching Josie.

"Oh daddy thank you so very very much."

"Look mama." It was a brown baby rabbit.

"Goodness Joshua, you den brought that girl another animal to doctor on."

Not paying much attention to the comments of her mother Josephine ran up to her daddy and gave him a big hug and then up to Uncle Elijah. She pulled the front door wide open and headed through the house. Julia jumped while shaking her head.

"I den told that girl time and time again about letting that screen door slam like that."

Elijah made his way onto the porch and leaned up against one of the thick wooden pillars that he himself had made. Joshua continued sharing his day.

"We ran into Big Ted on the way home, he says Fisher planning on opening up that spot of his in a few weeks time."

Gilda rolled her eyes and said nothing, but Joshua wanted more information.

"Hey Gillie, he say you and that Dot Manchester gonna be working the floor, is that true?" Gilda was caught off guard. "Yeah that's true."

"I will be working, but I won't be working no floor." Elijah in his deep, but irritated voice finally spoke out.

"Well Miss Gilda, where will you be working?"

"Excuse me Mr. Mason, you have no right to speak to me in that tone of voice."

Elijah shot back.

"Oh now you are concerned with my tone of voice." Julia interrupted. "Joshua, why don't you and I go into the kitchen?"

"You can help me fix us all a nice bowl of Peach cobbler and check on our dinner."

"In a minute Julia."

Julia put her hands on her hips and gave Joshua a steady gaze. When he looked back at her, he knew that it was best to do what his wife had asked and he followed her inside. Gilda continued, but now she stood up with her hands on her hips.

"Like I said I won't be working no floor!"

"I'm gonna be a barmaid is all, I'll get tips, good tips."

"Is that what Fisher told you?"

"Yes he did, and I trust his word."

"Is there any reason that you could not tell me about this yourself."

"Tell you, Elijah I haven't seen you."

"I've been working."

"Well, my life don't stop because you working Elijah." Gilda then returned to the swing on the porch. She knew how Elijah felt. Visiting Fisher's Place was one thing, but working there was another.

"Well Mr. Mason, aren't you gonna come over and sit down next to me?"

Not saying a word Elijah went over and sat down next to Gilda.

"It looks like you been working hard today."

"Yeah, I have."

"I'm sorry Elijah for snapping at you."

"It wasn't like I was trying to hide it from you or anything."

"I haven't seen you and hardly ever home anymore since you guys finished working on Fisher's Place." Elijah knew she was right.

"Are you angry that I took the job?"

"You've made it quit clear that you're your own woman."

"I'm not about to say that I'm excited about you working for Fisher."

"I don't know why you decided to do what you're doing?"

"All I know is that for the past five years we have had a very complicated relationship."

"What do you mean complicated Elijah?"

"I mean you don't know what you want regarding us; you know how I feel about you Gillie!"

Gilda became defensive; instead of listening to Elijah's testimony she began to point fingers.

"Well we won't mention the new company you have been keeping lately."

"What?"

Elijah began to laugh out loud.

"Are you referring to Colleen?"

Even though he knew it to be true, she was only a distraction from the loneliness that he was feeling for Gilda.

"Yeah we are friends, but that is all Gillie."

"I am in no way attracted to Colleen."

"Well I hear she makes herself available often enough." Elijah could not believe what he was hearing.

"Is Miss Gilda jealous?"

What Elijah really wanted in his life for good was Gilda. He loved her high spirit and the passion that they shared when they were together and it still lingered deep in his soul. She had stolen his heart and her indecisiveness was tearing him apart. Gilda didn't know that the many job offers that he had taken out of town kept his mind off of her. However, now Elijah had gotten to a crossroad and could no longer live his life waiting. He would have her and make her his. He knew that it would be a challenge, but he also knew deep down she was a loving passionate and caring woman. He also knew Gilda deserved someone with enough patience to help her find that tender side of herself again.

"I don't want to argue with you Gillie."

"The decision you made was one that you thought was necessary."

At that moment as if she had been listening for her cue to return, Julia stepped out of the door with two bowls of peach cobbler and Joshua followed behind with two more bowls.

"Are you two finished with your little spat?" Gilda leaned over and kissed Elijah on the cheek.

"Yes ma'am."

"Hear man." Joshua passed his brother a bowl.

"Man, I don't know about you two." After dessert Julia and Joshua left the two of them on the porch.

"Well Mr. Mason, do you mind taking me home at all?" Still slightly tight faced Elijah agreed. Gilda hollered in the screen door.

"Julia, Elijah is gonna take me home." Julia came to the front door wiping her hands in her apron.

"I swear chile, now I see where Josie get that stuff from."

"Don't you want to stay for dinner?"

"Naw not tonight, I wanna be back in town before it gets late.

"Okay Gillie I will talk to you later." Josie pushed her face through the screen door.

"See you later Auntie Gillie." Gilda blew her a kiss and followed Elijah off the porch. They hopped into the truck and took off into town.

Chapter 5

The ride into town was a quiet one. Gilda had fallen to sleep on the journey. Elijah looked over at her and then began to think about the secret that he held from back home. After the tragedy, he and his brother were forced to leave their hometown in Charleston, South Carolina. All these years he had carried with him the story of his father and the family's hidden fortune. Elijah had never spoken to his brother about the story that was once told to him. Before he and Joshua left home their father told Elijah he would know when the time was right to have the talk with his brother. Afterward he would then return home for what belonged to them.

When they finally arrived at Gilda's Elijah pulled the truck slowly in front. Battle began barking and startled Gilda.

"Whew, I must've dozed off."

Gilda pulled off her shoes and jumped out of the car barefoot. She went to the fence and let Battle out, he began jumping with excitement because he had not seen Gilda most of the day. She then picked up his food and water pans.

"Get down boy, I'm gonna feed ya."

"Elijah you hungry, I got some leftovers from yesterdays dinner in the pantry?"

"Yeah, I'll come in and share with you."

It had been almost two months since Elijah had spent any quality time with Gilda and smiled at the thought of being with her. Even if he had eaten a full thanksgiving dinner, he would eat again just to be in her company this evening. Elijah admitted to himself long ago under the moonlight of many half built houses that it would be impossible to live life without her. He missed her laugh, he missed looking at her and stealing kisses that made her blush beyond recovery. Elijah sat down in the big chair and turned on the radio.

Elijah sat for a minute just observing Gilda's place. Nothing had changed since the last time he was there. Even the fresh smell of lavender still crept through the living room window. He closed his eyes and laid his head back thinking about Gilda, thinking about their life. The sound of Johnnie Mercer and his hit tune, "Lazy Bones" crept through the radio and made the moment for Elijah that more delightful. He wanted to feel this way all the time. Elijah not realizing he had fallen asleep awakened to Gilda's voice calling from the kitchen. Gilda had freshened up wearing a soft white cotton dress and her house slippers.

Elijah cleaned himself up and sat down to have his meal.

"Ummm Ki'Somma that was delicious."

Afterwards Gilda removed and washed the dishes. Elijah then pushed himself from the table and grabbed Gilda into his lap. She softly kissed him on the lips.

"Mr. Mason wouldn't you like to take a nice hot bath."

"Only if you give it to me."

"I wouldn't have it any other way!"

"Good Girl."

Gilda had anticipated the day he would return and she was happy inside. However, she also struggled to keep this happiness. These feelings were so real to her, but they only temporarily camouflaged the void she felt in her life. It was quite frustrating not knowing what that void was and it affected her relationship with the only man she had ever truly loved.

Gilda filled the huge porcelain tub half way with cool water from the iron pipe valve and added the hot water from the stove. She then added a generous amount of lavender foaming oil.

"There that should do it."

Elijah watched as she prepared his bath and began to slowly stroke the back of her neck with his hands.

"That dress you're wearing is quite lovely my Ki'Somma." Gilda's smiled inside from his touch.

The coldness that recently covered her heart from his departure quickly began to disappear.

"I missed you so much little lady." Gilda said nothing as she pulled Elijah close and gently placed her lips on his. Elijah responded with nothing less as he took hold of her with pure passion and returned to her kisses in abundance. He gently lifted her and she wrapped her legs around his waist. Both began kissing and caressing the other neither could cease enjoying the others touch.

"Oh you smell so good." He whispered in her ear. Gilda moaned as she unbuttoned the top buttons of her dress. Elijah was pleased with the passion that consumed the woman that taken is heart hostage and he didn't hesitate to give her what she desired the most, his touch. Both shared a part of themselves slowly softly as if time had stood still in that moment. Elijah only wanted to please her and he did it effortlessly, kissing and caressing her.

Gilda fantasized many times about the love she had for Elijah. Her imagination would take them off to far away lands like those found in Miss Ann's books in her Library. The Moroccan king and queen in love gazing over the dessert sands in the full light of the moon.

"That's just the beginning my Ki'Somma." Gilda opened her eyes as Elijah spoke softly while slowly putting her down and then buttoning all but the top button of her dress.

"The night is still truly young."

Gilda nodded in agreement while trying to get her composure.

"Hurry baby and get in the tub, before the water gets cold."

Elijah began removing his clothes. Now the sounds of Bert Lown and His Hotel Biltmore Orchestra played "Bye Bye Blues" was now playing on the radio. The melody along with the presence of the man she loved had given Gilda a sense of peace. She closed her eyes and swayed to the sound of the music as Elijah slid his large body deep into the bottom of the tub."

"Ki'Somma come here and talk to me." Gilda sat down on the small stool next to the large tub. The aroma of Gilda's herbal creations filled the air

"The water smells good Ki'Somma, calming."

"I thought you might like it, I made it just for you." Elijah could not keep his eyes off of Gilda.

"I missed your beautiful face."

"Many nights I sat up wondering what you were doing, wondering if you could feel me thinking about you."

"Elijah, I didn't know that I had such an impact on your life."

"You've been quite busy with your business and all, I didn't want to interfere."

"Ki'Somma, I want you to know nothing would have kept me from returning home to you."

Gilda admired Elijah, he was a self made man and that gave her so much respect for him. Gilda took the thick cotton cloth and began washing his back.

"It's something else I wanted to tell you Gillie."

"What is it baby?"

"Man, after this conversation it just don't seem proper, regardless how good it is."

"Elijah what is it, you got another job?"

"Yeah, I'm afraid so, and it's a big one in Atlanta." Gilda tried to hold back her disappointment.

"Oh that's wonderful."

'What is it, and when do you leave?"

"Sometime next week."

"I met a man by the name of M.C. Vanlandingham, he's a black doctor over in Atlanta. He told me about this very wealthy philanthropist from Europe named Dr. Solomon

Rudger. Apparently, he was quit impressed with his research on Syphilis.

Gilda could remember hearing her mother and the women that came by the hair shop talk about the nerve sickness.

"Well this Rudger fella's is funding him to open up a medical office in Atlanta."

"Imagine that, and it will have everything needed to serve the needs of the people." Gilda could see that Elijah was really excited about this project and she showed her support.

"Oh Elijah that is so wonderful, I am very happy for you."

"It's good to know, even with all the obstacles that are thrown our way the race is still moving forward one step at a time."

"You should be proud of yourself Elijah, I'm very proud of you."

"How long do you think it would take to complete the project?"

"Well let's see, I got to round the crew up, probably take Joshua and Ted up with me."

"Mr. Johnson's grandson Tyler been inquiring about learning the trade, probably take him, and some more young men in town."

"I'm thinking it would do them all some good to get out of the fields."

"I've taking them on a few small projects and they catch on pretty quickly."

"With all that and breaks in between I say it should be finished in about two to three months time."

"I will be back periodically though, you know Atlanta is no where from here at all."

"We don't need to raise a frame, it's a standing building all brick, but we will do renovations on the inside."

Gilda felt content that Elijah would be returning home periodically; however she knew that he still felt uncomfortable with the fact that she would be working down at Fishers place.

After giving him his bath, Gilda grabbed for the large towel behind the door. Elijah stood up in the tub and as the water fell swiftly down his manly physique, Gilda wrapped the towel around his waist.

"Ahh that felt good."

Gilda smiled.

"I'm sure it did."

"I think I will air dry to cool off."

The two retired back to the bedroom and Gilda stood in front of Elijah while he sat on the stool near the window. She looked out into the night as the breeze blew softly across her face.

"It is a beautiful night tonight."

"I love the smell of the fresh country air."

"Yeah you are right it is beautiful out there, reminds me of home."

"You miss home Elijah?"

"Yeah sometimes, but mostly memories of my mom and pops."

"I remember how pops told me stories of how he met my mother."

"He married her after the Civil War."

"Your father was in the Civil War?"

"Yep Union army, he was a runaway couldn't have been no more than sixteen or seventeen years old when he fled."

"Oh you must be proud, you never shared that with me."

"Yes I'm very proud of him."

"He told us many stories about the war."

"Mostly me though, Joshua was not really that interested."

"He was young and always out being mischievous with my cousin Jerry."

Gilda was quite surprised that after all these years Elijah had finally opened up more about his past. Many times she encouraged the conversation, but she would find him changing the subject each time and eventually she gave up altogether.

However, tonight there was something different about Elijah and Gilda took it as an open invitation.

"Well since you are in the mood, please tell me more about your mother Elijah."

"Her name was Nadi it means *wise* in the Algonquin language and she was beautiful."

Elijah shook his head and smiled while reminiscing.

"She never let us forget our heritage either."

"My father didn't have a family and had met my grandfather, my mom and her sister Kimi in South Carolina."

"He said when he seen my mom it was love at first sight and he never looked backed."

"Very much like with you Ki' Somma." Gilda began to blush as Elijah continued.

"My Grandfather, Black Eagle was from the country near the great Red Mountains out west, but after the British settlers came in the government pushed them off the land. I never knew my Grandmother she died of the smallpox before I was born."

"Grandfather was rebellious and set out to find a place that he could continue to raise his daughters the Blackfoot way, without any interruptions, so he settled near the coast ."

"That's how he met my dad."

"Grandfather taught me, Joshua, and my cousin Jerry a lot about being one with nature."

"He taught us about hunting and defending ourselves other ways besides using a shot gun."

"Who is Jerry?"

"He's my first cousin my aunt Kimi's son."

Elijah laughed. "You would get a real kick out of Jerry." Gilda didn't have the slightest idea why he was saying that, but knew that somehow she would find out one day.

"Those where some of the best days of my life up until the scarlet fever came."

"My mother was the first to go and then grandfather not long after."

"My father, he took it really hard."

"He was never the same after that."

"You know Gillie, I am going to have to return home soon, very soon."

"I have some unfinished business that I need to attend to."

"I never told you why we left."

Gilda could see the sadness as his thoughts left there space for a brief time.

"My father was an outspoken man and had a great deal of integrity, but to some of the white folks in town, well they considered him uppidity."

"After an altercation with a man by the name of Gray he used his switchblade to defend his life."

"I knew our lives would never be he same when he came home that evening with blood all over him."

"He gave me a small pouch and forced me and Joshua to leave in the dark of the night into the woods and told us to run and not look back."

"We ran until we couldn't run anymore and when we did look back we could see the house filled with flames and at that moment I knew I would never see my father again."

"I need to go and see about my fathers business."

"I've kept in contact with my cousin Jerry."

"Wanna make that trip before harvest."

She understood the feeling of losing the most important people in this life. Those that brought wisdom and the comfort that no matter what, things would be okay. Gilda again begin to unbutton her dress and softly she kissed his

Adrienne Lynn Rutherford

lips. This time Elijah didn't stop her. Gilda's only desire was to show the deep affection that she had for the man she loved so dearly. As he softly stroked the curves of her body, she returned the gestures with intimate kisses upon his lips. Elijah stood up and his towel fell to the floor. Now, exposed to Gilda was the only man that she had ever known. Gilda smiled as Elijah lifted her and gently placed her on the bed. He then laid by her side in his fullness.

Then slowly and passionately she stroked his manhood and his moans of pleasure gave Gilda chills. She had given her love to him unselfishly and tonight would be no different than the others. At that moment she didn't think about him leaving nor did she think about his return. Her thoughts were only about right here and now.

Elijah began gently removing her dress and to his surprise she was bare underneath.

"You are so very beautiful."

Gilda cunningly smiled as she closed his eyes while Elijah softly touched her with his strong yet gentle hands. The shapeliness of her body always seemed to entice Elijah to insurmountable heights of desire for her. She reminded him of the beautiful Songhai Empress that he'd heard of in oral stories of the matriarchs of his home town. Elijah always enjoyed relishing in the beauty of Gilda and her cocoa brown skin. This is what pleased him; after all she was his Ki'Somma.

Gilda moaned as he moved his large hands along her hips and thighs while he kissed her softly and tenderly. She took it all in, this pleasure from this man who loved her in return.

"I love you my Ki'Somma."

Elijah whispered in her ear as she slowly opened her thighs to reveal her essence. He continued slowly but tenderly to pursue the fruits of her garden and partake of its sweet nectar. Soon the tide of her love exploded in a roaring wave as she cried out. "Elijah, oh Elijah!!"

Tears began to fill her eyes as Elijah slowly filled her with his manhood. Through the night he made passionate love to her, giving her all that he had to give of himself.

As the morning came into their presence, they embraced one another looking out of the window as the sun crept up over the horizon. To Gilda this sunrise was more beautiful than any other. Neither wanted to leave the other as both wished that this moment could last forever.

****

Later that morning Gilda finished packing a lunch for Elijah. They still had not really discussed her decision to work at Fisher's Place so she made one last attempt to see if his thoughts had changed since yesterday.

"Elijah, you still haven't given me your spill about how you fill about me working at Fisher's place."

"Gillie, I have nothing to say about that."

"I know that you are your own woman, and we're not married."

"I won't attempt to stop you if that's what you want to know and if you wanna know if I approve, the answer to that is still no."

Gilda said nothing. She gave him the lunch she packed for him and kissed him on the cheek.

"Love you Elijah."

"I love you too."

She then watched as he got in the pick up and drove off.

Even though Gilda's mind was made up, she was relieved that Elijah was willing to respect her freedom to make the choice.

As Elijah made his way down the dirt road the sun had fully shown its face and the humidity was high. He pulled out his handkerchief and wiped his brow.

"It's gonna be hot one."

After speaking with Gilda last night Elijah was anxious to speak to his brother. His father had told him that he would know the time and now he would keep his promise to his father.

The Mason men had known their share of hard work in their young lives even with the small fortune buried under the willow tree in front of the house. Elijah hadn't touched it as often as he had liked, because he knew the consequences and he didn't want attention brought to him and his brother. Elijah was glad that Joshua had a wife like Julia; she was humble and had a good heart. However, Elijah's main concern now was how he would tell the story to his brother. It had been almost eight years since they left South Carolina. It always bothered him a great deal that his father had to face the poison of racial hatred alone.

Elijah thought about Joshua and how he vowed to never return to South Carolina. He reminisced about so many others back home and the injustices they also experienced just for trying to make a better life for their families.

Elijah pulled his truck up to the house and saw Joshua standing at the woodblock with his hands above his head flexed as he strongly laid the axe down in the thick piece of wood. Elijah got out and shut the door.

"Wussup brother."

"Hey wassup, listen I need to talk to you."

Joshua, looking at the seriousness on his brother's face, stopped his chores and walked over to Elijah, while wiping his brow with this forearm.

"Is it something wrong?"

"No, I just have some things I need to share with you is all."

Elijah paused and took a deep breath.

"Well I don't know how to tell you, but to just tell you how Pop told me."

"I just want you to know I did what I did to protect the both of us, that's how Pop wanted it." Joshua didn't say a word; he only listened as Elijah continued. Joshua worried if something happened to someone back home, especially Jerry. The letters would only come every once and a while, discreetly addressed to Mr. Payton's home. Elijah responded only by stating that one day he would return to reclaim what was theirs. Both men retired to the shade under the tall tree in front of the house.

"Joshua, we left home at a young age, and we have done pretty well for ourselves in a short length of time."

"I was figuring that you have proved yourself time and time again since we have been here in Culloden."

"So my brother today is the day that I share some things with you." Joshua continued to listen attentively.

"Some of the things that Pop wanted me to keep."

"I feel like it should be told now because we have some things to do back home."

"What do you mean we, I told you Elijah I'm not never going back there."

"Joshua once I tell you what I need to tell you the decision is purely yours."

"I will tell you, I must go back home."

"Elijah where are you going with all of this."

"Okay, let me start from the beginning."

"You know how pop was a runaway and fought for the Union Army right?"

"Right."

"Well, while the war was coming to a close pops met a young white union solider named Fredrick Keeley."

"Mr. Keeley, he was a northern man from Massachusetts and he came from a very wealthy family. He didn't have to join the union because his family was rich, but this man felt he needed to contribute to the history of this country. Now because the army was segregated, there was not much interaction between black and white soldiers, even in the Union Army unless it was in passing. This pattern soon ended along the Mississippi River just outside of Mississippi.

Many men were killed and others taken and held prisoner by the Confederate Army."

"Some how Pop and this here man Keeley managed to get away. The two of them fled through the woods and into the swamp lands. They lived there for almost two weeks eating what they could find. Pop said they made the decision to lay low until it was safe."

"While they were attempting to find their way out of enemy territory the two came across a large plantation. It had been practically destroyed by the confederate soldiers who preyed even on their own because of the starvation and greed they faced in there own cavalries. He and Mr. Keeley went up to the huge deserted plantation house and he said it was larger than most that he had ever seen. The door was wide open and they yelled inside but nobody responded. Well they both decided to go into the house. He said it was really roomy with huge glass chandeliers, but the house had been ransacked and broken glass was everywhere. The furniture had been destroyed, and the kitchen had been completely wiped out."

"Pop said they knew they couldn't stay there long because it would only be a matter of time before the confederate army would return. He told me they picked up the thick wooden legs of a dining room chair and began roaming through the house for any signs of life and they did hear a sound, but it was very vague to the ear."

Knowing how keen their father's senses were both brothers begin to laugh. Elijah then continued.

"Pop and this Mr. Keeley went into the kitchen back to back, prepared to hit the first thing that would move. Then they heard the sound again, and noticed it was coming from behind a door. Pop said he opened the door and looked down the narrow wooden steps into nothing but darkness. They heard the sound again, but this time it was much clearer."

"*Help me, help me.*"

He said Keeley spoke to the voice down the stairs. *"Who are you?"*

"The name is O' Rielly, I am shot they left me hear to die in my own house."

"Please help me Sir."

"I have gold, anything that you want you can have it, just please help me out of this cellar."

"I don't want to die, not like this."

"Pop said they both looked at each other and one behind the other with papa in the front and Keeley covering his back they went into the cellar. He said that was the mustiest cellar he had ever been in, and the cob webs were thick as yarn."

"Here sir, I'm over here."

"So, they lifted him up on his feet and each took an arm and took him back up the stairs. He had been shot in the side, and pop said he had lost a lot of blood and he thanked them both. He was a short small framed man and he told them that his family was from Ireland."

"Pop told me he couldn't see the man having the nerve to use a whip on a horse let alone a slave, but the man wanted to show his gratitude to them both. He asked them to carry him out back behind the huge house and they helped him as he struggled to breathe. With their help he struggled and directed them to the stable house. There was one old horse left in a stable and he asked us to help him to get to it. Once he reached it his legs gave and he fell to his knees."

"All of a sudden, Pop said he started crying and just apologizing for everything that his brother, his father, and his grandfather before them had done to the African people."

"He told them that he always despised slavery.

"His brother had died of pneumonia before the war and he hadn't the heart to force the slaves to stay."

"Pop said Keeley asked him if he or his brother had any children and told them that he and his brother had taken two African women as mistresses not very long ago."

They had given each of them three children, but after his brother died he sent them both away with their Freedom papers and told them not to stop until they reached Canada."

Elijah and Joshua was suddenly distracted by the sound of Julia's voice *"Hey, you two guys hungry?"* They both responded in unison. *"No ma'am."*

Joshua then turned back to his older brother as they sat with their legs stretched comfortably in the grass like teenage boys. Joshua listened and waited patiently while still trying to figure out where Elijah was going with his story. He now was feeling a bit envious of his older brother, because at the time he hadn't sat long enough to hear such stories from his father. However, Joshua always knew Elijah had always been a better listener than he or Jerry and that made him a far better story teller.

"Where was I?"

Joshua reminded him.

"Oh yeah, so papa said this man took them inside the stable where the horse was and told them they could have the horse. He told Pop to pull the horse out of the stable, and the man struggled to make his way inside. He pushed all the hay to one side and underneath it laid a small wooden door. O'Rielly then tugged on it as hard as he could. Keeley asked the man to step aside and pulled the cellar door open. When it finally was opened Pops said he couldn't believe his eyes."

Elijah laughed aloud when he saw that Joshua's eyes had gotten wider, anticipating the next words to come out of his mouth."

"GOLD?"

"Did you say gold?"

Elijah nodded his head and suddenly all kinds of questions began running through Joshua's head. He couldn't get his thoughts together and his mind was racing.

"What happened then Elijah?"

"Well that old man gave it to the both of them, and told them it was all he had left that the confederate army didn't take. He told them he'd rather see it go to good folk than to let them find it. "Pop said he died right there and him and Keeley buried him and loaded the bags onto the horse and guiding it back into the swamps."

"Pop said he never been back to that place again.

"Soon after, the confederates as you know did lose the war."

"The funny thing is they were so preoccupied with salvaging anything of wealth, Pop said he and Keeley were able to make their way back across enemy lines"

"Pop said that was one of the saddest yet joyful times of his life, seeing so many slaves roaming the country side."

"He said some looked confused with no direction at all, while others moved faithfully with only a desire to make it north."

"Well eventually, he and Keeley found an area just outside of Charleston South Carolina."

"Pop and Fredrick spilt a sac and buried the rest."

"He and Fredrick returned to their regiments in silence and continued their duties, but later on Pops got word that Keeley was sent home with pneumonia.".

"When the war ended the United States government was kind enough to allow Union Soldier's, both black and white the opportunity to purchase land."

"Pop went back to South Carolina and staked a claim on the same land that he and old Fredrick Keeley had buried the gold coins."

Joshua was stunned he could hardly speak and he was almost afraid to ask the really big question, but he did.

"Where is the gold now brother?"

"Is it still there?"

"Well pop had spent some of it over the years, but at the same time he had to be very careful because he didn't want to draw attention to himself."

"You telling me we rich?"

"Something like that brother."

"You see, sometimes It's hard for white folks to see black folks doing good and that could be a dangerous thing for black folk, sometimes even death."

"You seen that back home for yourself."

"So pops wanted to be careful?"

"Yep, he built a home on that land and farmed it and used the gold only when it was absolutely necessary."

"Before we left, pop went into the floor board in the kitchen and pulled out an old black wool satchel shook it, and gave it to me."

"It's been buried here under the tree since."

"I didn't tell you because pops said not to."

I didn't understand myself, but he told me I would know when the time was right."

"I hope you have no ill feelings for what I have done."

Joshua looked at his brother.

"Brother how could I be angry with you?"

"You did what pops asked and I have to respect that."

"I would have done the same thing."

Joshua then laughed.

"Actually I don't know if I could have kept it this long." Elijah shook his head.

"Elijah, you know, I always wondered how we seemed to always make ends meet, no matter what."

"Shoot, I have no reason to be angry with you."

Afterwards, the brothers finally decided to take Julia up on her offer and went inside for dinner.

Chapter 6

It had been two weeks since Gilda and Elijah shared their love for one another. He was now down in Atlanta working on his project. Gilda met Battle at the front door because he was barking more than usual and she wanted to see what the commotion was all about. She stepped out on the front porch as two large shipping trucks rode past her little white house. She noticed Fisher was following behind them in a shiny black convertible with two other men. Gilda had no idea what Fisher was up to now. She did know that the two men he was with sure weren't from Culloden. Fisher shouted at the top of his voice while waving his hand at Gilda.

"It's here Gillie, come on down to my place."

Gilda for the past week had been thinking about her new adventure. She had never been a barmaid, but it seemed to sound quite exciting to her. Fisher had explained that she would be responsible for keeping up with the whiskey inventory, so she thought she might as well get dressed and go on over.

Dot on the other hand had been preparing in another way for her newfound career at Fisher's Place. She had stopped by Gilda's a couple of days ago just ranting and raving. Dot talked none stop as Gilda struggled through her thick hair. Dot had contacted a couple of lady friends from back home, Martha Porter and Jeanine Black .These young ladies also came down to get in on the action. Fisher told her he needed a few more dancers and Dot kept her promise. When the ladies arrived in Culloden, Dot took them straight to Gilda's. She couldn't stop bragging on and on about how Gilda was able to manage her intolerable head of hair. Gilda displayed her talents on both ladies and they were very pleased.

The ladies had been in Colluden for almost a month now. Martha, and Jeanine had grew up in a small town in Louisiana with Dot and it was obvious to Gilda neither of them were no strangers to the life.

The ladies had spent a lot of time in speak easy's and brothels most of their lives down in Louisiana's *Big Easy*.

Fisher had been waiting all his life to own his own business. However, he hadn't thought about the dark side that came with his self proclaimed success.

To Fisher, things were starting to look up for him. Big Paulie had been both a father and a friend, giving him opportunities that he otherwise would have never had. The ideal of a white man convincing Fisher that people were people no matter what color allowed him to finally see a small glimpse of good in the world.

Big Paulie spent a lot of time sharing his political views with Fisher. He felt the racial tension in America was due solely to the paranoia of those with the psychological need to feel superior. That need created a fear of losing what they had acquired because of their inhumane tactics of free slave labor and the unnecessary slaughtering of the natives to acquire land. He would always say: *"Fisher always remember it's all economics."*

He also explained to Fisher that many of the immigrants that came later on to the country shortly after it became a union took on this discriminatory ideology toward Blacks and Native Americans in order to be accepted by those who had the political influence that controlled the U.S. Immigration Department. For once in his life Fisher was able to put things into a world perspective. He had been given a subservient view all his life that crippled his self esteem. Big Paulie had taught him a lot and Fisher was grateful.

The driver of the truck pushed the dolly stacked with the crates of Whiskey inside the front door.

"Eh, Big Ted, show him where to stash the product."

Big Ted led the man down the hallway into the storage area. The man looked around as he observed the fine work done inside the place and he looked on amazed.

"Is that redwood?"

"Yes sir straight from California."

"I bet that cost a pretty penny."

"Yes suh, Fisher only get's the best."

"When y'all opening up?"

"This Saturday's the grand opening."

"Well I guess we may have to hang around for a spell."

The two men then returned to the front entrance as the other driver continued to roll in the goods. Big Paulie and Fisher sat on redwood stools in front of the bar. Big Paulie took a look around the a two story building, with its thick log railings that lined to entire second floor. There where chairs and tables all made of wood, they sat upstairs along the railings and down below in front of a small dance floor. In the corner near the entrance Fisher had purchased a grand piano it was shiny, black and waiting to be played.

"Things look really good Fisher, I'm gonna have to send Joey down to check it out, you did good son."

"You know Fisher; we couldn't get away with something like this up in Detroit."

"It wouldn't have been worth the trouble, too many eyes and ears, too many payoffs."

"Fisher, so you got to be discreet and that means no unnecessary trouble."

"You should do well, you may want to consider building some lodging quarters after a while, you know like a bed and breakfast."

"You may get a few folks from out of town once word gets out."

Fisher scratched his head.

"You know Paulie, that sounds like a good idea."

"Yeah I might even want to come down for a spell and see how things are going myself Fisher."

Both men began to laugh. However, Fisher knew better, Big Paulie was not one for crowds and especially those of a speak easy. He was a very inconspicuous man and because of this he was able to become a very wealthy man investing in businesses in Detroit, Chicago, Louisiana, and now Culloden Georgia. Big Paulie had lots of friends and Fisher was tied into it all.

"Hey and Fisher, don't worry about that sheriff, I got him covered."

"He won't be coming around here and neither will any of his back wood cronies."

"It didn't take much for him; these southern crooked lawmen are a lot easier to please when it comes to money."

Gilda walked into the door only moments later. She had on a white short sleeved shirt tied in the front and a pair of dark blue knee pants. Gilda came in spinning around looking up and then down toward Fisher and Paulie.

"This is Beautiful." Gilda knew that Joshua and Elijah were talented, but this piece of work she could not believe her eyes.

"I love it Fisher, you guys, Oh my goodness, did a great job."

"Fisher it is magnificent."

"Fisher these tables need place mats, lanterns, and chair cushions."

"We can get Miss Ann and Mrs. Johnson to do that."

"Over there you need some curtains for the windows." Gilda pointed to the stage area.

"No stage is quite a stage unless it has curtains as well, that is a very tall ceiling Fisher, but we'll figure out something."

"Gillie don't worry about that now, come over here I want you to meet somebody."

Gilda feeling guilty about her manners made her way over to the two men.

"Gillie this here is Big Paulie, he is the man that helped me get all of this together."

"How do you do Mr. Paulie."

"Oh Paulie's just fine, Gilda is it."

"Yes and thank you sir."

"Well fine." Big Paulie looked over at Fisher.

"Miss Gilda here is a very stunning young lady Fisher."

"Yes, I have been trying to catch her eye all my life."

Gilda hit him on the shoulder. Fisher rubbed his shoulder and smiled.

"Paulie, Gillie here is our bartender for the place."

"Wise choice Fisher, you need a beautiful woman behind the bar it will keep the men folk coming."

Fisher turned his attention back to Gilda.

"Gillie, go on behind the bar and get yourself acquainted to your space."

Gilda started for the bar and then turned around with a look of concern on her face.

"Fisher this is a really nice place, but what are you gonna do about Sherriff Bradford?"

"You know as well as I do they can be in some evil ways."

Paulie spoke up in a voice of confidence.

"Pretty lady there is no need for you to worry yourself about such things, all you need to do is keep being as pretty as you are and keep smiling leave the sheriff up to us."

Gilda paused a moment, nodded her head and changed the subject.

"That sure is a beautiful piano Fisher."

"Yeah I'm gonna go pick up Blind Jake an ole friend of the family, he will be playing for us and I'm gonna try and get some singers over from Alabama too!"

Fisher's place looked as if it could hold about 200 people or more. There was a brick oven and fireplace built into the kitchen and a back door that led out into the back of the building Elijah and Joshua had added two indoor bathrooms with flushing toilets and two sinks with running water thanks to the instruction of Uncle Rufus. Outback was a water pump and a small porch with a picnic table to match. There was also an open window from the kitchen to the back of the bar area for orders to be taken and delivered directly.

"Fisher who else did you hire to work for you?"

Fisher knowing how Gilda would respond hesitated for a minute.

"Well uhm lets see."

"Fisher, you already have a barmaid and dancers and you said you got entertainment on the way."

"Who's waiting tables and cooking in the kitchen?"

"I got me a waitress."

"Who Fisher?"

"Colleen."

"Colleen Grant?"

"Yep."

Amused Gilda continued. "How did you pull that off?"

Fisher pulled on his suspenders the way he does when he is feeling really good about himself.

"Well you knew she wasn't gonna have you working up in the place and she wasn't working here."

Gilda put her hands on her hips.

"How did she know I was working here Fisher?"

"Well I kinda told her."

"I seen her and her sister Connie at Johnson's Market while I was picking up some items and she approached me and I couldn't resist."

"Po, you sure are one slickster." Fisher began to laugh.

"Well sweetie a man's gotta do what a man's gotta do."

"I am the popular man in town these days you know!"

Fisher gave Gilda a big smile. Gilda thought she had just about heard it all until now.

"Colleen Grant the most holy and messiest woman in Culloden working in a Speak Easy."

Gilda knew that she was going to have to straighten her out sooner or later and sooner would be better than later she thought. Gilda spent most of the day talking with Fisher and becoming familiar with the liquor inventory, their names and how they would be served thanks to Big Paulie.

The inventory consisted of down home moonshine made right in Culloden and all types of Canadian liquor smuggled in via Detroit, as well as beer which was brewed in factories just outside of Chicago. Gilda stacked the bar and began preparing for opening day. She sent some of the young fellas from around town that Fisher had hired out back to the water pump to clean the glasses to be used at the bar. As Gilda prepared her work area she thought about Elijah. She wondered what he had been doing the past couple of weeks. He had promised to write but she had not received a word yet. Joshua had joined him the first week to help him instruct the younger men in most of the work.

After a full day of organizing and preparing for the grand opening, Gilda said her goodbyes to Fisher and Big Paulie. Big Ted offered to take her home and she accepted without hesitation. It had been an exhausting day and she was really not in the mood for the long trek back into town. Once home she thanked Ted and went to the mailbox, Battle as usual was waiting for her in anticipation. Gilda opened the gate to let him out and flipped through the mail and to her surprise Elijah had written her. She held the envelope to her heart then waved to Ted and quickly went into the house. Once settled in her grandmother's favorite big chair she anxiously opened and read the letter:

My Dear Ki'somma,

I know that it has been a while since you heard from me, I want you to know that you are in my thoughts and my heart each and everyday. The city of Atlanta is beautiful these days. The black community is really working hard to make things happen. There are a lot of professional

people here doctors, lawyers, teachers, and nurses of the sort. All graduates from the black colleges. Never have I seen such progress in so little time. The building is coming along fine. The young men are doing well in their training and have even added some of their own personal artistic talents to the project. I do not mind, it is giving them a since of self- confidence something that they can not get as easily in the fields. I do have to sometimes keep them focused, due to the distraction of the young girls in the city that attend the college nearby. Mr. Rudger seems very impressed with the progress and it looks like we will be finished sooner than expected. I expect to be home in about two weeks time. I have decided that this will probably be the last project I attempt to complete for a long while. I need to start getting my life in order and I would very much like you to share it with me.
Please think about it
Love Elijah.

Gilda sat in the chair for a long while and she was a little disappointed that she would not see Elijah for another two weeks. Nevertheless, she was happy to know that once this job was completed he would be returning home. The letter sent chills through her as she read every word. She imagined him speaking the words from his letter directly to her face to face. She imagined his handsome face and his masculine voice giving her his undivided attention. She could see his beautiful dreamy eyes and his luscious lips as they always compelled her to draw near him each time she laid eyes on him. She had realized that she truly missed his presence and now noticed that she was lonely without him. Even with the kind thoughts and words that Elijah had to offer, working at Fisher's Place made it a lot easier for her to accept the distance between her and the man that she loved so dearly.

Chapter 7

Finally, the night had come. Folks from all over town were talking about Fisher's Place and they came in their finest. Dot, Martha, and Jeanine had prepared themselves for weeks. They rehearsed what they thought was the most fantastic shake dancing routine ever seen in that part of the south. Gilda also prepared herself along with Fisher as well. Fisher surprised both her and Colleen with beautiful barmaid and waitress outfits all the way from New York City. Gilda wore a white sleeveless shirt embroidered with beautiful beads and pearls a black skirt that barely touched the knee, and two pair of shinny black slippers made especially for walking the soft cushion on the floor behind the bar. Colleen wore a white sleeveless tuxedo satin shirt with a black bow tie and the same comfortable shoes. Big Ted even got a few suits from New York City special ordered by Big Paulie. Gilda thought her outfits were far too beautiful for serving drinks, but Fisher insisted.

Before the doors opened, Fisher came up to Gilda behind the bar with a big box wrapped in what she thought was the most beautiful gift wrapping she had ever seen. "What is this Fisher?"

"Open it up and see."

Gilda took the box and began tediously opening the gift.

"Woman would you please just open that there box, It's only paper." Gilda smiled and then swiftly tore the paper off the box. She slowly opened it up and as her eyes grew wider Fisher began to smile. Inside the box were the most beautifully handmade head pieces she had ever seen, they consisted of pearls and other shiny ornaments including beads, and glass rhinestones. Gilda picked up each.

"These are beautiful Fisher."

"I am glad you like them, I figured they would give that beautiful short hair of yours a little extra style."

"They wear those up in Harlem, New York."

Inside were two more boxes much smaller than the first.

"Open em up girl!"

Gilda continued opening her gifts inside the first was a pair of beautiful pearl earrings. "Oh Fisher." she then opened the other and was a beautiful pearl broach

"How much were these Fisher?"

"They look awfully expensive."

"Fisher, you did not have to do this for me."

"Don't worry about it, you are worth each and every one of them Gillie."

"It's to show my appreciation for you throughout the years."

"As much as I love you, I know your heart belongs to another, but I need you to know how much you still mean to me."

Gilda teary eyed, leaned over the bar, and placed a kiss on Fishers cheek.

"Thank you Fisher so very much and I do love you too; you will always have a very special place in my heart." Fisher smiled.

"Okay, okay, enough of the mushy stuff just pick out one of dem their head pieces, put dem pearls on and get to work."

Fisher clapped his hands together as he spoke aloud to everyone in the place.

"Ladies and gentleman, this is what we have been waiting for."

"Let's make this here speak easy the talk of the South you hear."

Everyone shouted their responses and was amazed at the kindness Fisher had displayed. He had left no rock unturned in his attempt to please his employees. There was a very beautiful women's dressing room, but it was for all the ladies to use it had three vanity mirror sets as well as a couch, end tables and a full length mirror. While Big Ted looked like a million dollars at the front entrance. Gilda thought he looked good greeting the customers as they entered.

Fisher also asked Ms. King to cook in the kitchen, she was known throughout the town for her cooking. She had once owned a small restaurant that specialized in seafood and created her own seasonings, but after her husband died she gave up cooking for the public. After many visits and escorts to Sunday church service, Fisher was able to talk her into working for him. For tonight she prepared smothered catfish and cabbage; she also had chicken, Clam Chowder gumbo and also a fine southern tossed salad. Things were looking up for Fisher's Place. With the help from a few of the local men, Fisher threw up a two story cabin out back. The piano player Blind Jake came in the back hallway, tapping his stick along the baseboards ranting and raving about the piano being out of tune. Fisher had not even thought about getting that fine piano he bought tuned, so he and Jake began exchanging words back and forth.

"Just wait one minute Jake, I've had just about enough."

"I'm only one man and if you want to play in this here place, you will respect me you hear?"

"I will not have anybody working for me thinking they can say what they want in here." Fisher then turned and addressed the rest of the crew.

"Ya'll hear me?"

"I'm talkin to everybody, there's gonna be mutual respect around here."

"We all got a job to do, and that means no finger pointing."

"If problems occur, we will just solve them and keep it movin."

Everybody nodded in agreement. Fisher looked over at the other Piano Player.

"Hey Cleofis, do you know how to tune this damn piano?"

"Yes I do suh."

"Well friend, let's get this here piano tuned then."

Both men shook hands and everyone returned to their duties. Gilda had not spoken to Colleen since she had arrived that evening. Nevertheless, Colleen was anxiously waiting to approach Gilda at the bar. "Hello Gilda."

Gilda looked up into the mirror and saw Colleen's reflection. Gilda never had anything to say to Colleen, especially after all the gossip both her and her mother had stirred up about her family all these years.

"What is it Colleen?"

Gilda turned around to face her, irritated by the sight of her.

"I wanted to talk to you, and I will be frank."

"I'm sure that you don't want to bother yourself with Elijah, after all you have been putting him off for the past five years maybe even longer."

"I'm just saying that to say, if you don't want him step aside and allow a real woman to appreciate him for the real man that he is."

Gilda spent the past couple of days preparing for such an encounter with Colleen and she promised herself that she would not get angry at any stupid thing that would come out of her mouth. Colleen was known for speaking before she thought out anything. Gilda took a slow deep breath.

"My, My My seems to me you barking up the wrong tree."

"This here woman ain't got no ball and chain on Elijah, so if you want him take him."

"Let's see just how "real" you really are."

"Now if you excuse me I have things to do." Colleen turned red in the face while Gilda left her standing at the bar.

It had been awhile since she had seen Dot and Martha; they should have been out by now. She checked the kitchen and then went to the dressing room and opened the door. Gilda was speechless as she walked in because she couldn't believe her eyes. Martha sat on the couch nodding back and forth as if she was struggling to stay awake. Dot was on the stool at the vanity mirror with a piece of cloth tied around her arm. She turned around and noticed Gilda standing with the door wide open.

"Damn chile, don't you know how to knock when you come to a closed door?"

Gilda snapped back.

"This room ain't just yours Dot it's for all of us to use."

"Well, just don't stand there, can you shut it please." Gilda slowly closed the door.

"What are you doing Dot, and what the hell is wrong with Martha she sick?"

"Awww she alright, she just got her a little fix is all, she'll be just fine in a minute." Dot looked over at Gilda and smiled.

"Oh I keep forgetting you just a little ole county girl."

Gilda felt offended.

"What the hell is that suppose to mean Dot?"

"I may be a country girl, but I ain't no fool."

"I do know what that is and I know that it makes you sick, and can kill you."

Heroin had affected the lives of many dancers as well as singers and musicians during the prohibition era. Sometimes delivering a devastating blow to many careers ending in addiction and even death.

However, Dot paid Gilda no attention as she threw back the red curly locks and gently injected the needle into the crease of her arm. Gilda couldn't believe what she was seeing. She wouldn't have thought Dot could be so vulnerable to the world. It saddened her deeply to see these young beautiful women using heroin and heading down a road of self-destruction.

Gilda heard about Heroin from Miss Minnie. She shared her story about Paul Payton, the love of her young life while living in New York City. They were to travel the world performing together, but he could not tame his urge for the drug. The addiction had eventually killed him and left her with a broken heart.

"Dot you playing with death chile."

"Oh stop trying to be some kind of saint, this ain't got nothing to do with you Gillie."

"Do us all a favor and mind yo business, shoot you blowing my high."

"Oh is that what that stuff does to you Dot, have you talking all crazy."

Dot then spoke again this time slurring her words."

"Gillie, I'm sorry for yelling imma a little sick right now, don't mind me you hear?"

"Everything is fine, really, don't worry your little head about us."

"Just give me a minute and I will be good as new you'll see."

Gilda shook her head as she watched her friend nod in and out of consciousness. Dot looked back up at Gilda.

"We all gotta die one day, might as well die feeling good."

She began to smile as she tried to get out of her seat and Gilda watched her as she moved in slow motion. Dot finally managed to make it to the couch and flopped down next to Martha. She then floated off. Gilda left out the room shaking her head and slamming the door behind her. Drinking was one thing, but drugs were another. Gilda made a vow to herself that night she would concentrate on doing her job, watching after Fisher, and minding her own business. It was obvious that she would have to pay more attention to her surroundings after seeing what she seen tonight. If Fisher's Place attracted such things as drugs, other demons were sure to follow and she knew she would eventually have to get Fisher out of trouble.

Later that evening the moon was full and the doors opened to Fishers Place. It was the new hot spot and people drove in for miles to hear the sweet sounds of the blues and to taste the best kept secret around. There was good food and plenty of music and dancing.

The women and men were on the floor doing their thing and most could not resist giving their own impression of the shake dancing routine that Martha and Dot had performed through out the night. The dance however went to Jeanine who arrived later that night; she worked the floor and drove the men folk wild. Fisher could not believe his eyes as he watched Jeanine work the room. She had them hypnotized as she swayed her hips back and forth like that of an Arabian Princess. After her performance she received a standing ovation not from just the men but the women as well, this dance was not that of a typical shake dancer and it fascinated Fisher a lot.

Meanwhile Gilda stood behind the bar serving drinks and taking orders from Colleen for food. As she made drinks for Colleen she paid her no mind, it was too busy in the place to be concerned with Colleen and her personal issues. Fisher was walking around checking everything to make sure people were happy, he was a good host. His dream had finally turned into reality, he was a proud entrepreneur.

The next morning Gilda slept in, she was exhausted and just too tired to get up early. Battle sat at Gilda's bedside moaning. She awoke and realized that it was way past noon. She hadn't left Fishers until three in the morning. She slowly dragged out the bed and let Battle into the yard. Not long after there was a knock on front door. She went to the front room window and peeked through the curtain. It was Josie, and Julia was making her way from the truck toward the front porch. Gilda surprised opened the door.

"Hello Aunt Gillie."

"Hello baby."

Josie then grabbed Gilda around the waist and gave her a hug, then she ran out back.

"Don't' you break nothing you hear." Julia yelled out as she looked over Gilda.

"Chile you look a mess." Gilda stood at the door as Julia came into the house.

"Is that what the night life does to you."

"How did it go?"

Gilda smiled as she reminisced.

"Chile I had a ball."

"Met a lot of people from up north and out west."

"I don't know what Fisher was doing when he left here, but what ever it was it sure made him awfully popular."

"So did you make the right choice, taking the barmaid over the dancing job?"

"Well they both pay pretty decent, I suppose so."

"I made Forty dollars in tips last night." Julia was impressed "You did?"

"Yep, you should have seen me chile serving them drinks running from one end of that bar to the next."

"The fellas were tipping pretty good and even some of the ladies too."

"They told me about some really fancy places in Tennessee, Chicago, and Detroit."

"Some of the fella's even said I was the prettiest thing that they had seen, and I would be swimming in the money if I would come to Tennessee."

"Chile, you should have seen Fisher."

Gilda begin stomping around the living room holding on to her imaginary suspenders imitating Fisher's demeanor throughout the night.

"Chile he was walking around that place like a proud peacock greeting and socializing with all the folk."

Julia laughed. "So everything worked out then?"

"Well yes and no."

"What do you mean by that Gillie?"

"Last night I walked in on Dot and Martha in the dressing room."

"It was really ackward, because Dot wasn't acting like herself, real strange you know?"

"Martha was sitting on the couch nodding."

"I asked Dot what was wrong with her, she was fussing about busting in without knocking, and I told her that we share that room."

"I stood there and Dot, she shot up right there in front of me."

Julia covered her mouth in surprise.

"What!"

"Julia, I was so disappointed in her, but I didn't tell Fisher because I didn't wanna ruin his night."

"I thought she was smarter than that."

Julia shook her head.

"Yeah Gillie they got a problem alright, lord we just gotta pray for them."

"If that's what the city life is about, I reckon I will be staying right here in the country."

I don't want my chile growing up around nothing like that."

"That is just awful Gillie!"

Gilda quickly changed the subject and then pulled out the gifts that Fisher had given her. Julia was amazed at the detail of the ornaments. They both played in the mirror as they did when they were younger posing with the beautiful head pieces.

"You know Julia, Elijah say that Atlanta ain't all that bad though."

"He says black folks are progressing just fine, wouldn't you want to live somewhere they have paved roads to ride on for a change?"

"I like these dirt roads just fine, thank you very much."

"Aw chile come on just imagine it."

"Don't you want Josie to go to a good school?"

"Mrs. Johnson does just fine with the kids here in Culloden."

"I know Joshua told you about all those nice colleges they got up there in Atlanta."

"Yes he has, but I still say I like it fine right here." Gilda saw that Julia would not budge, so she changed the subject.

"Oh, I saw Colleen."

"You did, what happened?"

"Well naturally she had some old off the wall stuff to say, but I put her in her place."

Julia still stuck on the situation with Dot and Martha continued to question Gilda.

"I think you should tell Fisher about Dot and Martha."

"What if he doesn't know Gillie?" Gilda hunched her shoulders.

"What if he does, and anyway what am I suppose to say?"

"Hey Fisher you know your only shake dancers using."

"I have nothing else to say about that, I spoke my peace and closed the door."

"If he doesn't know, he will find out sooner or later."

"Besides, guess who had to stay over to help Fisher count up the money."

"You?"

"Yes, and I had to set up the bookkeeping."

"I really believe between him and Big Ted they're going to need all the help that they can get to keep things together."

"Julia, I can see this whole business thing turning into something much bigger than the both of them can handle."

Julia shook her head, she knew Gilda was probably right.

"Joshua sent a wire home today, just picked it up from Mr. Johnson's." Julia had been saving the real reason she came by to see Gilda.

"He said they had some problems." The look on Julia's face made Gilda uncomfortable.

"Everything is alright isn't it?"

"Yes and no."

"Elijah is fine, it's just that Dr. Rudger the gentleman that was funding the project passed away a few days ago. It was all of a sudden and his family is saying that they have no intentions on finishing the project."

"What!"

"Yeah, they shut the construction down and Elijah got pretty upset with his son."

"The cops came and he had to spend the night in jail, Dr. Vandlandingham bailed him out and he will go to court in the morning."

"He was lucky Gillie; it could have been a lot worse."

Gilda could not believe what she was hearing, just after she had read his letter. She knew how excited Elijah was about the project and now it had come to a complete stop. To him it was a very positive thing that he was doing.

"Well is Mr. Rudger son gonna get away with it."

"It all depends; they're waiting for the reading of the will."

"If there is anything there that states Dr. Vandlandingham is to receive some type of financial gift then they will finish the project, otherwise their hands are tied."

"Joshua said he would keep in touch about what's going on."

"That is the most awful thing Julia."

Gilda thought about the boys from town that Elijah took with him to do the work, she was sure they were disappointed as well.

****

The next two years would be a success for Fisher; he had folks from as far as Missouri to enjoy the entertainment of Fisher's Place. The money had gotten so good that he was able to hire Elijah and Joshua along with some of the young men in the town to complete a two story lodge. It had six rooms three on the first floor and three on the second floor.

Just as Fisher had anticipated word spread and with the support of his friends from up North they were coming in droves to check out the southern spot near the gulf. Performers were coming from all over the south and some parts of the north to hear and sing the sweet songs of the ole delta Blues. These people brought with them their fancy cars, fancy clothes and also some bad habits of the Speak Easy culture. Dot was right in the center of it all as she mingled with customers and enjoyed all the luxuries of being an in-house performer. The men fell to her feet as they spoiled her and supplied her habit.

Since the town was so small many people who visited Fisher's Place had began to lodge in neighboring towns. Gilda in all the excitement would be entertaining the customers from these far off places at the bar. She listened attentively to the stories they told about the big cities and the wonderful opportunities they had for black folk. To her it was a fairytale land mapped out by people who had lived it and she wanted to see it all for herself.

For the past two years the money was coming in fast at Fisher's place. Gilda found herself becoming both a full time barmaid and bookkeeper. She watched Fisher's finances grow, while making sure his books were balanced and Big Paulie received his share. Gilda constantly overlooked the social activities that came along with the business, the drugs the prostitution and the gambling. She found her solitude in the music and the entertainers. The sounds of the jazz and blues rhythms were the main ingredients to the recipe that kept Fisher's place popular and as a result the people kept coming. Finally, with Gilda's help he was able to pay off his debt to Big Paulie. As Big Paulie had promised, the place officially belonged to Fisher. He kept his end of the bargain as well and continued to purchase the fine Canadian whiskey and beer from Big Paulie each month.

Gilda would ponder many nights over the profits that he made along with the payroll that went out weekly. Fisher was becoming more distracted with the social scene and therefore putting more of the weight on Gilda. She begin to become frustrated as Fisher continued to hire and fire dancers, performers and musicians coming from all along the Gulf. Fisher was becoming a wealthy man very quickly. Gilda's irritation escalated as she watched him begin to excessively abuse his authority. He believed more variety would bring more customers. These employees were not as loyal as the others and would work sometimes less than two weeks at a time. Gilda begin to wonder why he was acting so strange. Something was bothering Fisher and Gilda just couldn't put her finger on it.

As events continued to turn for the worse Dot, Jeanine and Martha suddenly insisted it was time they returned to Louisiana. Gilda hearing the news tried to convince at least Jeanine to stay.

"Jeanine, I thought things were going so well now for you."

Regardless how much Gilda despised their extracurricular activities; she had also gotten use to Dot and Martha being around. Jeanine however, was very close to Gilda and from time to time helped her with the financial part of the business.

"Gillie, I best be getting on my way, but I'm sure I will see you again."

The two exchanged their goodbyes and Gilda watched Jeanine swiftly make her way to the train station.

Soon other orginal employees begin to quit, even Colleen after realizing that she didn't have any real desire for being a waitress. The afternoon before her departure, Dot stopped by Gilda's house for her usual hair appointment. She would be hitching a ride back to Louisiana after her visit. As Gilda begin combing through Dot's red hair she directed her over to the sink for a wash. Dot went on and on about how much she enjoyed her stay in Culloden

"Gilda chile, it has been fun; I never thought I would get as much as I did from this li'l ole town."

"My Aunt is doing much better now and my sister Clara say she healthy enough to take the trip north to live with her in Philadelphia."

"Me, I'm going back home to Louisiana."

Dot, Martha, and Jeanine was able to make a lot of money, and Gilda made plenty of money as well. However, Gilda was too busy keeping Fisher's books in order to realize how successful she had become.

"Gilda, watcha thinking about?"

"You hear me talking to you?"

"Oh Dot I'm sorry I was thinking bout something, what was you saying?"

"I was saying that you have been a real friend to me these past two years chile."

"I know I've been kinda hard to deal with at times, but I wanna thank you for everything."

Gilda couldn't understand the recent change of events. It was as if there was a little secret going on and she was not included. She still felt it strange that Dot and the others were leaving all of a sudden. Gilda even thought it more strange that Fisher was not convincing anyone to stay. Nevertheless, regardless of her suspicions, she finished Dot's hair and bid her farewell. Dot gave her an address in Louisiana and told her if she ever wanted to visit her and Martha to just drop a line.

Gilda soon retired her suspicions and decided to accept the fact that everyone had their own way of living in this life. She realized that Dot like herself spent the majority of her time trying to find her place in the world. The only difference between them was Dot risked coming to Culloden to find it.

Miss Gilda's Blues

Chapter 8

Culloden, Georgia
1933

Po Fisher had become quite successful in Monroe County by providing what others couldn't.

The 18th Amendment also known as the Prohibition Act established in 1910 prevented the sell and distribution of alcoholic beverages in the United States. This created an underground business that had made Fisher a wealthy man and he owed a lot of credit to Gilda. Now there was talk of ending Prohibition and new ideas where beginning to surface in government as well. These ideas were attributed to newly elected President Franklin D. Roosevelt. He displayed high aspirations for the promise of a "**New Deal**" which would finally bring economic relief to the country.

Fisher knew the times were changing and with it business relationships he'd established. It was not to his surprise things were beginning to get way out of hand with Lil Paulie. He knew for Gilda's safety, he would eventually have to let her go.

L'il Pauli's men were now in charge of the deliveries coming from Detroit. His men now begin to make it a habit to visit Culloden outside of scheduled deliveries. They were now more observant and enjoying the pleasures of Fisher's success under the leadership of Lil Paulie. Big Paulie had gotten sick in his old age. Fisher knew he was the glue that held his success together, without him and with L'il Paulie taking over the family business there would be consequences. Gilda had unknowingly gotten too deep and Fisher knew he had to protect her. He also knew that an opportunity like this one came only once in a lifetime for a blackman in these parts. Fisher had gotten a little wiser over the years and prepared for his future. The sheriff and local government officials of Monroe county were kept at bay thanks to Big Paulie. He'd set harsh examples of those who didn't accept his business offer. They were paid well for their cooperation, but were warned to stay away from Fisher's Place. Fisher knew if anything happened to him someone would have to know where he had been keeping his fortune and he decided that someone would be Gilda. He knew he could not trust the local bank, so he and Big Ted buried the majority of his fortune in a secret place. When Fisher returned home he knew the love that he had for Gilda all those years would never be. He'd come to the realization that what he and Gilda shared was unique. It no longer bothered him that her heart now belonged to Elijah.

****

Fisher could sense Gilda knew something wasn't right. She was very inquisitive and continued to ask questions he just couldn't answer at the time. However, Gilda continued to question his motives and finally Fisher gave in. He and Gilda sat down on the couch in the dressing room. Gilda knew her friend and it was obvious he was struggling with something.

Po Fisher put his hands in his head and begin reminiscing on his life to Gilda.

"Gillie, you know I come up hard."

Gilda shook her head in affirmation as he continued.

"Life been rough for me, especially after mama died and you been there all the way."

"Gillie, you, Big Ted and Julia was always there." Gilda grabbed his hand and held it inside of her's. She had never seen Fisher this way before.

"Gillie, from the very beginning, L'il Paulie has always had a thirst for power."

"He's done some awfully evil things to get it too, but things will work out you will see."

"I can't let you stay around her Gilda it's for your own good."

"But Fisher, I can help you, just let me help."

"No Gillie!"

He went over to his desk and opened the draw and handed Gilda two months salary.

"Here take this, it should hold you over for awhile, until I figure things out."

"Fisher?"

"Miss Gilda Harris, get outta here."

Gilda was furious about Fisher's decision and marched out with no words for her long time friend as he slowly closed the door.

Chapter 9

The time had gone by slowly for Julia, now seven months pregnant she felt hot, tired and ready to deliver her new gift into the world. Joshua had been a great comfort to her. She thought she was blessed to have the kind of man she had in him. Josie had always been a great help, she was getting older now and taking on some of the responsibilities around the house. She was also thinking up names to call her new brother or sister. Julia sat on the porch reminiscing on life as she gazed over the beautiful greenery of the land. The only worry she had was Gilda. *"Why can't she just settle herself down, she had a man who loved her dearly, and would even die for her."*

"What else could that chile possibly want?"

Nevertheless at the same time in many ways Julia admired Gilda's free spirit and noticed that it had even rubbed off a little on Josie. Julia was distracted by Joshua's truck coming up the road and when he pulled up to the house; to her surprise he had Gilda in the passenger seat.

"Hey babe, look who I picked up in town." Gilda hopped out of the truck. "Hey Julia."

"Hey Gillie."

"Lord have mercy whatcha been eating chile?" Julia struggled to get out of the chair with one hand reaching out to Gilda for help. She grabbed her as Julia pulled herself up. "Ahh lord have mercy Jesus, thank you Gillie."

Gilda stepped back and put her hands on her hip while observing her dear friend.

"You show you seven months?"

"Shoot you may have twins in there."

Josie ran from on the side of the house.

"Auntie Gillie!"

Gilda gave her a big hug.

"How's my baby?"

"Fine."

Gilda went in her dress pocket and pulled out a small glass vile, it was her Honeysuckle bath oil that she enjoyed making.

"This is for you sweetie and make sure yo mama let you put a little in your bath water tonight okay suga."

"Okay, now get and put that up, I don't want you to lose it, me and yo mamma gonna talk big girl talk."

Josie ran into the house and the screen door slammed behind her, Julia practically jumped to the roof.

"I keep telling that chile to catch that door when she running in and out the house, it just works my nerves when she does that."

Both women sat back down on the swing chair.

"Gillie, if you get thirsty you best be getting it yourself chile, because I'm hot and I'm tired of moving around in this here heat."

"I try to do everything early in the morning while it is still cool."

"I've gained so much weight."

"How am I gonna get this stuff off of me?" Gilda laughed.

"Shoot chile you crazy, all the moving you do around here that should be the least of your worries."

"The only time I see you sitting down this much is when you pregnant."

"I know and let me tell you something Gillie, I don't think this here body gonna last for two more months."

I had been thinking about Joshua getting a message out to Doc Norman to come have a look at me. He was just here last month and said everything was going fine, but you know a mama knows."

Joshua passed by the ladies and hopped into the truck. "Baby I'll be back, I'm still finishing up that shed for Mrs. Johnson, shouldn't be to long." Julia blew a kiss at her husband and waved him on. Then she turned her attention back to Gilda. "What's on your mine chile?"

"You know Julia, life is a very unpredictable thing."

"You can be the happiest person in the world and then something can happen that would have you think it ripped the very soul out of ya."

"I miss my mama, and my grandma so very much and I just fill like I was cheated sometimes."

"I never really knew what it was like to have a daddy."

"My life has been a puzzle with a whole lot of missing pieces in it and I have been spending all this time trying to find them pieces."

"It just gets so frustrating trying to fill those empty spaces in my life."

Julia looked on attentively, she knew that Gilda had been feeling lonely since her mother passed and nothing not even Elijah was able to fill that space for her.

"I understand how you feel Gillie, but I don't want you to fill this way."

"Things have to take time and we just got to keep on living."

"The lord has brought us both a long way chile and I just don't think he gonna leave us now."

Julia plucked a rose off her bush hanging over the porch and gave it to Gilda and she smiled.

"Chile and that Josie, she so crazy about you, thanks to you she got them same free-spirited ways too."

"I don't know what imma do with her."

"I can say for sure though, we all got each other."

"And anyway, you got a man that show is crazy about you."

Gilda turned to Julia.

"That was real good how you just slid Elijah in there Julia."

"What you talking about?"

"Go head on Julia you ain't slick."

"Well I just can't understand the two of you is all, y'all are something different I tell you."

"Joshua tells me to mind my own business every time I bring it up, but I just believe you two is just two stubborn old fools in love."

"Hey, I just thought, whatcha doing up and out this way so early in the morning?"

"You didn't work last night did you?"

"Naw that's what I wanted to tell you, Fisher fired me."

"What?"

"Yeah, and boy was I hot with him."

"You would think after all I have done for that man."

"How long it's been?"

"A couple days."

Julia folded her arms on top her stomach.

"Gillie, and you just telling me about this?"

"I ain't had any time to get around to it, I've been meaning to get out here."

"I'm here now."

"Anyway, I spent most of the weekend doing hair and last night I spent the night at Miss Ann's."

"What'd you do up there?"

"She asked me to help her pack charity boxes for The AME Missionary Society."

"They received a shipment of clothes and shoes from a few special organizations up North."

"She was so excitied too, because the A.M.E Missionary gives those charity boxes to needy families all over Georgia."

"Anyway chile about Fisher, I was so angry at first."

" Even after he spent a long while explaining to me what happened when he was up North."

"But afterward, he told me that he no longer needed me and that's what got me so fired up."

"Chile I was so hot at him and left him standing in that office and I didn't say a word."

"Gillie, after all you two have been through, I'm sure he had a good reason to do what he did."

"Yeah I know."

"Anyway, I got to walking home and I thought about it, no more long nights."

"I can rest my mind and my body."

"I believe it done aged me a few years." Both women started laughing.

"Gillie you is crazy girl, I don't know bout you sometimes."

"You know you gonna have to apologize to Fisher don't cha."

"Yeah I know."

"I will soon enough, but right now I gotta start taken care of myself."

"I might wanna have some children some day." Julia could not believe what she was hearing. She didn't know how long Gilda would have the notion in her head, so she decided to encourage the thought and put Fisher on the back burner.

"Wow, that explains it then."

"Explains what Julia."

"Elijah."

"What about Elijah, Julia?"

"Gillie, I must tell you I thought you had given him the cold shoulder, but now I know you weren't there last night."

"Julia, what on earth are you talking about?"

"Elijah, he left here last night headed for Fisher's Place to see you before he left outta town this morning."

"He must've stayed there anyway, because chile when he came home he was wasted I tell you."

"He was talking about how much he loves you, and why can't he seem to make you understand that you two belong together."

"He woke us all up, even Josie out of her sleep telling her how much he loved all of us."

"He then started hugging on Joshua so hard I thought he was going to squeeze the life outta him."

"He told me how proud he was of me and Joshua for continuing their family legacy and wishing that he too could do the same one of these days."

"He was busy last night chile."

"He kept saying something about us never having to worry about anything, that he was gonna see to it that we all would be safe and be happy." Julia then smiled at Gilda.

"I told Elijah, that's a lot of responsibility for one man, why don't you go lay down and get you some sleep." Both the girls chuckled, and Julia continued.

"Chile I woke up this morning to get breakfast started and that man was gone gone gone."

"I said to Joshua, I be darn that man is gonna lose his mind." Gillie looked over at Julia she understood what Elijah had seen in both Julia and Joshua.

"You okay Gillie?"

"Yeah, I'm just proud of you too is all."

"You, Fisher and Miss Ann the only family I really have."

"Gillie what are you saying?"

"You don't understand Julia, when I go home there is no one there but me and Battle to keep me company."

"You and Joshua, you guys have each other."

"Gillie that is the silliest thing I ever heard."

"Did you ever think that it's that way because that's the way you see it?"

"Even if you don't see a future with Elijah, there are plenty of fine decent men around these parts that would love to share their life with you."

"That is just it Julia I don't wanna be all cooped up, I wanna travel and see the world." Julia sat back in the chair. *"This woman is crazy and stubborn as a mule."*

Julia with her patient nature could practically put up with everything that Gilda did, but sometimes she would get that look that made Gilda feel as guilty as a misbehaved child.

"Gillie, I just want you to be happy that's all."

"Julia, you know I love Elijah, you know that better than anybody, probably even me I suppose."

"I just haven't made it to that point yet."

"Gillie all I know is that the lord been good to us."

"I feel blessed and you should too."

"I just don't think you should feel like you being hindered because someone wants to love you and take care of you."

"Yes I may cook and clean and I have children, but on the same hand Joshua he cook and he clean and he help me take care of his children."

"It's just living Gillie that's all, just living."

"Look around you Gillie, folks out here starving with no place to go."

"I mean literally starving on the road, these same roads that we ride and walk to and from town on."

"You know, sometimes me and Josie go up yonder a couple of miles by Wylie River, there is a women and her daughter living just like that."

"Her name is Pearl and her daughter is Coral, she goes to the schoolhouse with Josie."

"They come her all the way he from Mississippi on foot, her and her daughter."

"I was so hurt for Pearl when she told me her story all I could think of was that being me and Josie."

"I take her food when I can and shoes for her daughter."

"Pearl is a very proud women and she keeps her rifle close by too."

"Could you imagine living like that in the woods Gillie, and with a child?"

"She even told me that they found a man hung deep in the woods and she say poor little Coral saw him too."

"Gilda I felt so bad for that child."

Gilda shook her head at Julia and reminded her of that dark day that stole their innocence forever. It was a hot Georgia afternoon and as usual they had walked in the woods searching for worms and bugs for fishing bait. They had wondered much deeper than they were allowed to go and came upon an awful smell and there before their eyes was a man swinging from a large oak tree.

Gilda could remember the stench was unbearable as they both stood in a state of shock watching the body swing to and fro. Julia stood stiff as a board, she couldn't move. Gilda screamed her name to follow her, as she began to run as fast as she could. Julia began to wale and scream out as she recognized the young man. It was Pryor he had been nearly five years their senior. He was the only child to Mrs. Robinson, who had also lost her husband to a lynch mob almost fifteen years earlier. They continued to reminisce about her too, remembering how she had lost the strength to carry on.

"Lord Julia that was the day we grew up to this world."

"Yep, but Beauty knew exactly what to do."

This was one of the many incidents of lynching's that occurred in Monroe County. Gilda's mother Beauty had encouraged both girls to write letters to Mrs. Ida B. Wells-Barnett Founder of the Associated Negro Press in Illinois. She was a head strong activist that spoke out blatantly and with courage against lynching throughout the south. Ida had been a patron of Beauty's and close friend. She met Mrs. Wells-Barnett at a rally while living in Pennsylvania.

Mrs. Wells-Barnett had become a correspondent for several black newspapers that attacked the South's failure to acknowledge the reconstruction laws after the removal of U.S troops in 1887. Mrs. Wells-Barnett focused her attention on lynching, an effective tool for quieting resistance of the white supremacist group, the Ku Klux Klan.

Mrs. Wells-Barnett responded to the girls letters and traveled discreetly to Culloden Georgia. She interviewed each of them as anonymous eyewitnesses and investigated the events that led up to the lynching. The results of the investigation led up to the physical assaults on white women, whom Ida B. Wells-Barnett could see nor find. In turn she publicly attacked officials in Monroe County and other surrounding counties in Georgia. When questioned, these county officials had insisted that the lynching were reluctantly imposed punishment required to protect white women from promiscuous black men. However there hadn't been any proof in the matter. Her efforts were courageous and the girls held her in high regard. Mrs. Wells-Barnett explained to them the need for them to be fearless and strong in any event regarding injustices against of the black race. She also explained to them their need to understand as black americans in this country they were entitled to the same rights and privileges as white americans. The world had recently lost the powerful voice of Mrs Barnett the year before, but Gilda and Julia felt previledged to have known such a courageous women.

"Gillie, I tell you I've been thinking since the last time we talked about it, I really wouldn't mine leaving this here town after all."

"I haven't mentioned it to Joshua, but if we could I would like to move out west. Take my babies somewhere that we could live in peace and get them a good education."

Gilda sat quietly as tears begin to run down her face.

"Gillie, Gillie, you alright Chile?" Gilda turned to Julia. "What on gods green Earth is wrong with me Julia?" Gilda reached in her dress pocket and pull out her handkerchief.

"I don't know if I am coming or going."

"Sometimes I sit back and I think about life and all kind of things."

"It's so frustrating because I can't seem to come up with a solid plan that will stick."

I think working at the joint helped to keep my mind off of things."

"Lord knows it wasn't one of the holiest places to find peace, but I did find some comfort there."

"Gillie, listen, you don't have to be involved in a whole lot of nothing to find no peace."

"Somebody looking at my situation would swear I was just a plain ole country girl and that I may be, but that is not all I am."

"I'm saying that to say, you have to be still."

"Gillie sometimes you just have to be still, you have been avoiding a lot of things for a longtime, things that I know would be good for you if you just gave them a chance."

"There is a man that loves you and I mean what I say when I say that."

"If you just sit back and be still the god lord will reveal some things to you I promise you that."

"Look around Gilda I been with Joshua a long while and we haven't never wanted for nothing."

"What are you waiting for?"

These Mason boys are something else I tell you, smart too."

" I think about all those years they took contracting work out of town."

"We both know that these white folks ain't paying them what they worth, but you know what, I don't say nothing, it ain't my place."

"I do know Joshua and Elijah are god fearing men and whatever they have been doing to keep this family safe I believe it's with a good conscious."

Gilda took a real long look a Julia. It was much more to her than just a house-wife and mother. Julia carried a quiet strength and pride in her family. Gilda wanted those same things for herself one day, but had a difficult time figuring how she could make it to that point. She was beginning to realize that she could no longer make up excuses any more. There were some things she just had to learn on her own. Gilda gave Julia a big hug, wiped her eyes and stood up.

"You wanna go to church with me Sunday." Julia struggled to her feet, if I don't have this child of mine I will go to church with you on Sunday." Gilda gave Julia a big hug.

"I love you Julia."

"We love you too Gillie."

"You ain't gonna wait on Joshua to come to take you home?"

"Naw, I think I'll walk, it will be good for me."

"We'll be expecting to see that Elijah real soon, to him you probably been missing in action far to long."

Gilda gave her a big smile.

On the walk home Gilda continued thinking, since they had grown older the tables had indeed turned. It use to be a time when Gilda was always pulling on Julia to keep up, now Julia was doing the pulling, life was sure strange sometimes.

Chapter 10

That next morning the weather had become a little milder as the end of the summer made its way into Culloden. Gilda looked around her yard as she admired the beauty of her home. The pecan tree had finally ripened and without hesitation she pulled a few off the tree and stuck them in her dress pocket. The hills across the road where Miss Ann lived showed off it's wildflowers in full bloom. The smell of the fresh air gave her a since of peace and tranquility as well as the birds who visited her each morning for their daily bread. Gilda's thoughts then turned to Fisher. She had not spoken to him since their falling out, and she knew she would have to make things right. Gilda knew friendship was much stronger than a petty disagreement and after all, Fisher shared some very intimate details about his experience with her, things he shared with no one else. Gilda realized that Fisher trusted her far more than she could have imagined. She always knew from the very beginning there had been some strange things going on at Fisher's Place.

"Could Fisher be in trouble?"

Gilda knew L'il Paulie could be very dangerous, but she never let on how she felt to Fisher. She decided to drop by and see Fisher to patch things up with him. After all, they had known each other all their lives.

That evening as the sun set Gilda made here way to Fisher's Place. The place was full of laughter, song, and dance as usual. The music was food to Gilda's soul and to her surprise Blind Jake had returned.

Blind Jake was a talented Piano player; he had been a friend of Po Fisher for many years. Jake was from the Georgia Sea Islands the place that Fisher's mother had grown up. These were a few of the many Islands that blacks resided on within the southern region of the United States. These islands inhabited the descendents of African slaves who worked the land on plantations of these same sea islands not long ago. Gilda always thought Blind Jake was very special; god had given him a great gift. Being blind had not interfered with his passion for music, as a result he became quite popular up and down the delta. Jake, escorted by Fisher also traveled to Chicago and Detroit to play for many of his business acquaintances. Jake was a decent god fearing man with a love for the blues.

Gilda walked over to Big Ted sitting inside the door with his hat cocked to the side.

"Hey Gillie how you doing?"

"I ain't seen you in a minute."

Gilda gave him a big hug.

"It's good to see you Ted, you seen Fisher around?"

"Yep, he out back in a meeting with them Italian fellas."

Before Gilda could walk away Ted lightly tugged on her arm.

"Hey Gillie, be careful cause between me and you, something real fishy's going on round here."

"I don't trust them fellas too much."

"They always walkin round here with that shady look, you know, like they up to something."

"I hate Fisher have to do business wit em, they even hang around at closing now to watch him count the money." Finally for Gilda, everything was coming together now. She came to one conclusion; Fisher did what he did to protect her.

"Gillie, you know things were just fine until ole man Paulie died."

Fisher hadn't told her that either.

"After Big Paulie past away I could see pressure being put on Fisher, he between a rock and a hard place now and I don't think he know how he gonna get out."

"He ain't been himself Gillie, you know when the ole man was here he had protection from the sheriff."

"L'il Paulie is controlling everything now and he ain't nothing like his father."

"Ted, I really need to speak with him."

"Go on back, I'm sure he would love to see you."

"Maybe you can make some sense out of what is going on round here."

"Gillie be careful."

"I will Ted, thanks."

Ted had been the strong arm for Fisher and he had been with him since the beginning. Ted was loyal with a heart of gold and Gilda knew if anything were to happen to Fisher he would be the one to make things right.

However, before she could make it to the back she was summoned again, but this time from the stage as Blind Jake spoke. "I here my favorite girl is in the house."

The crowd began to applaud as Blind Jake hit the keys of the piano and began talking to his favorite Georgia girl:

"I was bitter she would not hold me."
"I was bitter she would not scold me."
"I was bitter why you do me that way."
"Knowing that I would be the love that she would need one day."

Gilda replied.

"Who loves that man more than I do?"

Blind Jake began to smile.

"That's my Gillie the love of my life, come on gal would you be my wife?"

"My heart aches and stays in pain since you been gone things just ain't the same."

The crowd began to applaud. Gilda walked over and got on stage, she gave him a big kiss on the cheek, popped herself on the hip with here hand. She through her hands up and blew Blind Jake a kiss.

"Ohhh how I love this man."

Big Ted looked at Gilda and began to laugh.

"Gal you ain't gone ever change, you will always have that fire."

"Honey chile remember, ain't nothing like the Blues."

Ted returned the smile.

"No ain't nothing like it, you show right about that."

Gilda gave him a big smile through her hand up high waved good bye and disappeared into the busy corridor. Inside she could see Ms. Kelly preparing the evening menu.

"What's cooking this evening Ms. Kelly?"

Gilda made sure Fisher took care of his employees, encouraging him to do the honorable thing and share the wealth since he was doing so well. So for the past two years Ms. Kelly worked hard to support her daughter's efforts to get her grandson off to college in Atlanta. "Today is Friday chile, and on Friday we have smothered pork chops with rice and cabbage, and I'm topping it off with some of my mean hot water corn bread."

"Ohh that sounds good."

"Ms. Kelly how is your daughter and grandson ?"

"Oh he doing mighty fine, he sent for his mother and she will be staying up there cooking and cleaning for them at the dorm on his college campus."

"They were looking for someone to clean up after them boys and cook for them."

"I told her to get on up there quick before they ask somebody else."

"She left this past Thursday."

"Oh that is good news Ms. Kelly, what about you?"

"You plan on going over to Atlanta to be with the two of them?"

"Well me and my daughter talked about getting a place once she got settled in."

"I told her I wanted to stay here just a little longer build up my nest egg yah know, because every little bit counts."

"So Gillie, if the good lords willing I will be moving to Atlanta to be with my family one of these days."

"Well I tell you Ms. Kelly, we sure will miss ya cooking."

Ms. Kelly blushed as she always had.

"Gone get out my kitchen, Ill fix you something to take home wit cha, and I'll put plenty in here for that crazy man friend of yours too."

Gilda blushed at the comment and did as she was instructed.

As she finally made her way to the end of the narrow hallway to the office door, Gilda could over hear Fisher and Paulie discussing money. Fisher didn't sound too comfortable with the conversation that was taking place. Gilda softly put her ear to the door. She knew that snooping wasn't proper, but she figured that this was an emergency. If she was going to get a full understanding about what was going on she would have to do a little investigating.

"Man I can't afford that, if I pay you that, how am I gonna to keep the business running?" "I got expenses I need to cover and I got people that gotta be paid."

Lil Paulie shook his head.

"Now Fisher haven't we been good to you."

"Well no, Big Paulie's been real good to me."

"You on the other hand have been a thorn in my side."

Soon after the comment Gilda jumped as she heard Fisher take a blow.

"Well it seems as though you forget how good I have been to you too."

"My pa took real good care of you when you didn't even have a pot to piss in and he sent you all the way back here to this little ole hick town with that dream of yours now didn't he?"

"Yes suh he did, but I paid him back all the money that he invested in me."

"I did that before he died and you know that was the agreement we made."

"Yeah, but times are changing and you still need protection don't you boy."

Adrienne Lynn Rutherford

I understand the white folk down here just don't take too kindly to upiddity niggers."

"Isn't that what they call you down here Fisher?"

"You know I spoke to that sheriff, it appears the two of you have a long history."

"He waiting for you and his temper sorta reminded me of one of dem ole rabid dogs wanting to get at a piece of raw meat."

"But, see if you pay us good, I promise you, we will keep a leash on that mad dog capeche."

"Now I need you to remember Fisher, it's hard times around here, you know with the depression and all."

"Now what do you think will happen if the Sherriff stops getting his money and we decide to take him off that leash of his Po Fisher?"

"I guess, I'd be a dead man running." Gilda covered her mouth with both her hands.

She'd heard enough and softly knocked on the door.

"Fisher, you in there it's me Gillie."

Paulie gave Fisher a cynical grin.

"Looks like you got company Fisher, don't just stand there invite the little lady in?"

Fisher gave Paulie a long evil stare and whispered to keep her from hearing.

"Paulie, you leave her out of this, ya here?"

For Gilda, Fisher could see himself killing Paulie with his bare hands. Paulie looked on with a little grin as the door slowly swung open.

"We gonna be heading back up North, our train leaves in an hour."

I decided to leave old Sonny here behind, just to keep a watch over things do you mind Fisher?"

"I expect I don't Paulie."

"Good, by the way the sheriff will be taken care of, for the time being that is."

With that said Paulie exited the door while Gilda stood tall as she could against it. Paulie tipped his hat to her then he and the two gentlemen walked down the hall and disappeared around the corner into the corridor.

This was nothing new for Fisher, all his life at different levels, he had prepared for counter attacks. It was a part of his survival mechanism. He knew he had to make some serious moves and he had to make them fast.

"Come on in Gillie, its real good seeing you."

He extended his arms and Gilda gave a long and needed hug to her childhood friend.

"What brings you back around the devil's den?"

"Well I came by to see you and to see how things been fairing these past few days without me breathing down your neck."

"I also wanted to patch things up between the two of us and to let you know that I don't feel angry anymore."

"I thought long and hard about everything Fisher and I want to apologize for saying those things to you that day. Fisher gave Gilda a slight smile, it was all he had left considering the events that had taking place.

"Gillie, you know I could never stay mad at you, I forgave you before you hit that door."

"I was wrong too; I should have given you some type of explanation."

"I must tell you though, there's a lot going on right now, more that you could possibly know."

"I didn't need you around here because I don't know what is gonna become of this place."

Fisher sat back down in his chair and offered Gilda a seat as well.

"I've worked so very hard you know."

"Hell I'm still a young man and with all of this I got going on around me, I don't see no future no more for myself at all, not here in Culloden."

"Gillie, you couldn't possibly imagine what it feels like to see no future at all."

Gilda got up from the chair and peeked out of the door. Once she seen the hallway was clear she softly closed the door and turned to Fisher in a whispering voice

"Fisher, I ain't blind you know."

"I know something going on, something that ain't good."

"I understand why you sent me away now, but I wanna help you get out of this and I want you to stop all that talking about having no future."

"That's just plain ole nonsense; shoot and it don't sound like the Fisher I know."

"Gillie, there ain't no way out of such things when you doing business with the mob."

"There has got to be a way Fisher, shoot black folks been through way worse things than that old rattlesnake Paulie."

"We've overcame many many years of slavery, your spirit is stronger than that Fisher."

"You are a freeman remember that."

"Gilda look, nobody knows that better than me."

"I know that I'm a freeman, and I've never been more free than when I left hear on that freight train."

"I made a way out of no way for myself, you know ain't nobody ever gave me nothing!"

"Everything that I have, every piece of wood on this place, very table, every chair, every liquor bottle that roll through that back door out there, I paid for!"

"But Gillie, you have to understand I made a deal with the devil a long time ago when I ran into these folks."

"When Paulie was living it didn't seem like a bad idea and everything was going just fine, but times are changing and they changing fast."

"Everybody in the business who played the game right was doing good, but time is running out and pretty soon there won't be any prohibition at all."

"Those folks who have spent their life making a living from prohibition will have to find themselves another way and Paulie knows that."

"That's why he's down here trying to strong arm me for anything that he can."

"The little gambling spots that he has set up In Chicago and out west aren't making him a lot of money, hell even the black folk up in Harlem are doing better than him with the numbers racket."

"He doesn't have a chance up there and his dirty heroin business isn't paying off like he planned either."

"Once his cousin's up in Chicago find out about that, among other things he will answer for it too."

"Over the years L'il Paulie has crossed a lot of people, good people that I know who want him dead."

"Prohibition has made me a lot of money, more than I could have ever imagined years ago, shoot I consider my self lucky, we as a people we suffering."

"I'm not blind Gillie, I see us out their in the woods and along the back roads living in tin roof houses and tents, times is hard."

"I've done well not just for myself, but for every person who has ever worked or came in contact with me around here."

"I had an opportunity along while ago to run into a man like big Paulie back up in Detroit and I will always be grateful for that."

"I helped him make a lot of money rowing the boat back an forth from Amherstburg Canada running liquor across the Detroit River to the states and he believed enough in me and my dream to help me return home and start up my own business."

"It was what he called a gentleman's agreement."

Adrienne Lynn Rutherford

"Now, even though that agreement was settled, things are still going bad."

Fisher stood up and looked out of the curtain window into the night. At that moment Gilda saw a glimpse of satisfaction on his face, he then smiled.

"Those were the times I tell you."

"You know me and L'il Paulie's younger brother Joey, we pulled some capers up there in Detroit, we were the closest I tell you."

"He was just like his Pa, very fair and a loyal man, cause for them it wasn't about the color of a man but the integrity and character of a man."

"Joey never let color come in between our relationship, unlike his brother."

"What happened to him Fisher?"

"He was murdered!"

Gilda grew tense from just hearing that word. Fisher bowed his head; his suspicions had become part of his very existence in the past couple of years.

"That damn Paulie, he was jealous of his own brother."

"After I returned home, a few months later they told me Joey had drowned in the Detroit River, said somebody had dropped a dime on him."

"He and his crew were coming back from a routine run from Amherstburg with a shipment."

"You know what Gillie?"

"Our shipments would never come in until way after midnight."

"The cops who walked the beat down by the river that time of the night were on the payroll."

"I always knew it was something strange about that."

"I believe to this day that Lil Paulie killed his own brother."

"Joey was the one taking care of all the business for his father."

"Paulie was too hot headed and obsessed about being the boss, but never seemed to make a good businessman."

"He always rubbed folk the wrong way and that didn't sit well with Big Paulie."

"When I was there, Paulie was partying and spending up all his father's money on gambling and women while me and Joey, we kept the business going."

"Big Paulie, he never spoke on it, but always kept it business."

"Joey had workers, but not like the grimy gophers that Paulie carries around with him."

Fisher then hit his fist against the wall and Gilda jumped.

"He's a coward and he knows I know it."

"Fisher, is there any way you can prove Paulie killed his brother?"

Fisher began pacing the floor reminiscing on the events that occurred.

"Remember when Big Paulie came down to check the place out?"

"Well he told me that he was sick then, and he didn't know how long he was gonna live."

"He explained to me that Lil Paulie had come to him in a rage of anger a couple of weeks before they found Joey along the river bank dead."

"He said Lil Paulie went on about how he couldn't understand how he could have passed him up because he was the oldest son."

"He felt he should be the one to take care of the business if anything happened to Big Paulie."

"Big Paulie went on to explain that L'il Paulie had slowly turned a few of his trustworthy workers against him promising a better situation so to speak."

"All accept their cousin Franco and a few more loyal members of the family."

"Franco is a good man."

"He also hates Paulie and he knows that Paulie killed Joey too."

"Franco returned to Chicago after Big Paulie died and he had a few successful investments out west and over seas."

"He sent me and Joey out west a few times too."

"He always told us he could trust us far more than Lil Paulie."

"Anyway, Big Paulie told me many times over the years that things were becoming unsafe, his fear was not for himself."

"It was for Joey."

"He said he'd mentioned it to Joey at times, but Joey just shook it off."

"Instead he defended his brother and told his father Lil Paulie was just a hot head and he couldn't hurt him because he was his only baby brother."

"He was wrong."

"Joey had planned to come down to Culloden but he never made it Gillie."

"That was the last time I seen Big Paulie alive, but before he left he told me one thing that stuck with me, he said: *When there is no loyalty in the business the business crumbles.*"

"I will never forget that."

"Lil Paulie is a very greedy man Gillie; I have been preparing myself for this day for quite sometime. I knew it was just a matter of time."

"Fisher, what do you plan on doing now?"

"You can't keep living like this, its crazy."

Fisher looked over at Gilda as she stood up against the wall of the office.

"There are some things I will need you to do later, but as for now stay away from here you hear?"

Gilda nodded her head like a school girl.

"Gillie we can't talk here anymore."

"I want you to meet me out by the pond behind the church on Sunday and we can talk there."

I believe there are some things I will need you to do for me just in case something happens to me."

"You will know what to do and don't worry about me."

"Now you go on home."

Soon after Fisher went in his desk and began writing a letter.

Chapter 11

Gilda took what she thought was the shortest, but turned out to be the longest walk home that she had ever taken from Fisher's Place. In that moment in time her mind was wrapped around nothing but Fisher.

Ms. Kelly had prepared Gilda a meal as she promised. Gilda wondered for a long time how he pulled off establishing such a business. Fisher was right he had gotten the best of everything including some of the most popular blues singers like W.C Handy, Scrapper Blackwell and how could she forget Ole Lucille Logan. Both she and Fisher also saw the darker side of the live bands and glamorous nights of the business. One thing kept resonating in her mind, Fisher stating he'd made a deal with the devil. The thought gave Gilda chills. She would talk to Elijah; he would know what to do in a situation like this. *"We have to help Fisher some kind of way."* She thought.

Meanwhile, Elijah was enjoying the summer breeze as he made his way from Gainesville, Florida to Culloden and all he could do was think about Gilda. He hadn't seen her and he had truly missed her. While he was away in Florida he'd purchased a beautiful handcrafted locket of pure white gold for Gilda. On the back he had it engraved:

>To my Ki'Somma, the light of my life
>My heart belongs to you forever.

The women shoppers in the Jewelry store with their fancy clothes and hats looked on in envy while he purchased the expensive gift. When he returned home Julia told him that Gilda no longer worked at Fisher's Place. Elijah was relieved at the news, but didn't concern himself with the reasons. After his outburst everyone in Culloden knew how he felt about Gilda. After speaking with Julia, he was glad that she and Josie had not been terrified by his outburst before departing. His patience had just about run out and he was determined to have Gilda, because just loving her all this time was no longer enough.

Elijah didn't hesitate to make his way to Gilda's after hearing the news. He was anxious to hold her once more and wanted to give her everything that her precious mind and heart could ever want. However, his past still haunted him and he had to settle it once and for all. Elijah had never imagined leaving the South, but the thought was becoming more and more convincing. He knew it would be impossible to live in peace with their fortune, especially in Culloden. He also would never be able to return home to live. Elijah knew it had been the grace of the lord that he and his brother made it safely out of his home town. The reality of his father's death had awakened Elijah many nights as he tossed and turned in his sleep. He knew whatever plans he and Joshua would make; he wasn't going to leave without Gilda.

Gilda's house had cooled off a bit with the night air coming through in the screen door. After relaxing in a nice lukewarm lavender oil bath she prepared to see Elijah. The meal Ms. Kelly packed for her during her visit at Fisher's was warming in the stove. After what she'd seen and heard today she didn't have much of an appetite.

Gilda wanted to speak with Elijah tonight about what was going on with Fisher. She turned on the radio to the songs of her favorite Delta Blues; the echo of Bessie Smith filled the front room of the house. Gilda vowed every time that she heard this woman on the radio that she would soon make it to Louisiana on her annual trip back to the South. There was a stern knock on the front door. Gilda saw Elijah looking in the screen while she sat in the chair next to the radio. "Whatcha looking in here for, come on in babe." Elijah gave Gilda a big grin and walked inside. He was dusty from head to toe.

"What you been into sweetie?"

"Well, I went down to Gainesville to check on the boys." "They've been good apprentice."

Some of them have started their own businesses and wanted me to come checkem out."

"Now they know what it's like to work for themselves."

"Well Elijah you did teach them everything that they know."

"You should be very proud of yourself."

" I feel really good about it, my main concern was letting them know they have options in this world."

"Anyway, after that I went by Mr. Payton's to fix his porch, but the porch job turned into the door job, and the door job turned into the barn job and the barn job turned into the truck job and here I am."

"I don't mind though he been awfully good to me and my brother, but I tell you if he had a son born and raised in that house he would work him to death."

Gilda laughed.

"How's Mrs. Payton?"

"Miss Ann told me that she was under the weather these last few days."

"She's doing much better and believe me; Mr. Payton wouldn't let her lift a finger."

"He even tried to cook some fried chicken, he offered me some I took one good look at that chicken and it took everything in me not to burst out in laughter."

"Well Mr. Mason I have you a nice lukewarm lavender bath ready and I brought you dinner from Fisher's if you hungry."

"Ms. Kelly sends her love."

"Look at your clothes Elijah." Elijah pulled at his pants they were filled with sawdust and oil

"I know."

"What you gonna do for clothes I can't wash that out this evening those need a good soaking."

Elijah began to blush like a school boy.

"Ki'Somma no need to worry, Mrs. Payton knew I was coming straight here to see ya after I left."

"She insisted that I take a pair of ole trousers and a shirt her brother had left behind." Gillie waved her hand at Elijah as she blushed over the comment.

"Boy oh boy that Mrs. Payton, she show ain't changed one bit, she is something else I tell you."

"Yes she is."

Elijah followed Gilda down the hall, to the bathroom and she lit the oil lamp. Elijah leaned down and inhaled the sweet smell of her skin as he slowly began to gently kiss her on the nap of her neck. Gilda could feel his manhood and it made her insides flutter. She had desired him for far too long.

No other man had made her feel this way, no other man could touch her deep down in side the way Elijah had. There were many wealthy men who came through Fisher's Place, but none impressed her enough to give up the feelings she had for Elijah.

"Ki'Somma I have a very special surprise for you."

Gilda looked up at Elijah with the joy that was his primary quest. Elijah went into his pocket and pulled out a small box. Gilda's eyes lit up as he handed it to her.

"Well aren't you gonna open it."

Gilda turned to Elijah and tears came to her eyes.

"My Ki'Somma why are you crying?"

"I don't know Elijah, It's just that you always make me feel so good inside and this time I can't contain myself is all."

"Well open it." Gilda opened the small box.

"Oh Elijah it's beautiful." Gilda's hands were shaking and Elijah slowly took the box out of her hand removed the locket out and turned it over to read the inscription on the back. Gilda didn't hesitate she reached up as high as she could stretch her arms grabbed his cheeks with both hands and lowered his lips into hers and softly kissed him.

"I love you Elijah."

"I love you too."

Elijah then took the locket and put it around Gilda's neck.

"It looks beautiful on you."

"Ki'Somma, I desire you and only you."

Gilda slowly begin unbuttoning his shirt and slid it off his large broad shoulders. Gilda stepped back as he took off his boots and unbuckled his pants. Elijah stood in the nakedness of his manhood in the presence of the woman that he loved so dearly. He reached down and returned the same desirable kiss that she had given him. Elijah tested the water and then slowly eased himself into the tub. Gilda passed him a clean wash cloth from off the shelf. She then grabbed a pillow off the small chair in the corner and put it under her knees as she knelt down next to the tub. As she made herself comfortable, Gilda noticed that Elijah had been watching her every move. He gazed into her eyes, and gave her a quick wink, which made Gilda blush even more. She always felt good around Elijah. From the first day they met, Gilda always wondered what was it about this man that had her so mesmerized. It was the first time she had realized that love was a powerful thing between a man and a woman.

Elijah sank his large body deeper into the tub.

"Ki'Somma, there are a few things that I would like to talk to you about."

"Baby, I have something I would like to discuss with you too."

Elijah was very careful not the reveal to much to Gilda this soon. Things were complicated and he needed to sort out a lot of it himself. If she had any questions or concerns about the situation he wanted to be confident in the answers that he would give her.

"Me and Joshua were talking about selling some of the land."

"A couple of folks from down by the river offered to work the land and I accepted."

"We told them they don't have to give us anything just yet, but if they promised to take care of it we would sign the deed over to them now."

"Oh dear heart that was a wonderful thing the two of you have done."

"I know you made a lot of people so happy."

"The good lord will bless you for it."

"Gilda had seen the struggle that many of the black folks had experienced during the depression and she was proud of the man she loved for his generosity."

"Gilda there's something else."

"Yes dear heart."

"I love you and I wanna start a family."

"Now before you go on giving me all the reasons why you can't, let me tell you I will not take no for an answer."

"Gillie, we've been at this courting thing for a long time now and It's about to make me lose my mind."

Before he could continue, Gilda softly placed her finger on his lips.

"I know Elijah, I know how you feel about me."

"You don't think I been knowing all this time your intentions for us?"

"I also know how you been acting around here when I'm not around, but it's okay because I wanna be with you too."

"I love you and no man has ever made me feel the way that you make me feel."

"I don't think I could go on with a peace of mind if I let you walk out of my life Elijah."

Elijah could not believe what he was hearing and he continued to listen attentively to Gilda as she opened up fully to him. He grabbed her gently by the face.

"My Ki'Somma, I will make you happy and you will never regret loving me I promise you."

Gilda took the wash cloth from him and slowly begin washing his back. "Elijah is that what you had to talk to me about?"

"No there is something else, I will be returning home to straighten out some unfinished business, as soon as I hear from my cousin Jerry."

Gilda didn't not know what Elijah meant by unfinished business, but she did know that whatever it was it must have been important if he was uncomfortable about it.

Gilda was never good at hiding her emotions and Elijah could see the concern on her face.

"Everything is fine, trust me on this okay."

"I will explain it more once I hear back from my cousin Jerry."

Gilda rinsed the wash cloth soaped it up really good and continued to bathe Elijah's wide chest. She then slowly ran the washcloth down the center until she made it gently underwater.

"Lil lady you better watch yourself, you making it hard for me to relax in this here tub of water."

Gilda smiled.

"Ki'Somma, what about you, what is it that you needed to talk to me about?"

Gilda did not want to interrupt the mood, but she really needed to talk.

"Well it's about Fisher."

"What about Fisher?" Now Elijah had straightened himself up in the tub.

He knew that Fisher had been soft on Gilda as long as he could remember and Elijah was not good at hiding the jealousy he felt about their peculiar relationship.

"Well I think he's in trouble, big trouble."

"I do believe something is going to come to a head."

"He fired me while you were away and I was so angry at him for doing that."

"We had a big falling out."

"Anyway, then later on after I talked with Julia, I thought it was the best thing to do, considering the long nights."

"Things were getting even stranger around there for awhile anyway."

Gilda passed Elijah a Towel as he climbed out of the bath tub.

"Strange like what?"

"Well First Jeanine just picked up and left for no reason and then a week later Dot and Martha left in a big hurry."

"They didn't give any reason?"

"No, but Dot did give me this crazy excuse while I was doing her hair, but I ain't crazy, it's more I tell you."

Elijah dressed himself and listened attentively as Gilda continued.

"Anyway, I decided to go and see Fisher because I wanted to apologize to him for the way I acted."

"When I went back, I overheard him talking to Paulie."

Right away Elijah knew why Gilda felt a little anxious about Paulie. Elijah had played poker them and Big Ted had told him all about the business connections with the sheriff and the Major. It was the first time Elijah saw what a little muscle and money could do in a small southern town like Culloden.

This all seemed to work out in Fisher's favor because he was the least of the small town's concern. Many of the folks had their attention focused on the political issues surrounding indictments by the Federal Government for the covering up of lynchings in the south and the economic effects of the depression. Fisher, even with his popularity and overnight success with his underground business to his advantage had not merited much legal attention.

Liquor had eased a lot of the economic hardship for those who had the resources to distribute it. As the speak easy's grew in popularity many folks in the north and south had no idea how much money was really being made during the prohibition years.

Gilda had no problem sharing with Elijah the details of the events that unfolded at Fisher's Place. She was eager to help, but had no clue as to how.

"Elijah that Lil Paulie is an awful man, he was speaking to Fisher as if he owned him."

"I heard him threaten to let the sheriff lose on him, if he doesn't do what he says."

"Did he say what it was he wanted him to do?"

"No, he didn't say, he didn't even know I heard the things that I heard."

"I told him that he needed to do something!"

"That Paulie also left one of his watchdogs behind, he called him Sonnie."

"He's suppose to be keeping an eye on Fisher and watch the money coming in until Paulie comes back to town."

"Elijah I am awfully worried for Fisher, if you would have seen the look on his face."

"I'm really afraid he is going to do something really foolish to get himself hurt or even killed."

Elijah gave Gilda a long look and he could see the concern on her face. He knew that Gilda was concerned about Fisher and he had accepted that. Elijah also knew that she had promised herself to him and he was grateful for that. If she wanted his help he would give it to her.

"What is it that you want me to do?"

Gilda thought for a minute she knew how hot headed Elijah could get in a situation. She didn't want him to get directly involved with the likes of Paulie and possibly risk his life. It was bad enough Fisher had to deal with those crooks and to bring another person into this that she cared so much about would simply be unbearable.

"Elijah I don't want you to do nothing, not just yet."

"Fisher wants me to meet him at the pond behind the church this Sunday."

"I guess at that time he will tell me what it is he plans to do."

Elijah looked deeply into Gilda's soft brown eyes. "Ki'Somma, everything will be fine, Fisher is a grown man."

"He knows what he is doing, he's been around those guys for awhile."

"If anybody knows how to deal with them it's Fisher."

"He will do what is best."

Elijah got out of the tub and wrapped the towel around his waist. He then reached down for Gilda's chin and consoled her with a kiss.

"He will." He said.

Gilda nodded with a smile of trust in Elijah's words and reached up and returned the kiss. Elijah lifted her in his arms and took her to the bed room. He laid her down softly on the bed and soon began to relax her tense body with his hands.

"Elijah, what about dinner?"

"Ki'Somma you are my dinner."

He then began to passionately kiss her softly and Gilda didn't speak a word, but only moaned with pleasure. Elijah then gently relieved her of the soft white cotton gown. It had been tempting to him since he had walked in the door. He observed the nipples of her breast protruding beneath. Elijah slowly continued down her body with his masculine hands caressing the loveliness of her as he slowly opened her thighs giving her intense pleasure.

Elijah had sorely missed the touch of the woman that he loved so much. He gently grabbed her around the waist and propped her up on his lap and with her legs around his waist he caressed her breast tasting the sweetness of each, giving no less attention to the other. Gilda closed her eyes and enjoyed the pleasure that Elijah enjoyed providing her. Slowly he entered her and in that moment Gilda fell back in the comfort of his arms. She closed her eyes enjoying the love of her life as Elijah, now deep inside relished in her essence pleasing her with soft strokes of his manhood. Gilda put her hands around his neck as he held her tightly caressing her and feeling her womanhood. Simultaneously they burst with pure passion as they enjoyed one another over and over again into the night. Each had missed the other so dearly and they made love into the early morning.

Chapter 12

Sunday didn't come fast enough for Gilda.
It was 7:00 am; she jumped out of the bed and began her prayers.

"Dear God, please forgive me for not visiting your house like I should, I am a God fearing woman you know that because you know my heart."

"You also know I am supposed to meet Fisher around the back of the church by the pond after church services today."

"And Lord, you also know what is going on with these city slickers too dear Father."

"I know I have not been talking to you lately like I should, but please watch over all of us."

"I feel that there is going to be some even worse times than this before things get better, dear Lord I pray for your protection, discernment, and wisdom and above all your guidance Lord Amen."

Gilda got off of her knees and went into the closet. She pulled out a pretty pink cotton shirt with lace at the collar and a black skirt. Gilda then got her shoes and lightly sprinkled cornstarch in them. She then pulled out her hair with the pressing comb and afterwards used the curling irons. She looked herself over in the long mirror. Gilda had not been cutting on her hair for the past few months and noticed that it was beginning to grow back. Gilda then went to the bathroom with her clothes to freshen up and before long she was dressed. She arrived at the church and the first person she seen was Colleen. Elijah had warned her that Colleen had returned from visiting her sister up North.

"Well good morning Gilda, fancy seeing you here." Gilda didn't want to make a scene because that is exactly what Colleen always enjoyed doing. Therefore, she didn't waste any time responding to her comment in a sarcastic manner while waving her fan to combat the early morning heat. "Well I'm just so delighted that you fought your way through all this here crowd of folks to visit with little ole me Colleen."

"You know Colleen; it is a real good thing that the Lord is forgiving now isn't it?"

"After all we both know what Proverbs chapter 6, verses 16-19 says right?"

"You do still read your bible don't you Colleen?" Colleen and her small entourage looked at Gilda wide-eyed. It was evident that she was not the same woman they were use to dealing with. Gilda was more reserved in her attack on Colleen nowadays as if she was addressing a child. Colleen, embarrassed by the comments made one last attempt.

"Indeed I do, which leads me to wonder, how's the Juke Joint Gilda?"

"Oh I wouldn't know."

"I was fired for being such a darn good worker."

"Imagine that!"

Now even Colleen's entourage could not fight off their grins to Gilda's sarcastic humor. Colleen had finally had enough; She rolled her eyes and proceeded into the church with the rest of the congregation. Reverend Brown had given a good service that morning. Everyone left out with their spirits lifted. The children came out singing the songs that they had heard while listening to the choir. Little Josie was one as she ran past her mother and Gilda standing out front. Gilda had told Julia everything. They were passing notes during services like they use to when they were little girls.

"Gillie, I sure hope you know what you are doing."

"Julia, I need to know what is going on before I can even decide if there is anything I have to do."

"Fisher just wants to talk to me about some-things. He doesn't want me involved, he said that to me himself." Julia folded her arms across her growing stomach.

"Well how does Elijah feel about all of this?"

"Well, he said that Fisher was a grown man and he could handle himself and that he he's been doing business with them a longtime, so he knows what he's up against."

"Well Gillie he is right."

"I know that Julia, I never denied that, but Julia you, me and Fisher, come on now we been friends along time, even before Elijah and Joshua."

"If he needs my help, I can't turn him down."

Gilda and Julia turned their attention to Fisher who was coming out of the church conversing with Reverend Brown. Gilda watched Fisher as he waved his hand at a black convertible on the side of the road. "Julia something really strange is going on, look over there."

Julia discreetly turned around and saw in the car.

"You think they're here for Fisher?"

"I believe so; I hope we get a chance to talk like we planned."

Gilda wondered had things gotten worse since the last time she had spoken to him. Fisher acknowledged the three men in the car and then approached Gilda and Julia, he gave each a kiss.

"Good morning ladies."

"Good morning Fisher."

"Fisher, me and Julia here are worried."

"What in the world is going on?"

"Gillie, just be quiet a minute and listen."

"Remember how we use to hide our treasures back in the woods when we were kids?"

Gilda nodded in confirmation.

"Well, I need you two to remember this: Wylie River Woods follow the signs Gillie and then dig four feet on the north side of the tree."

"Fisher, you alright?"

Fisher didn't respond, but only gave them both a hug.

"I love the two of you, I am leaving town and won't be back."

"I tried to get Ted to come with me."

"He has never left Monroe County."

"I left him some money and a train ticket out of Barnsville and he promised me he would follow, but I know him better."

Gilda and Julia could see the sadness in Fisher's eyes. He really didn't want to leave Big Ted behind.

"Please check on him for me, there have been a change of events and I really need to get outta town right now."

"Ladies please look happy for me, I don't need any sad hearts for me."

"You hear?"

"Just remember what I told you, watch for the signs."

Fisher walked over to the shiny car. The man on the passenger side got out and let Fisher in the front seat, he slid in the back and afterwards they drove off. Gilda and Julia watched as the car lifted the dust from the dirt road until it was out of sight.

"What was all that about Gillie?"

"I don't know, maybe that is what he wanted to tell me.

"Let's get over to Fisher's Place."

"Gillie, we can't go over there."

"It may be dangerous, the sheriff or anybody may show up."

"Julia I need to talk to Ted."

They both hopped into the truck, Julia struggled as she got in. Julia waved to Miss Ann to look after Josie.

"Something awfully strange has gone down Julia, I can feel it."

"How did they know he was coming to the church Gillie?"

"I don't know Julia, they must've followed him."

All kind of thoughts started rushing through Gilda's head and none of them were good. It took them what seemed like forever to get to the other side of town to Fisher's Place. Gilda had hoped that Ted had not run into the sheriff. If

Fisher had told them that he needed to go right away, that was what he'd meant. The girls sped down the road and the red Georgia dust wavered at every turn. They soon heard the sounds of sirens going off.

"Damn!"

Gilda looked in the rear view mirror.

"It's the sheriff Julia."

He pulled along the side of them and directed them off the road. Once they had stopped, he pulled in the front of them and got out of the car. He held his hand on his gun holster and walked up to the driver's window. "Where you two girls going in such a hurry?"

Julia rubbed on her round stomach.

"I'm feeling mighty strange sherriff suh, it's almost my time and I wanna get home is all."

"Is that the problem?" The sheriff looked over at Gilda. Gilda shot him back another look. "That is correct suh."

"Well good then, for a minute there I thought maybe you two girls was fixing to run into something that ain't any of your business."

"You know strange things happen to folks around here that go meddling in other folks business; you know what I mean Gilda?"

Gilda gave him a cold stare.

"I have no idea what you are talking about sir, but I will keep that in mind."

"Well all is good then girls."

"I think we have an understanding, you know it's good to have an under-standing."

"Good day." The sheriff tipped his hat got back in his car and pulled off.

"Gillie, I'm getting awfully worried now, this is serious."

"Did you hear the sheriff?"

"Yeah, I did and I smell a rat too."

"So what now Gillie?"

"Well, we're going down to Wylie River like Fisher said and find out just what he been up to."

The ladies headed toward Wylie creek. On the way they ran into a small tent community. Julia asked Gilda to pull over and Julia slowly got out of the truck, she was feeling a little nauseated from the ride. "Gillie, im'ma see if Pearl got some sassafras tea." As she walked into the small tent community a short stout women approached her.

"Good morning Julia."

"Good morning Pearl, how you doing these days."

"Julia it looks like I should be asking you that question." "That baby of yours is sitting awfully low."

"Yeah and I feel like I'm about to burst."

"Pearl I want you to meet someone; This here is my sister-friend Gilda, but we call her Gillie."

"Hello Miss Gillie it's a pleasure meeting you."

"Same here, but Gillie would be just fine." Pearl smiled at Gilda's reply. "Well Gillie and Julia, what brings you out this way?"

"We just passing through gonna take a walk down yonder, but I wanted to get some of your sassafras tea, I'm feeling a bit nauseated today."

"Oh sure Julia come on over here and have a seat I'll fix you right up."

"Julia, while you sit here I'm gonna take this way down to the creek."

"Julia nodded at Gilda as Pearl gave her a tin cup."

"Here this should make you feel better."

"Ah thanks Pearl."

"Now Gillie, you be careful chile of dem dare woods, it could be dangerous, dem snake bites and such."

"One of the men here had gotten bitten by one of them snakes back yonder."

"If it wasn't for sister Gracie here he probably wouldn't be with us."

Gilda looked over at Gracie. She was a stern looking woman; her skin was dark as coal, her hair snow white and her eyes blue as the sky. She had been a runaway slave just before the war. Gracie and many others like herself lived in the swamps of Louisiana in order to stay alive. It was in those same swamps that she learned to use the healing herbs of the earth to combat diseases that plagued her people. Now she shared those remedies with Pearl.

Gracie gave Gilda a long observation, but said nothing. Gilda nodded her head and turned the attention back on Julia.

"Oh Pearl, don't worry about me, I'll be fine."

"Julia is the one that we have to watch."

Gilda excused herself and began her journey down near the river. The sound of the birds and fresh water running down the stream brought back memories to Gilda.

"I just want to pin point exactly were Fisher was talking about."

It had been a long while since she'd gone that deep into the woods. Gilda walked slowly stepping over snake holes as she checked the tree barks on the trail.

"I know this is the way."

After a few minutes she begin identifying the fresh symbols that Fisher carved into the bark of the trees one after another. This was one of the skills passed down from their ancestors. It was one of the many methods used to help runaway slaves during the Underground Railroad. Many folks now would use this secret skill as a way to safely hide their personal valuables. Gilda studied the markings carefully, it had been awhile since she'd played this game with Fisher. Finally she found the large tree that fisher had spoken of. Gilda pulled a handkerchief from her skirt pocket, tore a piece and tightly wrapped it around a branch.

"There, that should do it."

Gilda quickly made her way back toward the small tent community. There she found Julia and Pearl sitting down talking and finishing up their second cup of tea.

"Gillie girl look at you."

"I know Julia; I need to get outta these clothes."

"It was such a pleasure meeting you Pearl and you too Miss Gracie."

"You too Gillie."

Gilda helped Julia as she struggled to get up.

"Gillie I was just talking to Pearl."

"I offered her a job to come and help me around the house."

"Oh that sounds good; she could sho use it right about now Pearl."

"So Pearl I guess I will see you and Cora out to the house tomorrow."

"I'll be there, and thanks again Julia."

"No thank you."

Afterwards Gilda dropped Julia off and headed back to town.

Chapter 13

Early the following afternoon Gilda caught a ride with Mr. Payton to Julia's to fix Josie's hair. She also wanted to talk more with Julia about the events surrounding Fisher.

When she arrived Pearl was there hanging laundry as she had promised and was being helped by Josie and her daughter Cora. Gilda fixed both of the little girl's hair. When she was done, the two of them looked liked angels with ribbons holding their long pony tails in place. As the mid-afternoon creeped in Gilda and Julia sat on the porch vigorously waving their fans against the summer heat. Julia had the radio playing and the sweet sounds of the Delta Blues were ringing out the front window. Gilda began nodding her head and snapping her fingers.

"Chile I just love this here song."

"Any word from Big Ted Gillie?"

"Not yet, and I'm worried, I was sure he would have contacted us by now."

"Well, Folks been saying Fisher's Place been closed down."

From the distance they could see Elijah's truck coming up the dirt road fast. The two of them knew something was wrong. Gilda got up and stood at the edge of the porch. Elijah and Joshua pulled up to the house, jumped out of the truck and went directly toward the barn. They walked pass both Gilda and Julia without saying a word. When they returned, Elijah had an axe and Joshua had his shot gun.

"What on earth is going on Joshua?" Gilda looked into the eyes of the man she loved.

"Elijah what's wrong?"

She could see the anger in his face.

"We found Ted strung up from a tree just outside of town this morning." The two women looked on in horror.

"Me and Joshua gonna help get him down."

"Billie Ray and John are over there waiting for us, just so the birds don't get at him." Gilda fell back into the swing on the porch and began to cry.

"My God, my God!"

Julia looked at Joshua with tears in her eyes.

"Julia baby, don't worry we will be back soon."

The men jumped in the truck and sped off the same way they had come. During the commotion Pearl made her way to the front part of the house.

"Is everything okay up here?"

"No, they've killed Ted." All the women sat on the porch not saying a word.

Julia suddenly began to wail with pain.

"Oh my God!"

"I think it is time, someone please get Doc."

But there was no time, her water had already broken and the ladies helped her into the house. The girls ran in behind Gilda, only to be turned away.

"Go on outside we will call you if we need you, go on now!"

"Gillie, I need the doctor, please I don't want to lose my baby."

"Just relax Julia, ain't gonna be no babies lost here today becasue me and Pearl are here with you."

"I promise we won't let that happen will we Pearl?"

"No Julia."

"We won't let that happen I promise you."

"I've delivered plenty of babies in my time, shoot even delivered my own."

"Be still honey, just be still now."

"Gillie, I need you to go and get me some fresh towels and some linen; As many as you can find and put the towels in some hot water on the stove."

Gilda did as instructed and returned momentarily with the linen and later retrieved the warm towels from the stove.

"Gilda, looks like she's going to be a fighter, I need some rope to tie her legs."

Gilda ran back out of the room to the backside of the house. She went to the clothes line and began to snatch it down. From outside she could her Julia's screams.

Josie, listened in horror but was soon comforted by Cora. Cora had seen her mother do this work many times. When Josie began to cry, Gilda consoled her on the way into the house. "Everything is going to be fine sweetpea."

"Don't worry, it hurts an awful lot to bring a child into the world, your mama will be fine."

The girls went to the back of the house to the bedroom window and stooped low so they could not be seen. Gilda returned to her best friends side. "Gillie, where are you?"

"I'm here Julia."

Julia was sweating profusely and complained often of feeling hot. Gilda as instructed left her side briefly to tie her legs to the bottom bed posts as Pearl stuffed the pillows behind Julia and pushed her body as close as she could to the foot of the bed until her knees were fully bent and legs spread apart. "Okay honey, you gonna have to help us get this baby out."

Gilda had known to do many of these things. As a little girl she too watched her grandmother deliver Mrs. Payton's grandchild Perry. Both women encouraged Julia to push and as she screamed out in pain. Pearl raised the pillows behind Julia's head and Gilda kneeled at the foot of the bed waiting.

"No sign of the head yet." Julia took a few short breaths and Pearl shouted.

"Okay Julia try to make this a long one sweetie." Pearl lifted Julia up and again she screamed in agony pushing even harder with more force than the time before. Pearl began wiping Julia's face with a cool wash cloth.

"You are doing good honey, just fine."

"Owww, it hurts Pearl."

"It's supposed to hurt chile, now come on push." Gilda's eyes widened and she begin smiling with excitement.

"I see it, I see the head Julia, come on chile push."

Pearl lifted Julia up again and a sharp pain went down the center of her back as she screamed

"Lord help me please!!!"

Gilda shouted.

"Come on Julia one more time sweetie." Julia pushed again. Soon cries of a baby covered the entire house.

"Julia, it's a boy, it's a boy." Julia began smiling and Pearl slowly laid her head back down.

"Congratulations."

Julia and the ladies were all laughing and crying at the same time. Pearl grabbed the warm face bowl filled with sterile water to clean her and the baby up. Gilda had the honor of cutting the umbilical cord. The two girls ran through the house to the back, but were stopped in their tracks at the bedroom door. Pearl sent them both for more cotton linen while Gilda continued to wipe down the wailing baby.

"Wow! It's a boy."

"Joshua's gonna be so happy."

When Josie returned Julia waved her hand for both her and Cora to come into the room. Gilda laid the baby boy in his mother's arms and immediately he quieted down at the sound of her voice. "Look at your little brother isn't he beautiful."

Julia had a son and his eyes were wide open and they were the color of honey.

"Look at his eyes Mama they are the color of honey, just like Daddies."

Julia smiled and gave both her children a kiss. Gilda and Pearl left them in the room and went out on the porch. "My goodness what a day."

"Yes Lord, it is tuff work bringing a life into the world Gillie."

Doc Norman arrived a few hours later and gave a bill of health to Julia and the baby. He also congratulated Gilda and Pearl for a job well done. After Pearl and Cora left for the evening, Gilda and Josie sat on the porch while Julia and the baby slept. Gilda wondered where Joshua and Elijah were. They'd left to see about Ted and were gone since early afternoon. Gilda held on to the locket around her neck thinking about Elijah and the plans they had made. Soon the truck slowly made its way up the road. Joshua couldn't get out the car good before, Josie ran up.

"Daddy, mamma had a baby boy."

Joshua looked up at Gilda for confirmation and she pointed to the door.

"They're in the house resting now and the Doc's been out here too." Joshua nodded and went into the house. Gilda turned her attention back to Elijah as he slowly pulled the tools and shotgun out of the bed of the truck.

"What happen with Ted?"

"We been waiting all day for ya'll." Elijah closed the truck bed door and walked over to Gilda. He put his hands around her and gave her a big hug. Gilda knew her man, it was an embrace filled with pain and anger.

"Let's go into the house Gillie."

Gilda went into the house behind Elijah and she then peeked in on Julia and Joshua. She smiled as he stood holding his son.

"Julia you are so very strong, I am so proud of you"

"Thank you Gillie, just look at your godchild."

"Yep that's my boy." Gilda could see how very proud Joshua was.

"Have you named him Joshua?"

"Of course I have, he is Joshua Theodore Mason Jr. named after me and Big Ted.

 Elijah stepped into the room. "Where is my Nephew?" Joshua held him up to Elijah so that he could get a look. "He's handsome isn't he Uncle Elijah?"

"And that he is." Elijah then looked over at Gilda. "How long will it be before you let me marry you woman?"

"I have been waiting for sometime now." Elijah got on his knees in front of Gilda. "Haven't I proved my undying love to you?" Startled Gilda looked around the room and noticed everyone was watching her. Elijah lifted Gilda up off her feet.

"We got lots of catching up to do."

"They're already up two." Elijah didn't want to damper the joy Julia and Joshua shared so he and Gilda headed out the door.

"We're going into town, we will be back tomorrow." When they left, Gilda attempted to get information out of Elijah about Ted. He refused to speak with her about it until they were at the house. When they arrived, Gilda made Elijah a shot of Canadian Liquor that she kept stashed away in her cubbard for emergencies. When they settled in on the couch and Elijah explained how dangerous things had gotten.

"Gillie, I don't know what is going on around here, but the sheriff and his deputies are on the rampage."

"Billie Ray said that Big Ted told him that he and Fisher had a plan and he was suppose to leave when it was time."

"Ted promised Fisher that he was right behind him, Billie Ray said Ted told him he just couldn't leave."

"Ted went over there and burned Fisher's Place down to the ground."

Gilda covered her mouth with surprise. "Oh my God?"

"That's not the half of it either Gillie."

"It appears afterwards late last night he got a visit from Paulie, the Sheriff and his lynch mob."

Billy Ray followed them just outside of town"

"Gillie, he risked his life."

"He saw everything and when it was clear, Billie Ray went by John's."

"He said he hid all night till the last truck pulled off." "Me and Joshua were at John's helping him with the roof of his barn when Billy Ray got there this morning."

"He told us everything and took us to Ted." Gilda sat on the sofa with tears in her eyes as she listened to the events that occurred.

"How could they be so cruel?"

"Ted never harmed a fly, and he was a good man."

"I guess since they could not catch up with Fisher, they went after the one closest to him."

"It appears that way my love."

"Billie Ray told us Ted fought back before they could get a hold of him."

He killed two of em with his shotgun."

"He must've run out of ammunition and they were finally able to get a shot in because, we seen the bullet wound in his shoulder."

Elijah didn't want to share everything with Gilda, it was too much. He didn't want to mention that they had tortured him before they shot him while he was still hanging from that tree. He and the others vowed it would be their secret to keep amongst brothers for Ted's dignity.

"We picked up a wooden casket from Mr. Wallace and we buried him Gillie."

"You know we gone have to start making plans to leave this here place."

"I don't know how much more safe its gonna be around here."

"I got a feeling that the sheriff gone be snooping around."

"It's a good possibility that the sheriff and his deputies want to get anyone who they feel might be tied to Fisher, maybe even you Gillie!"

Gilda realized the things that Fisher shared with her in his office that day had finally come to past.

"I know why they went after Ted."

"They were getting a pay off and had been living off of Fisher's success for sometime Elijah."

"Ted burning down Fisher's Place was a slap in their face."

"Paulie has no need for em, so now the money is gone." Fisher had left just in time and she only hoped that he was safe.

However Elijah's concerns were only for Gilda.

After a warm bath the two sat on the couch. Gilda was anxious to hear the sounds of the new night time syndicated Blues broadcast on the radio. Some how with all of the commotion, Gilda found a way to settle her mind and she found comfort snuggled inside Elijah's arms. The sweet smell of her vanilla bean body oil never failed to entice is manhood. "You are the most beautiful woman that I have ever laid my eyes on."

"You, my dear heart are the most wonderful man inside and out."

Elijah even in his down mood managed to smile for Gilda.

He gently touched her face with the back of his hand.

"You are the only women that I want to spend the rest of my life with."

Gilda blushed because she had always felt the same way about him. He slowly pulled her closer to him and began kissing and caressing her. He kissed her lips lusciously and unbuttoned each of her buttons on her gown and with every button loosed he softly kissed her. Gilda laid back in his arms open to all that he wanted to explore. Elijah picked her up into his arms and took her into the bedroom. There he laid her down gently Gilda looked on in desire at the man that she craved all her life. Both were hurting deeply about the events that had occurred and needed to be comforted by the others touch. Neither thought about tomorrow only what they shared together at that moment of time.

"Ki'Somma."

Elijah whispered as he gently kissed her neck, moving slowly down to her nipples caressing them to stiffness as she moaned in ecstasy. Gilda moaned with pleasure as she felt the erotic throbbing in between her thighs. She slowly began caressing the nap of his neck as he continued his exploration over her body. Like a traveler he toured her world savoring the taste of her. His journey continued down to her navel kissing her softly. Gilda felt as though she was going to explode. Elijah did not stop, his desire was to be her every thought, and he made that his primary mission in life.

"How do you feel?"

He whispered in her ear with his deep voice."

"I want to bring you to love my Ki'Somma."

He repeated his journey over her body.

"Oh how passionate this man is."

She thought to herself. Slowly he continued to kiss and caress her gently moving his tongue around her waist until he had found her treasure deep below. He played with her in a soft way showing his expertise in loving her fully. Gilda moaned continuously and began calling his name.

"Oh Elijah."

Slowly he slid his manhood into her and gently he gave her loving strokes. Soon they were together moving toward one another. The strokes became thrust as Gilda gave out soft moans of pleasure. He held her close to his body not letting her go. Gilda closed her eyes as the feeling became so good it overwhelmed her to tears. Gilda had been the first to show Elijah the gentleness that he had for love. He made no secret of it each time he made love to her. After a time, together they reached the pinnacle of their closeness. Elijah looked down into Gilda's eyes feeling like a king making love to his queen. He began kissing her all over her face and along her neck until she began to giggle

"Mr. Mason what has gotten into you?"

"You my Ki'somma you've gotten into me."

The two stayed in bed the entire night holding on to each more closely and savoring the love they felt for one another. Gilda knew after that night their lives would never be the same.

Chapter 14

The memorial for Ted had been the saddest since Gilda's mother had passed. She and Julia had insisted on acknowledging his life even though Elijah and the others had buried him. Gilda and Elijah sat together in the pew and he held her close while she mourned for her dear friend.

Gilda, Julia, Big Ted and Po Fisher had all grown up together in the little town of Culloden and it was as if she had lost a brother. They all had shared some good times together now life was taking charge and swiftly catapulting them into places Gilda could have never imagined. Ted had no family. His only family was Fisher and he had disappeared. No one had heard from him since that day at the church. Julia sang a beautiful tune of "Precious Lord" while leading the church choir. Tears fell from her eyes as she looked over at Joshua holding their son. Josie was with Miss Ann, who had not attended another funeral since Gilda's mother had passed. When the service was over the four of them went back out to the Mason house. They all sat on the porch quiet and motionless. Julia looked up from nursing the baby.

"Y'all know what?"

"I'm getting awfully tired of living around this here place."

"There has been nothing here but death, hate, and misery."

"The white folk around here can be so cruel to the black folks."

"We're human just like them and we breathe the same air as they do."

"They know better than most that we bleed the same blood too."

"We're supposed to be free, but we ain't free, worrying whether today is the day we just may get strung up from a tree."

"It just ain't right."

With all the commotion, Gilda and Julia finally had the opportunity to tell Joshua and Elijah about the large tree by Wylie River. The next morning Elijah and Joshua grabbed a couple of shovels and took Gilda back to the wooded area. This time Gilda had no problem remembering the trail and after a few minutes of walking she pointed to the handkerchief.

"There it is."

Joshua and Elijah started digging.

After about thirty minutes Joshua came across a large potato sack and hit it with his shovel,

"This must be it."

"Elijah, help me get it out."

Elijah with all the strength he had pulled at the sack.

"Look man it's another one."

One had been stacked neatly on top of the other. Elijah took his pocket knife and made a small cut into the mesh of the sacks. The first was stuffed neatly with money stacks and the much heavier one contained individual pouches. Elijah grabbed one and handed it to Gilda. She opened it up and her eyes grew wide with surprise.

"Good lord it's gold!"

"This is what Fisher was trying to talk to me about; he had stashed money and gold?"

The only thing going through Gilda's mind was how, when, and why.

Joshua took off his hat and wiped his brow.

"Hmmm looks like ole Fisher, was saving up for a rainy day." Elijah bent down and grabbed a piece of paper and handed it to Gilda.

"Well, what do you want to do Gilda?"

"I can't do anything that's Fisher's money, and his coins." Elijah spoke sincerely.

"I think he had you come here for a reason, what does the note say?"

Gilda looked down at the envelope it had been addressed to her. She opened it and read its contents while Elijah and Joshua listened;

Gilda,

If you are reading this letter I am probably dead. I want you to split this with Julia and Ted, send Ted out west so he can start a new life; he always talked about going to California.
Fisher

Tears filled Gilda's eyes; it was just too much to bear in such a little time. Elijah held her as Joshua began pouring dirt back on top of Fisher's treasure.

"He did listen to me, I always told him to put a little up for himself just in case."

"I would tell him just in case."

"Elijah can we move these."

"The money can be moved, the gold on the other hand will be difficult."

"Me and Joshua would have to come back for it."

"It's just too heavy to carry without equipment."

"You two will have to keep it out to the house because I just don't feel comfortable with it being at my house."

After quickly loading the sack into the bed of the truck they made their way back to the house.

****

Elijah finally received word from back home from his cousin Jerry.

The deed to his father's land was sold and released to a man by the name of Foster Keeley. Keeley was the youngest brother of Fredrick Keeley. Fredrick had shared his adventures many times with his brother. He was very ill when he returned home and had no desire to return to South Carolina. He passed away months after returning home. Foster Keeley arrived in South Carolina looking for the Mason's and his brothers half of the gold. Foster was an alcoholic and spent several years on a drinking and gambling rampage out West. Foster had lost nearly everything and decided to search for the man who shared the story of his brother's unclaimed fortune. He traveled to South Carolina in search of the Mason's. Foster became outraged when he discovered that Joseph Mason was deceased and his land tied up in taxes. Foster Keeley spent a portion of what was left of his inheritance to purchase the one hundred acres of land in the hopes of finding a treasure.

 Foster figured that the gold had to be buried somewhere on it and spent the last few years digging. He decided to hire the two brother posse by the name of Gray. The two had known the history behind the Mason's and had informed Foster about Elijah and Joshua and why they left South Carolina. Foster figured they couldn't have possibly taken the gold. The Gray's convinced him it would have been impossible. The short time they had to escape the hands of the lynch mob would not have allowed it. Therefore, Foster had full confidence in the investment he'd made up until now.

 Elijah looked over the letter from his cousin. After talking it over with Joshua they decided to leave for South Carolina in two days time. Joshua encouraged Julia to stay with Gilda.

 The Gray boys were known for their affiliation with the Ku Klux Klan. They despised the Mason men, holding on to the belief that Joseph Mason had killed their father in cold blood. Elijah knew that it was a possibility that a lynch mob would be organized once word had gotten out of their return The treasure left back home was their father's life savings.

Joseph Mason had sacrificed his life for his family and there was no way they were gonna leave it behind.

In a lot of ways Elijah understood Gilda wanting to get away to a better place. There were too many bad memories that dwelled in her home town. After all, he had memories of his own as well. *"Maybe we could move west."* He thought to himself, after all they would have more than enough to survive on once he returned home.

It had been a few days since Gilda helped Elijah and Joshua unload Fisher's sack of money. Joshua buried it under the house and there it would stay for the time being. Today however, Gillie sat across from Miss Ann helping her sort clothing donated to the AME Church.

Miss Ann felt it was her duty to get as many clothes and shoes for the needy children in town as she could. Even with the financial state of the country there were many folks that managed to come together through their churches and social clubs to provide for the needy. Miss Ann was always excited about the new shipment.

"Oh the children are going to be so pleased."

Miss Ann began to notice that Gilda was more quiet than usual.

"Gillie is there something the matter sweetie?"

Gilda shook her head and Miss Ann put both hands on her hips.

"Now Gillie why would you sit there in front of an old woman and tell a bold face tail like that, I can see chile."

"I may be old but I can still read folks."

"Is it that Elijah?"

Gilda shook her head.

"No ma'am it is not, I just have been doing a lot of thinking lately Elijah asked me to marry him, but I do not know if that's what I want."

"Do you love him chile?"

"Yes I do."

"Shoot you don't have any problems then."

"It's never good for such a young girl like your self to worry bout things so much because you have your entire life ahead of you."

"The good lord only blesses you with one life."

Miss Ann slapped her knee and laughed.

"So when you get old like me you can spend the rest of your days thinking about all the good times you had."

"What ever is due to you the good Lord going to make sure you get it, you can believe that."

"You here me chile?"

"Yes ma'am."

"Miss Ann you have been knowing me since I was a child."

"Yes and a busy one at that."

Gilda had to smile.

"You knew my mama and my Grandma too."

"Yes, I surely did!"

"Sometimes I feel like I got cheated out of spending more time with them."

"Thinking maybe my life could have been a whole lot different if I would have had them with me a while longer."

"Chile the Lord works in mysterious ways and everybody is put on this here earth to do an assignment for him and chile he got so many, some big some small"

"Yes you lost the two most important people in your life so very young, but the good lord got better things for you in the future."

"You just gotta be patient."

"He never gives us more than we can handle, you remember that."

"Ain't nothing wrong with you or your life Gillie, you just living."

Miss Ann continued.

"Being able to get up and see another day is another chance to figure out what the Lord expects of you, and you can't figure any of it out without faith."

"He made it that way and that's the tricky part that gets us all riled up inside, so while we are living we are also encouraged to develop trust in him."

"So don't spend time being sad, because sadness doesn't change the situation faith will do that."

Gilda thought for a minute. Miss Ann was wise in her age and always seemed to give her a clearer picture of life.

"Now that young man Elijah, he is a nice looking fellow and he been sweet on you a long time Gillie."

"I may be an old woman, but I got two half good eyes to see."

Gilda looked astonished, could it have been that obvious she thought.

"Them other girls around here, I see how they use to chase after him and they were in their right mind to do so too!"

"Shoot if I had been fifty years younger I might have even tried for myself." Gilda placed her hand over her mouth to cover her grin, "Miss Ann."

The two ladies laughed.

"Are you blind chile?"

"Men like that are rare I tell you."

"You know Gillie, I never told you this but I once had a lover, his name was Conrad and he was from Texas, oh and handsome he was."

"I met him in California while visiting my Aunt Barbara Jean."

"He was rugged, tall, and did I say handsome."

"He was so sweet on me and we did everything together."

"That was one of the most wonderful summers in my life." Gilda listened attentively.

"He proposed to me, but I was so wrapped up in all the what ifs." Gillie looked confused. "What do you mean the what ifs?"

"You know, what if it doesn't work, what if my parents don't approve, what if, what if, what if, that's what I am talking about."

"When I seen him again it was about five years later, he had acquired a sizable amount of land in Oklahoma and was cattle farming."

"Sad for me though, he'd gotten married and his wife gave him three children."

"I promised myself that next time a strong man with a good heart approached me and gave his love and passion to me, I would take him and run for the hills."

"Now don't get me wrong I had others after him, but none, none could have ever compared to Conrad."

"Do you follow me Gillie?"

Gilda knew exactly what Miss Ann was trying to tell her, it was the same thing that Julia had been speaking to her about. Some people are just made for one another.

Elijah was no stranger in her life; he had been there through it all for her. She began looking back on all the times that he appeared when she had needed him the most and even at times when she didn't he was still there. Gilda grinned as she also thought about the times that he opposed some of the decisions that she had made in her life, like working at Fisher's.

"Boy did he raise the dead about that."

She thought, but he always supported her by always being there. Gilda's thoughts were interrupted.

"Gilda, you still there chile?"

"Oh yes Miss Ann."

"Keep good thoughts chile, the way the world is we need to keep good thoughts." The remaining afternoon the women continued talking about love, life and dreams to come.

Chapter 15

It was early Wednesday morning when Elijah and Joshua loaded the truck for their trip home; each had mixed feelings about going back. The sun had not come up yet, but Gilda and Julia still watched as the men packed down the bed of the pick up truck. They would have to travel through dangerous areas before reaching the border of South Carolina before daybreak, so leaving early was a benefit. Julia handed Joshua a basket of food for the road. She'd prepared fried chicken, corn muffins, and also put fruit preserves and some raw carrots and celery inside from the garden. "How long do you think it would take you before you get there?"

"It shouldn't take us long, about eight or nine hours."

Gilda looked at Elijah; she had spent the night at the house and had stayed with Elijah in his quarters. The two of them stayed up all night talking and playing checkers. He loved Gilda down to the depths in his soul.

Elijah gave Gilda a wink.

"When I get back you will marry me, so start looking for a wedding dress."

Gilda smiled and blew him a kiss.

"I will be waiting for you Mr. Mason."

The men hopped up in Elijah's truck waved and soon they were gone into the darkness.

****

Elijah and Joshua had arrived home at high noon. Right away they headed for the post office to send word for Mr. Johnson to inform the girls that they had gotten there safely. Elijah looked around the small little town. He noticed right away not much had changed since they left years ago. Mr. Harper was the Grocer in town and he also ran the postal service. Right away he recognized the men and greeted them with dismay.

"Whatcha two boys doing back here, you know them Gray boys find out you back there's gonna be trouble."

"You know they blame you two for killing their papa."

Joshua stepped up to Mr. Harper.

"Now look here Mr. Harper, don't be going around here spreading no rumors and such, we didn't kill that man."

Elijah pulled his brother back and stepped to Mr. Harper.

"Sir, I don't mean no disrespect to you or your business, you knew my father and you've been knowing us since we were boys."

"But, I would suggest that you keep those types of comments fairly to yourself."

"We're grown men now and I suggest you respect us as such, because we don't want no trouble sir."

"I wanna apologize about that Elijah; it's just that it ain't been any peace around here since that guy Keeley has been hanging around."

"He got folks in an up roar not to mention those Gray boys he's got on his payroll."

Mr. Harper continued as he expressed his concerns more properly, as the life long friend that he had always been to their father. He offered the men a drink in the back pantry and then asked the men what happened that tragic night. Elijah and Joshua took turns explaining how Mr. Gray came by the house with his boys and a couple other men with a noose looking to hang their father. Joshua spoke out, "what were we suppose to do just stand their?"

"The Gray boys, they know what happened that night." Mr. Harper's temperament changed.

"We just don't want no trouble son and that's all."

"Folks have gotten older around here and most of the young folks have moved up north for work."

Elijah understood, but he thought it more important to focus on their business and nothing else.

"Ain't gonna be no trouble sir, you just make sure that message gets to were it needs to go, come on Josh."

The two hoped in the truck and then drove to meet their cousin Jerry.

"We can't stay here to long Elijah, it's gonna be dangerous once they find out that we're back."

"I wanna be out of here before it gets dark."

"Elijah, the story ain't gonna never get told right you know that."

Elijah looked over at Joshua.

"I came here for one thing and for one thing only, what belongs to us."

"I promised pop and I'm gonna do just that."

After what seemed like hours they finally came across the land. The house that once stood there just off the road was no longer there. They got out of the truck and looked over the beautiful green hilly land. The trees prevented them from seeing the landscape that laid on the other side. Both men now realized how much land their father had acquired, but now it had been lost. Lost to hatred, like so many others had.

They didn't want the land anymore, but would claim what their father had promised. Suddenly the men heard a strange sound of the past. Joshua smiled and responded.

"That must be Jerry."

Elijah got into the truck and rode over the grass into the trees so that it couldn't t be spotted.

When he returned, cousin Jerry landed on both feet from the tall oak tree.

"Hey fella's."

Elijah and Joshua had not seen their first cousin since that terrible night. While they were coming up the three could not be separated, because they were the children of sisters. Jerry had a strong a resemblance to both Elijah and Joshua.

He stood a foot taller than Joshua and a foot shorter than Elijah. He wore two braids also that fell at his shoulders and a round brim buffalo hide hat. A hat he had received from their grandfather when he was just a boy. Elijah would laugh at him in his youth because the hat was so large it swallowed his entire head, now a man he had grown into it perfectly just like his grandfather Black Eagle had told him he would. Jerry was upset that his family had to leave, but he was anxious to have finally been able to contact Elijah when it was safe to return home. The men carried on like youngsters as they rustled and punched at one another.

"Man, it sure is good to see you guys."

"I had to hold the young ladies down all by myself."

"What's up?" Both exchanged a high five with Jerry. "We good, we good, what about you Jerry?"

"What's up with you, what's going on around her man?"

"Man I tell you these Charleston sheriffs have gotten worse."

"We need to do this and get out of sight before dark."

"They're night riding all the time now, it's terrible."

"That Sam fella that I wrote you about, crazy man."

Jerry began to laugh while shaking his head.

"Man, they been out there digging their hearts out." Elijah and Joshua also begin to laugh.

"Man, you should have seen them, cursing one another and that Keeley fella, was so disgusted because they haven't found a thing."

"Uncle Joe sure knew what he was doing when he put that Gold away." Elijah went to the truck and got his rifle and Joshua did the same.

"You packing?"

Joshua asked Jerry.

"Of course."

Jerry pulled out his sling shot and Elijah smiled, while shaking his head

"You still playing with that thing huh?"

"Yep, saved my life many times, I call it my silent killer."

The men had been taught to use a sling shot as young boys while growing. Grandfather Black Eagle taught them all to use many hand made weapons to hunt small game like rabbit and squirrel in the woods of South Carolina. Elijah always favored the bow and arrow more, but chose the rifle because the bullet was always swifter. Jerry was eager to get down to business.

"Do you remember where Uncle Joseph told you he buried it?"

Elijah nodded his head.

"Yeah how could I forget that?" Well come on, you lead the way man cause I have been waiting on this day all my life it seems."

"I've been waiting to see it too."

"I wanted to look at it, but mamma told me that it was sacred ground and should not be touched until it was time."

"I tell you them Gray boys would be digging forever trying to locate it."

"Come on fella's I got the tools all ready"

Jerry and Joshua followed Elijah as they began their hike into the past. After about fifteen minutes of walking, the surroundings started to become familiar to Elijah. He began recognizing certain trees and pathways that his father had brought him through. "We have to go this way he said, I think we're getting close." After a few more minutes the men stopped. "Yes right here." Joshua looked at Jerry, they were astonished. "The Grays or Foster Keeley would have never thought to look here." It was the grave of their grandfather Black Eagle.

Elijah stood proud of himself for remembering the exact location. It was a small grave stone, it was marked with Blackfoot language markings, these grave sites had been common along the Delta Bayou, many tribes had buried their dead all over the delta in this same fashion. "Elijah, our pop sure was a clever man."

"Yes he was."

"Do we have to disturb the body?"

"I believe so."

While Jerry and Elijah were talking, Joshua wondered off to another grave site. He read the inscription on another small stone. It belonged to their mother and father. Also, a small stone with their mother and fathers name on it. Elijah and Jerry walked over to the site. "

"Me and P.J. buried uncle after you left."

"At the time I didn't have the heart to tell ya."

"He told me not to, said you would come home and it was just too dangerous at the time." Joshua began to collect tears in his eyes. He recalled the last time he and Elijah had seen their father, they were on the run for there life. Elijah held the tears back he had done his mourning when he was forced to leave his father. He was proud of his heritage and proud to be the son of such a courageous man.

The men returned to their grandfather's grave and begin working on the tombstone. It was very difficult and very heavy at first but after an hour or so of prying, pushing and pulling they finally loosened the stone out of the soil. Slowly, Elijah and Jerry gave a big push and down below was an elegantly crafted coffin. Jerry handed Elijah the crow bar and he grabbed the narrow wood handled shovel and begin digging around the coffin until the surface was exposed. Spooked by the act, Jerry spoke out.

"What are you guys doing, are you going to open the coffin?"

Neither said a word as they continued to complete the job. Suddenly the trees begin to dance in the wind as a large dark cloud hovered over the wooded area. Joshua looked up and watched the sky and trees as their leaves were forced to the ground by the strong winds. Elijah never looked up from the ditch, but took the crow bar and shoved it into the entrance of the coffin and began to pry. After several forceful attempts the coffin door popped open. He moved backward and looked at the sky as the cloud moved and the sun returned through the tops of the trees. Elijah looked up at his family "It is done!" He then climbed out and Joshua went down to slowly open the coffin. Jerry finally gathered enough nerve look down into the open coffin.

"Good lord man, that's grandpa?"

Jerry was astonished.

"No, it's just a shell; he's far from here now."

Joshua, unaffected by the sight of the gruesome skeleton put on his gloves and went along side of the corpse with his hands. He pulled out a satchel, then another and then another there were four total. He tossed each one to Jerry and then one to Joshua both needed two hands to catch the heavy sacs. They looked inside and just as Elijah had said there were pure gold coins. Elijah looked down at the corpse and said a small Blackfoot prayer over his grandfather. Then Joshua said his spill.

"Thank you grandpa, for watching over the family's inheritance."

Afterward the men fixed the grave back and placed the stone back in its place and made their way back to the pick up. Unknowingly they had spent well over two hours at the grave site.

"You fella's go on ahead back to your truck and I'll bring my truck around and meet you on the west side of the woods."

Jerry passed his satchel to Joshua and they proceeded back to their truck. Once they reached the truck, Elijah opened the passenger door and he and Joshua took all 4 sacks of gold and placed them neatly in the small compartment beneath the floorboard below front seats. Elijah backed the truck out onto the grass and then onto to the road, but to there surprise stood three men. Elijah and Joshua had recognized two. It was the Grays and they had slightly aged in the face. Percy the eldest had gone bald in the top of his head. Both assumed the other must had been Keeley.

"Well what do we have here?"

"Do you two boys know you're on private property?"

Elijah turned his attention to the unarmed man standing with his armed folded while George the eldest smiled displaying his two front rotten teeth.

"Mr. Keeley these here are the Mason boy's, ole Joseph Mason's sons."

Foster Keeley was an almost completely bald, tall and frail man. He reeked of alcohol and held a cigar in the corner of his mouth. "What you two doing on my land boy?" Elijah did not say a word while Joshua sized up the small framed man.

George pulled his flask out of his back pocket and turned it up, while trying to hold his balance and his rifle.

"Keeley, these two half-breeds help their daddy kill my papa."

"Left em in a puddle of blood and then ran like the cowards they are."

"That's a lie and you know it George." Elijah looked over at Joshua.

"Hold your peace brother."

George smiled again.

"Never mind, the sheriff been looking for the two of you for a long time.

"He gonna be real happy to know that you back in town."

Elijah responded in a still yet calm voice.

"Don't know why, because we both know that he and your father rode together under them white sheets."
"Everybody knows how your daddy harassed the black folks around here, including my father."

Percy shot back.

"Get cha hands up, the both of you before I blast your black hide all over this here place."

Miss Gilda's Blues 181

Foster Keeley stood watch and studied the two men, they were hardly what he expected. Both were strong and fearless and that made him quite uncomfortable.

"There is no need for all of this nonsense."

"I'm sure it's all a misunderstanding right fella's?"

"I'm not interested in this family feud that you have going on."

"I'm a businessman is all."

"I have one question and one question only."

"Where's the gold?"

Both Gray men stood with the barrels of their guns pointed at both Elijah and Joshua.

"We don't know what you are talking about."

Percy Gray then took the handle of his gun and hit Joshua in the stomach.

"You speaking for the both of ya?" He bent over in pain but managed to regain his composure. Elijah was furious but waited patiently.

"You heard the man where is the gold?" Keeley finally spoke.

"Now, I know your daddy was a wealthy man."

He walked up on Elijah.

"I know the whole story, pretty exciting too."

"Only my brother Fredrick could be so lucky."

"Now Elijah, I know you a rational man and we don't have to spend a lot of time discussing something that we both know you have the answer to."

"If you give me that gold I will sign the deed to this here land over to you and our business will be finished."

Elijah looked the man in the face coldly and then over at the Grays. He knew that if they hadn't been armed he and Joshua would have killed them both with their bare hands.

"We don't have any gold."

George Gray looked over at Foster Keeley.

"I betcha I can make em talk boss."

Giving him a stained tobacco grin.

"Percy, check the truck."

Percy went over to the truck and laid his shot gun on the door. He began rumbling vigorously through the back bed of the truck. Elijah had enough tools and supplies to keep him looking for a while. George was feeling really sure of himself, and continued to bring up the past.

"You know I thought we would never see y'all boys again."

"You gotta lot of nerve coming back here thinking you was gonna get away with what you did."

Foster Keeley looked over at George.

"Would you shut your drunken trap."

"I will be glad to get rid of you two once this thing is over."

George looked over at Foster while scratching his head. Joshua looked over at Elijah; to him it appeared that the three had been spending a lot of their time in the bottle

"Oh, now wait a minute Mr. Keeley you got business to settle with me and my brother."

"Who ya talkin bout getting rid of?"

George then pulled his tooth pick out of his ear and stuck it in his mouth. His concentration had completely left the Mason's and now he was aiming his rifle at Keeley. He then hollered over to his brother.

"Any luck?"

Percy hollered back.

"Naw not yet!"

Elijah could not believe what he was seeing, here they were being held hostage by three drunken men and two were armed. He looked over at his brother and not to his surprise they had been thinking the same thing. All Elijah could think about was Jerry's location. Where was he when he needed him. George called Percy out of the truck.

"Ole Foster here is expectin to get rid of us once he gets the gold, whatcha think about that?"

"Oh is that so huh?"

Foster looked over at Elijah and Joshua.

"I've just about had it up to here with this place."

"You know how many years I have been traveling back and forth to this god forsaken town, looking for this damn gold my brother spoke about in his journal?"

"Hell, I'm starting to believe it doesn't even exist."

"I've covered this entire hillside digging, searching for this damn gold."

"I'm sick of this place and I'm sick of you two." He pointed angrily at the Gray men."

George gave him a cold look and out of the blue took his rifle and shot him in the chest. Elijah turned his head and Joshua looked in amazement as his blood scattered against the dingy t-shirt of George Gray.

"Now there, he doesn't have to be sick anymore now does he?"

He and his brother begin to laugh. Quickly George's attention returned to Elijah and Joshua.

"Now if'n you don't tell me were that gold is I'm gonna let you Elijah, watch your brother here die like uh rabid dog." Elijah finally gave in.

"Okay, okay, we know were the gold is, it's over yonder in the woods."

"You better be telling the truth boy, I will shot you."

"Go on, move along then."

Percy and George both shoved at Elijah and Joshua and they went into the woods. Elijah and Joshua both were waiting for their cousin to surface. As the men went further in Elijah begin to hear a familiar sound, a sound from their childhood. He and Joshua continued walking as the Gray boys constantly pushed there barrels in their backs. Out of no were, a rock hit George in the side of his temple and he dropped his gun. Percy turned in confusion toward his brother. Meanwhile Elijah quickly grabbed the gun from the ground.

"Whose grinning now, tell your brother to back off or I'll kill you both."

"Percy, you know I will do it."

Percy attempted to fire a shot anyway, grazing Elijah in the arm and Elijah shot him through the chest. He fell on the ground moaning as the blood seeped from his body. His brother cried out to him in anguish as he took his last breath. Then George looked over at Elijah.

"You will pay for this I promise you."

"I will hunt you down and kill you like the dog you are, just like I did your father." Elijah struggled to raise the shotgun to shoot again but before he could George dropped his gun and held his head while he screamed in pain. Soon he fell dead next to his younger brother. Joshua went and grabbed it as he watched him take quick breaths until his breathing ceased. Elijah looked high into the tree.

"Damn Jerry, what took you so long man?" Jerry took a long leap and landed feet first to the ground. "Man, I thought I was losing my touch."

"I seen everything, even when the Gray's shot Keeley these here boys were crazy man."

Jerry with the fine precision taught to him by Grandfather Black Eagle swiftly targeted the temple of George's head with a solid cement rock. This, if done correctly would cause an automatic seizure to the brain. Jerry looked around.

"Fellas, we gotta get outta here, we can't stay."

Joshua observed the concerned look on Jerry's face. "What about baby sister and Auntie Kimi?"

"None of us can stay."

"I don't trust anybody around here; they will be looking for somebody, anybody, any of us including mamma."

"I can't guarantee that people will be quiet around here either, especially Mr. Harper."

"He will sing like a bird if the opportunity presents itself."

"One thing for sure, we got a little time before word gets out about you two, because anybody if given the opportunity could have gotten at the Gray's."

The three of them did not waste anymore time. Elijah and Joshua followed Jerry to his mothers and dropped off his truck. She hadn't seen Elijah and Joshua in many years and she hugged them until Jerry had to pry her loose. On there way out Jerry gave his mother a sack and when she opened it her eyes grew wide.

"You and Codi pack some things quickly and take the truck up to North Carolina to cousin Mattie's right now."

"Stay put until I contact you."

Startled, she began asking him questions. He explained the situation briefly, but had no more time to answer. He kissed her, said his goodbyes and went out the door.

"Y'all boys be careful, I'm praying for ya."

The Mason boys along with their cousin Jerry jumped in the truck and headed back for Culloden.

Chapter 16

After Elijah and Joshua left for South Carolina, Gillie and Julia spent most of the day in town. Julia packed her and the children an overnight bag to stay at Gilda's. Later in the afternoon, Gilda sent Josie and Cora over to Mr. Johnson's Market to see if there had been any word from Elijah and Joshua. They were surprised to find out they had arrived earlier than expected and both prayed that they would make it home safe. The afternoon sun was not as hot as it had been the prior weeks before. "Chile I can feel it cooling off a bit." Julia looked up from nursing the baby.

"It's about time, that summer heats been a scorcher." Josie and Cora played in the huge yard that Gilda had always been so proud of. It was her solitude; this was where she spent most of her leisure time during the day.

"Chile you have a mighty fine garden out here."

"Look how those Honeysuckles have bloomed; I could smell them from the house too."

"I want a piece to take home with me so I'll have it for next year."

Gilda laughed as she waved her hand at Julia.

"Julia you say that every time you come over here during the summer months and you never take a root."

"Just remind me chile."

The girls ran up to Gilda.

"Auntie Gillie do you have a jam jar, we wanna catch some bumble bees look they are all over the flowers."

"Oh yes that is a sweet one over there the honey bees love Jasmine."

Gilda directed the girls into the house.

"Go there in the pantry by the kitchen sink; I believe I have about three or four jam jars left in there."

"Be careful not to break them sweetie."

Gilda loved her oils and she always looked forward to the blooms in her garden. The process seemed to keep her close to her mother and grandmother. Julia lifted the baby from nursing and put him over her shoulder and slowly began patting him on his back. She then gave her attention to Gillie.

"So Miss Gilda, you getting married."

"You know he will be home soon and when he gets back you gonna be his priority."

Gilda looked at Julia with a small grin.

"I know, I know, whatcha think should I have a big wedding or something small here in the backyard."

"You ain't gonna have no time chile for no big wedding that man don't care nothing about all of that."

"All Elijah want is to make you his wife."

They noticed the tall young boy walking on the side of the fence, it was Colleen's nephew. He was a very nice young man and enjoyed playing with Josie.

"Boobie, come here." The handsome boy came into the fence.

"Hello Miss Gillie and Miss Julia."

"My have you grown son."

"How's ya mama?" Julia asked.

"Oh she doing well."

Gilda was still looking the young man over and chuckling to herself as she soon realized she and Julia had become both her mother and Miss Minnie.

The girls stopped what they were doing and went over to the patio.

"Hey Boobie."

"Hey Josie."

Josie with a bright smile on her face continued her conversation.

"You wanna catch some bumble bees with us?"

"Sure."

Josie returned from the pantry with another glass bottle and Gilda stopped her.

"Josie, how old are you now baby?"

"Eight years old auntie Gillie."

"You and Boobie, how long you two been friends?"

"Ummm since we were about four years old, you know when I started school auntie Gillie." She then ran to join her friends.

Josie was a pretty girl, but it brought back memories to Gilda.

Josie would be a different kind of girl she thought to herself. She had her mother and father, but also her and Elijah. There were people around to support her and to Gilda this just seemed to be the most important thing for a child's thinking.

"I'm gonna go lay the baby down, he's fast asleep."

Julia went inside and into the bedroom and laid little Joshua down on the bed. She returned to the porch with Gilda and they watched the children play in the yard.

"Chile I talk and I talk with that child, you know about how me and her papa met, and how she got here."

Gilda looked at her startled and Julia nodded her head.

"Yes I did girl."

"You think I want my baby to make the same mistakes I made?"

"Shoot no."

"I tell her that this here is girls talk, because if your daddy finds out about it he'll have both of our hides."

The two women burst out into laughter.

Soon the sun had gone down and the ladies retired to the front room of the house and the children were sitting on the porch laughing and talking.

"I'm expecting Joshua and Elijah will not get back until way past midnight sometime."

"I'm sure they will pass through town on the way home."

"He'll see the truck out front and Pearl knows that Cora's with me." Gilda then turned her attention to the children and spoke to them through the window.

. "Boobie your mama know where you are, if she don't you best be getting home."

"Its getting dark outside and I don't want you walking the road alone."

"Yes Miss Gillie."

Boobie said his goodbyes to the two girls and left the porch with his head down kicking dirt. Soon, the sound of sweet blues filled the front room of the house as Gilda nodded with the music on the radio.

"Girl times may be hard, but the blues oh the blues is like medicine."

While Julia was helping the girls get ready for bed Gilda sat in the chair and snapped hr fingers to what she called magic. Since the new syndicated broadcast had come to Culloden, Gilda was able to hear the latest recordings of both the Blues and Jazz. Also, between music selections on Saturday nights there would be dedications giving to the listeners from the listeners via the weekend national broadcast. The announcer began another dedication.

"This is a special dedication going out to the most influential ragtime artist known to the music world." The radio announcer continued: *This is for you Gillie from a friend who is able to survive even when it seemed that death was so close. Love you, your Louisiana man.*"

The music selection was a song by composer Scott Joplin, the well known ragtime pianist and composer. Few people had known how much she had favored the music of this great man. Gillie jumped out of her seat she could not believe her ears. Julia stood in the doorway in disbelief.

"Oh my god Julia did you here that?"

"There are only three people in this world that know how much I love Scott Joplin."

Your standing here, one is on the road, and no it couldn't be Julia." Gilda looked over at Julia.

"Do you think?"

"Oh my goodness it must be."

Julia shook her head.

"Well Gillie you know Fisher is a real slickster, I wouldn't put nothing pass him."

Gilda put here hand over here mouth. She knew that one had heard from Fisher, and Paulie had not showed up back down in Culloden after Ted had destroyed the juke joint.

"Could Fisher really be still alive Julia?"

"If he is alive Julia, he must be close by because how else would he be able to give me a message over the radio broadcast."

"Chile them waves can travel, that station just outside Atlanta and that broadcast is national every weekend."

"It's playing all down the Delta."

"I hear they also taped to Gillie, so that message could be weeks old."

Gilda knew Julia could be right.

"Julia, I believe he is trying to tell me something, he reaching out for help."

"Maybe he wanna come back for his money and the gold"

"Gillie, he knows better than that, if he comes back here the sheriff will kill him sure enough."

"I got an idea Julia, maybe we can go down to Louisiana ourselves do some poking around maybe we will get lucky."

"Dot and Martha are there, maybe they can help."

"Wow, I don't know about that Gillie."

"You haven't seen them girls in a while and we don't know what they're up to."

"Besides, I can't just pick up and leave the children."

"I will go alone."

"What, Gillie are you outta your mind!"

"No I'm not; I will get in touch with Dot."

"She told me anytime I wanted to come down to New Orleans that I was welcome."

"I don't like it Gillie, I just don't like it."

"I don't' think you should go stomping yourself down to New Orleans with all that money, because it's just too dangerous."

"Okay fine I will leave it here with you."

Julia started shaking her head as Gilda tried to convince her of another one of her spontaneous ideas.

"Gillie, don't put me in this."

"Did you forget your suppose to marry Elijah when he returns, what you think he gone say if you go on some wild goose chase down in Louisiana looking for Fisher."

"C'mon Julia I will be fine, but I don't want you telling Elijah because you know he will only try to talk me out of it."

Julia could see that Gilda was not going to bulge, so she told her she would not say a word to Elijah.

"Gilda I ain't promising nothing, you know how that man is."

"I just want you to stall him is all, I'm coming back and besides he will understand."

"Umph, you trying to convince me or yourself chile."

Gilda started rambling through the dining room draw.

"I got Dot and Martha's address right here 204 West Lincoln rte 44 New Orleans Louisiana."

Gilda knew Julia wasn't good at keeping a secret, so she made her promise again.

"I mean it Julia, not a word to Elijah."

"Not until I find out what's going on."

"Okay, Okay, I said Okay."

Later on that night a little after midnight the men arrived into town, and as Julia had expected they identified the truck parked out in front of Gilda's. Elijah knew that his brother had missed his family.

"Joshua, you wanna stop?"

"Naw they're probably sleeping I'll come back in the morning"

The men returned to the farm and after sharing a toast with Fisher's finest the men retired until early daylight.

Gilda awakened to the brightness of sunshine and the smell of eggs and bacon frying in the kitchen. The girls had already been up and Gilda could here them out back playing in the yard. She had spent most of the night up thinking. She had been completely taken by surprise by what she heard the night before. Now there was a possibility that Fisher was alive after all.

After freshening up Gilda went into the kitchen and Julia greeted her at doorway wiping her hands on her apron.

"You here that horn out front Gillie?"

"That must be Joshua, watch the stove for me." However, after hearing all the commotion out front Gilda turned the stove down and made her way to the front porch. To her surprise there was Elijah with his upper arm bandaged up.

"Elijah, what happened to you?"

"Nothing much just had a little accident that's all, it's just a flesh wound I'll be fine."

"How are you beautiful?"

"Oh I'm good."

"Hey Joshua."

"Hey Gillie."

Gilda noticed the young man leaning against the banister with the large cow skin hat.

"Hello, you must be cousin Jerry."

"Hello, and you must be the infamous Gillie" Gilda extended her hand to greet the newcomer.

"It's a pleasure meeting you, welcome to Culloden."

Gilda looked over at Elijah and he quickly hunched his shoulders.

"Well, whatever Elijah has told you it's only half the truth, the rest you can get from me."

"Well he told me he had found the love of his life, and I been knowing this man since he was a child, and he ain't never spoke on a woman like that."

"Hmm, well I guess he has covered everything then."

Elijah laughed out loud.

"You see what I mean now Jerry?"

Gilda could fill her insides warm as Elijah softly grabbed her around her waist and placed a kiss on her lips. She was no longer fighting the energy that he brought into her life. Last night was a change of events that left her wondering. Even as much as she loved Elijah and decided she wanted to spend the rest of her life with him it wasn't enough to convince her not to look for Fisher.

Gilda made up her mind; she would take her journey to see Dot and Martha in New Orleans. She figured maybe they could answer some of the questions she had about Fisher. Gilda and Elijah had made plans to marry and she knew he wouldn't let anything come in between that, not even Fisher.

Although it was not normally the way Gilda would do things, she thought this an exception to the rule. Fisher needed her and she felt it was her obligation not to let him down. He had no one left in this life but her and Julia she thought and because Julia was not able, Gilda was going to make sure that she did all that she could to make sure he was safe.

It had been a week since Elijah and Joshua had returned from South Carolina with their cousin Jerry and he fit right in. The word had gotten out that Elijah and Joshua had a cousin visiting. Jerry soon had his hands full, as the young women of Culloden still hoping to settle down with a Mason begin stopping by. The women brought with them their best recipes of peach preserves and down home cooking specialties. Julia had given up and all she could do is shake her head.

Julia sat on the porch swing thinking about Pearl, she had been such a big help and had become a dear friend. Pearl was overwhelmed with tears of joy when the family had decided to help her and Cora start a new life. Julia paid her as promised, but gave her more than enough to start her life over again. Pearl always wanted to go out west and spoke to Julia and Gilda about her dream for a better life all the time. Joshua made her dream come true when he bought her and her daughter Cora tickets for the train. Josie was sad losing her friend but they said there goodbyes knowing that they would see each other again.

Meanwhile, Gilda sat down at home and began her letter to Dot and Martha.

She would let Elijah in on it just as soon as she could pin point what was going on.

Dear Dot and Martha,

How are you girls, it has been a while since I have seen you I am sorry that we could not talk more since the business down here went bad. I would like to come and see you both. Maybe you could take me on a little tour of Louisiana. I here the Delta Blues scene is really popping.

Drop me a line to set a date
See you soon.
Gillie

After completing the letter Gilda didn't wait and she took the letter right away down to Mr. Johnson's to be mailed. She would then anticipate the response.

Elijah had finally tied up unfinished business in town and got confirmation that his mother's sister had gotten to North Carolina safely. He made his way to check on the love of his life. Gilda was not home when he arrived so he sat on the porch pulled out his harmonica and waited patiently as he blew his favorite tunes of Jolly Roll Morten. He figured she could not have been far because the front door was open and

Battle was lying on the living room floor. Gilda was returning from Miss Ann's when she heard the tunes of Elijah's harmonica. She smiled as she saw Elijah sitting on her porch. She walked along the side of the white picket fence rhythmically moving to the tunes of his harmonica. Gilda made her way to the porch and gave him a kiss.

"You make me fill like dancing Mr. Mason." He then returned the kiss

"Hello Ki'Somma, you looking mighty fine this morning."

"Well thank-you Mr. Mason, how are you?"

"I'm great now that I've seen you."

"How is your arm sweetheart?"

"It's coming along and healing very well."

"Elijah will you ever tell me what happened down in South Carolina?"

"No need, everything is taken care of and it's now the past so you don't have to worry your head about that."

"Well what about Jerry, he staying here with you and Joshua?"

"I don't believe so."

"His mother and sister are in North Carolina now, so he will probably eventually head that way."

"He's is a renegade you know."

"South Carolina only held him because of his mother and sister."

Gilda could see that Elijah pretty much didn't want to go into the details of the events that had occurred back home, so she changed the subject.

"Did you hear about the writers down hear from up north up near Barnesville."

"Yeah, Julia was giving us the spill on it back at the house before I left this morning but I didn't get any of the details."

"Well they're trying to finally organize and get the word out about what's going on with these lynching's in the south, thanks to Mrs. Wells-Barnett." They are determined to carry on her legacy."

"They want to get bothh black and white women down here to support her organization against lynching:

The Association of Southern Women for the Prevention of Lynching." Elijah was impressed.

"That sounds promising; we have lost so many black men; young and old down here for reasons that are so very senseless."

"It's never too late to fight for justice, especially when it deals with human life." Gilda agreed as she continued to listen to Elijah. She was impressed that he was conscientious of the efforts in the fight for freedom and equality.

"We all have the right to live free of prejudice and injustices and not be judged because of the color of our skin."

"I like the spirit of this Ida B. Wells-Barnett."

"When did they arrive Gillie?"

"A couple of days ago, the southern states are looking mighty bad to the people up North."

"They have gotten the federal government involved by writing them about people like the Sheriff."

"The Governor and many other political leaders have made the pages of the northern papers about their insensitivity to the cries of injustice of Black people all over Georgia.

"Elijah, you know that's probably why we ain't seen much of Sheriff Bradford and his deputies lately."

"You could be right Gillie, but my Grandfather always told us, just because a dog is lying quiet don't mean he sleeping."

Elijah then took Gilda's hand and the two of them went into the house, as usual Gilda reached for the radio, Elijah gently grabbed her hand and put it on his chest.

"Do you feel that?"

Gilda could feel his heart beating strong and fast.

"That is what you do to me when I am with you."

Gilda held her head up and smiled.

"Do I make you nervous?" Elijah laughed.

"No my Ki'Somma I don't think it is a nervous condition, I just think that you bring joy to my heart."

Gilda felt the same thing, but once more she held back. Elijah reached for her other hand.

"Dance with me."

He held Gilda close to his heart and they danced to the sounds on the radio. Gilda closed her eyes and savored the closeness that she felt in the arms of the man whose love for her held no boundaries. At this moment in time both her mind and heart were at peace.

"Ki'Somma?"

"Yes Elijah my love."

"We are only days away from spending the rest of our lives together."

Gilda knew that once Elijah found out about her plans, he would certainly object and it would tear their relationship apart. If they married now, she would never get the opportunity to find out about the message behind the music. Gilda knew Fisher and she figured that he was reaching out to her the best that he knew how. It was too dangerous any other way because people talk and they would talk even more for the right price. Gilda savored the closeness to Elijah as they moved to the music.

"Dear Elijah, please forgive me for what I'm about to do."

Gilda decided she would take her chances; she wasn't going to wait for a response from Dot or Martha she was going to Louisiana.

That following morning after another heavenly night with the love of her life, Gilda got dressed, packed her a couple of bags, stashed a roll of notes in the center of her brassiere and she and battle headed to Mr. Johnsons. She asked him to take her to the train station and to look after

Battle for awhile. Gilda also made him promise not to tell anyone were she was, especially Elijah.

Mr. Johnson promised, but only if she would let him and Miss Ann know that she had made it to her destination.

"Now Gillie, you know Elijah gonna be awfully angry once he finds out you gone and he gonna be even more angry to know I knew and didn't tellem."

Gilda gave him a sigh; she knew it to be true, but after explaining to Mr. Johnson how important it was that she do this, he eventually gave in.

That afternoon after work Elijah went to Gilda's, only to find the house locked up. He checked around back and whistled for Battle but he got no response.

"Something strange is going on, this ain't like Gillie."

Jerry sat in the truck and watched the gestures of his eldest cousin.

"Everything okay man?"

"Naw, something's not right Jerry."

"Gillie's not here and Battle ain't here either."

"Well come on man, lets go out to the house maybe she's on her way there or something."

The men arrived at the house and Elijah hopped out of the truck. Julia was hanging clothes out back.

"Julia, Gillie been by here today?"

"No I haven't seen her."

Julia looked at Elijah; he showed worry on his face.

"What's wrong Elijah?"

"I've been by the house twice today and I haven't seen her."

Julia looked over at Jerry and he hunched his shoulders. She then turned her attention back to Elijah.

"Well, no use of worrying she couldn't have gone that far, you were just with her last night right?"

"Yes."

"Well, what did she say?"

"Only that you two were going to a meeting at the church on Wednesday for the anti- lynching committee, let's see, and we listened to some music then I came home. "Nothing to explain this though."

Julia put her hand on her chin; she was trying to get in the mind of her good friend, but knew she'd promised not to tell anyone about the radio situation.

"Well maybe she is up to Miss Ann's."

"No I checked with Mr. Johnson, Miss Ann been gone since this morning."

"She's over to Barnesville visiting with her cousin and she won't be back until tomorrow, so I know Gillie's not with her."

"I'm telling you something ain't right."

Julia's mind started racing again. "*I hope that girl has not gone and left here going to Louisiana.*"

Julia watched Elijah and she knew she'd promised Gilda, but it was going to be much harder than she thought to keep it from him. He waited as if he'd read Julia's mind anticipating the response he wanted to hear.

However, Julia held her friends secret as promised and continued to convince Elijah she would turn up.

For the next three days Elijah was a very difficult man to deal with. No one was able to talk to him, while he communicated with only grunts and growls. Today they were supposed to go to Florida to be married, but still no Gilda. Jerry was concerned because he had never seen his cousin this way before.

"Man, Elijah is awfully touchy."

Joshua smiled while shaking his head.

"Yeah don't mind him Jerry he get's that way about Gillie."

"How long has he been this way man?"

"Hmmm, let's see ummm since the first day he set eyes on her."

"I'll have to tell you the story one of these days."

Jerry was surprised because he had always admired the way Elijah handled the women back home and he even found himself taking after his eldest cousin. He would have never believed the ladies man would get this uptight about one woman.

"*She sure must be something special.*" He said to himself.

Julia looked over at the two sitting at the kitchen table as she prepared dinner

"Oh ladies men, were you?"

The look on her face was a sign to Joshua he should explain.

"Well babe, back home Elijah was what you call big for his age."

"Even the older women would make passes at him."

Joshua then began pulling on his suspenders with a smile.

"You know, we all were awfully big for our age, in height of course."

"Many times though them single women, they went out their way to get at Elijah because he was the eldest."

Julia stopped and put her hands on her hips and looked at Joshua.

"Baby I'm just saying." Jerry shook his head and began to laugh at his cousin.

"He's right Julia, we were never boys always men."

"After grandfather died Elijah just emotionally detached himself from everything and everyone."

"No woman could penetrate him no matter how they tried."

"That man out back, I don't know who he is."

After awhile Elijah approached Julia while she was preparing dinner.

"Okay Julia you are being too calm, we haven't heard from Gillie in three days and she's is not in Culloden that much I have figured out."

"I seen Battle down to Mr. Johnson's he finally confessed."

"He said she left three days ago."

"Where is she Julia?"

Joshua looked at Julia and she looked back at Joshua and soon all the men had their eyes on her.

"Okay Okay already."

While chopping green pepper on the chopping board Julia stopped and threw her hands up.

"She must have gone to Louisiana."

"WHAT?"

"For what?"

Elijah's voice echoed throughout the small kitchen and it was so loud Julia almost jumped to the ceiling. Joshua looked over at his wife with his arms folded. She now felt guilty about holding the secret that she confirmed with Ms. Ann days ago.

"Do tell sweetheart."

"Well, while you guys were away, we were over to Gillie's listening to the radio and she thought Fisher had left her a clue to his whereabouts."

"It said he was safe as a dead man could be or something like that."

"Anyway, the announcer started playing some Scott Joplin ragtime tune and Gillie swore it had to be from Fisher."

Elijah shook his head in disbelief; he couldn't believe what he was hearing.

"Are you kidding, that is the most ridiculous thing I have ever heard Julia."

"How'd she come to that conclusion?"

"Julia and you encouraged that nonsense?"

"Well, not exactly, I asked her the same thing Elijah and she said that there were only two people in this world who knew how much she liked that song and that was you and Fisher."

"She figured you didn't send it, so it must've been Fisher."

"I must say I heard it myself, it sounded convincing." Now Elijah was furious, Gilda had run off and said a word to no one in search for a possible dead man alone."

Gilda had never been that far away by herself and Elijah became concerned for her safety. It was apparent to him that their plans for marriage were a joke.

"Julia, did she tell you where he was going in Louisiana?"

"Well, not exactly."

"What do you mean, not exactly?"

"I mean not exactly."

"She mentioned New Orleans because that's where the broadcast originated from, plus Dot and Martha are there too."

"She said they told her to come down anytime."

"Gilda talked to me about going, but that was all."

"I didn't think she would actually leave and say nothing, especially with the wedding and all."

"I'm sorry Elijah."

Elijah got up from the table and practically pushed the front screen door off the hinges and Jerry looked at Joshua and Julia.

Julia observed the confused look on Jerry's face and tried to explain.

"He is always like this about Gillie; you'll get use to it." Julia then took her apron off and threw it in the chair.

"I don't know what get's into her."

"If she knew how that man acted about her she would haul him off and marry him and save all of us the torture."

After Elijah cooled off he came back into the house, went into his room and soon returned with a suitcase. It was obvious that he had not packed very well because his clothing was hanging out of the sides of his suitcase. Elijah went back out the door and Jerry jumped off the porch behind him.

"Where you going?"

"I'm going to Louisiana."

"Well you can't go alone, I'm coming with you."

Elijah looked over at Julia standing on the porch with her hands folded.

"Well?"

"Well what Elijah?"

"C'mon Julia give it up, you have proved your loyalty far beyond the point of necessity."

Joshua looked over at his wife.

"C'mon' Julia give it up."

Julia went into her bedroom when she returned she handed Elijah a small piece of paper.

"Thank you sister."

Jerry shouted as he climbed in the truck with Elijah while he was pulling off.

"We'll contact you just as soon as we get to New Orleans."

Chapter 17

New Orleans, Louisiana

Gilda arrived in the late afternoon at the New Orleans Train Station. This was a different place than Culloden. It was a much bigger city and Gilda couldn't believe her ears as the sounds of Blues and Jazz were everywhere. When she stepped off the train there were musicians set up at the train station playing for coins. They were young and old alike.

However, Gilda was quickly reminded that she was still south of the Mason Dixie line as signs of open segregation where prevalent at the public bathrooms and water fountains. Gilda while pulling her luggage to the main street looked for someone who could help her find Dot's location. Soon she ran into a gentleman who called himself Scuffie Wilson. He was a talented young man and stood at the street corner doing a tap dance. He took his hat off of his head and greeted Gilda with a smile.

"My my my what do we have here a little birdie out of its nest maybe."

"How can I help you?"

"With your fine self, you know you show is fine."

Gilda begin to smile, he reminded her of the musicians that had entertained at Fisher's place.

"Thank you Sir, I'm looking for a lady friend of mine."

"Well young lady, I know just about everybody who is anybody down here in New Orleans."

"This is where the fun starts and this is where it ends right here."

Gilda continued.

"Do you know a woman by the name of Dot Manchester?"

"Dot, everybody knows Dot."

"She just up the way there at Lincoln Rte 44."

Mr. Wilson then gave Gilda a long look from head to toe.

"You don't look like you looking for work young lady?"

"No, I'm just visiting; can you show me the way?"

"Listen here young lady, I can't move off of my corner, but I will show you how to get there."

After receiving directions from the gentleman Gilda was more confused than ever.

"That sounds like an awful long way Mr. Wilson."

"Oh it is a bit out of the way if you plan on walking to get there."

"You may get lucky and catch a ride with one of these city slickers going that way, or hey look ova yonder see that lady."

Mr. Wilson pointed across the street.

"That's Sophie, Sophie sweet thighs Lewis yes suh."

"Hey she got some wheels and she can help you get there."

"Hey Sophie, come here for a minute I want you to meet somebody."

Gilda took a good look at Sophie, she was an older women, yet very beautiful and high spirited much like Miss Minnie.

She was dressed in a powder blue satin dress that revealed her cleavage, a pair of powder blue satin high heel pumps and a large powder blue hat trimmed in white lace that matched her dress perfectly.

"Hello honey."

"Hello, Sophie this here is, what did you say your name was?"

"Gilda, Gilda Harris, but you can call me Gillie."

"Hello Gillie, I'm Sophie and its pleasure meeting yah."

"Sophie, Gillie here is looking for Dot."

"Oh yeah, where you from Gillie?"

"We use to work together down in Culloden at Fisher's Place."

Sophie smiled.

"Po Fisher, hey that was the man."

"I came down that way a couple of times."

"Fisher really brought that Bayou swing to life down in that l'il ole town of his and he sure knew how to throw a party yes suh."

Gilda couldn't understand why she spoke of Fisher as if he was dead.

"You a friend of Fisher?"

Sophie surprised at the question began to laugh.

"Yes, actually I was and we was closer than most."

"It seems as though you speak of him as if he was dead."

"Well word around town here says he is."

"You know anything different suga?"

"Oh no, not at all."

"I haven't heard anything about Fisher since his place closed, it's just a surprise to me to hear such a thing is all."

Gilda was very careful not to reveal too much of what she knew. She would get more details once she spoke with Dot.

"Well I'll tell you, we loved him a bunch down here in New Orleans."

"He helped a lot of people get up North to make a lot of money."

"It's such a tragic thing that happened to him though."

Sophie grabbed hold to Gilda's bag.

"Well come on chile if you need a ride to the Red Velvet you better be coming."

Gilda tipped Mr. Wilson, got in the car with Sophie and made her way to the Red Velvet.

On the drive down the narrow road Gilda witnessed the landscape of the Louisiana Bayou. There were weeping willow trees that swayed low along the roadside giving shade from the heat of the sun. There were large gated fences that housed the ruins of the Spanish-American War.

The sights that struck her the most were the large old dilapidated plantation houses and their graveyards that sat off of the road.

Sophie glanced at Gilda and began explaining as she noticed her interest in the view.

"Yeah those are what's left from the Spanish American wars and see over yonder, that there is an old slave cemetery."

"We passing route 23 now, and it is a true reminder of our tainted past down here."

"You will see a lot; you just keep a watchful eye."

Gilda had never seen grave yards with tombs that sat above the ground. Sophie explained the issues surrounded the sea level of Louisiana being the reason they were unable to bury their dead underground. Sophie passed her a handkerchief.

"Miss Gillie, you'll be just fine, this here is the delta honey the deeper south you get the more bitter the history."

The ladies arrived to their destination and to Gilda the Red Velvet looked like a palace. There were beautiful red rose bushes lining the entire front of the house.

All kinds of fancy cars and extravagant horse and carriages were parked out front. Across the field was a riverbank with boats large and small docked alongside of it. People of all walks of life, languages and colors covered the landscape.

Gilda thought she had stepped into another world because she had seen nothing like it.

"This is the Red Velvet?"

"Yes chile, welcome to the Red Velvet Blues and Jazz Enchanted Paradise the jewel of New Orleans."

The landscape was beautiful with highly manicured trees and shrubs that stretched to the river's edge. There were cement walkways and tall lantern poles that stood between each. Along the paved walkway Gilda also noticed benches with men and women coupled up, talking and laughing.

The front doors to the mansion where tall and made of a beautiful oak wood and above them were draped beautiful Red Velvet panels. There where six tall pillars that accentuated the front of the house and the steps made of stone with red carpet covering the center.

"Sophie this place is beautiful."

"Yes, I thought so to."

"You wanted to find Dot, well this is where she is."

Sophie laughed at Gilda's surprised look.

"Chile, if you know Dot, you knew you wouldn't find her picking no cotton or cleaning up no white woman's house."

Gilda shook her head, because she should have known better. Dot was a hustler and was always about the money. Dot always wanted the best and did what she thought it took to get it.

"Okay Sophie show me the way."

Gilda grabbed her suitcase out the car and followed Sophie up to the house. The people standing outside were looking with curiosity at this young country girl making her way into the Red Velvet Brothel and Enchanted Blues and Jazz Paradise. Once inside she could see the beautiful artistic designs. The staircase was the most beautiful with its huge pillars and separate staircases that joined at a large platform above. There were red velvet curtains that draped to the floor in the hallway just outside the parlor walkway. Gilda looked up in awe at the chandelier that hung from the ceiling. It was grander than Miss Ann's back home. As she turned around admiring the view she found herself bumping into folks at the same time and soon realized just how much of a country girl she really was. Sophie continued guiding her through the house passing several parlors filled with men and women dancing and enjoying themselves. There was the blue parlor, green parlor and purple parlor all identified by the furniture inside of them and the velvet sash that hung above each of the doorways. Gilda dragged her luggage behind her, stopping time to time to gather her strength to proceed through the thickness of the crowded hallway. There was a gentleman playing the piano in the main atrium. Gilda looked again.

"No, it couldn't be."

Gilda excused herself from Sophie for a moment and walked over to the man. As she thought it was Blind Man Jake.

"Oh my god Jake it's me Gilda."

Jakes smile lit up the room.

"Gilda, my one and only love."

"What you doing down here in these parts darling."

"I'm here to see Dot, whatcha doing down here man?"

"Well the girls brought me down to make a little money you know."

"I felt so bad about what happened to Fisher." Gilda gave him a hug.

"How long will you be with us Gillie?"

"I don't know."

"I haven't seen or even talked to Dot or Martha yet."

"Okay, come back and check for me."

Gilda agreed, said her goodbyes and Sophie continued guiding her through the crowded mansion. Finally after making it to the rear of the house the ladies went through a narrow hallway that lead out to the large back porch. Outside Gilda the view was much closer than before and that much more beautiful. In the center of the grounds was another band playing in a large gazebo. Sophie then pointed to Dot.

"Well this is where I let you go sweetie, I've got business up front."

Gilda thanked Sophie and made her way toward Dot.

Dot was having a goodtime a usual and sitting on the lap of a finely dressed gentleman. Gilda sat here suit case down and walked over to the Dot and the neatly dressed gentlemen. "Excuse me Madame."

Dot took one look at Gilda and jumped right off the gentleman lap so quickly that she almost startled the poor man to death.

"Gillie, what on earth." Dot gave her a big hug.

Gilda assumed that she had not yet received her letter.

"What the hell are you doing down here in these parts chile." Dot turned her attention back to the Gentleman.

"Excuse me Dr. Reynolds, this is a very dear friend of mind sweetie, do you mind."

The gentleman gave his approval and Dot pulled Gilda into the back door of the house.

She led her back through the crowded rooms while she went on and on about how happy she was to see here. Gilda asked her how everyone was doing, but she ignored the question and she continued talking and helping Gilda carried her luggage up the large staircase. They walked down the hall and Dot stopped at two large elegantly engraved wooden doors. She turned both knobs and Gilda could not believe her eyes as she entered the elegant parlor.

It was elaborately decorated with lovely blue velvet curtains and the finest French furniture. Dot opened another door and it led to a bedroom. The bed was fit for a Queen with large Oak wood pillars on each corner. The sheets were made of a Blue satin with huge pillows attacked atop of it. Lying across the top of all four pillars was a large piece of beautiful white chiffon that fell on all sides of her bed.

The dresser stood taller than both women and in the corner was a beautiful large Chifforobe with all kinds of perfume and several candles.

"Do you like?"

Gilda nodded in agreement to the question.

"Who's house is this Dot, where is Martha?" The two of you left together." Dot looked over at Gilda and smiled while she lit her cigarette.

"You haven't changed a bit Gillie, always the questions!"

"There is plenty of time for that small talk chile; would you like something to drink?" Dot walked over to the wall and there was a small box, she pushed the tiny button on it and a gentleman responded on the other end. Percy can you please bring me and my friend some wine, and some fresh strawberries with chocolate dip please."

"Si senorita Dottie."

The voice on the other side of the door responded.

"My goodness, Dottie is it?" Gilda laughed. Once they settled down Gilda told Dot about the events back home. Including Big Ted's Death and the radio broadcast from who she thought could have been Fisher. However, Gilda was no fool, she didn't mention the money or the Gold. Fisher didn't mention that he had shared anything with Dot so she wouldn't either.

Gilda found out that the house belonged to a Creole woman by the name of Marietta Fallsworth .

Miss Fallsworth had spent most of her life in New Orleans as a mistress to a very prominent French Merchant who courted her many years. In his old age he returned to Paris for good and offered to purchase Marrietta a home. She chose Route 44 and legend has it he paid for it in pure gold coins. Gilda listened to the story and was amazed.

Gilda took another look around Dot's place.

"Is all this space yours?"

"Yep, but I share the parlor with Martha." Dot, picked up her cigarettes and lit one with her silver lighter, she then took a long drag, and while blowing out the smoke begin to speak to Gilda.

"So Gilda what have you been doing with yourself sweetie?"

"Chile did we have some good times back in Culloden or what?"

"Man, I sure do miss Fisher's Place."

"How is that man of yours?"

"What's his name?"
"Elijah right?"
"Oh he's doing fine."
"You two haven't tied the knot yet?"
Gillie thought for a moment.
"Oh my god, how could I have been so selfish."
She had left without informing anyone not even Julia and Elijah had probably washed his hands of her for standing him up days before there wedding day. But the whole situation about Fisher was bothering her, and she needed to know exactly what was going on. This decision would be the only way that she could live the rest of her life in peace with Elijah, if he would still have her

"Gilda, where you staying?"
"I haven't thought about that yet."
"I came right here from the train station."
Dot stood up.
"Well enough said, you can stay here with me as long as you like."
"But, just so you know when Lady Marrietta returns from Paris she's gonna want to know why a beautiful lady like yourself isn't working."
"Gillie, you go on and settle in, I'm gonna let Martha know that your here, she will be surprised to see you."
"If you need anything, you just push this here button and Percy will bring you what ever it is you need."
"Thanks Dot."
"Chile don't you worry your head about that, you family it ain't no problem, just enjoy your visit." Dot pulled the double doors closed behind her. Gilda laid down on the couch and fell asleep. She was exhausted; it had been a long train ride from Culloden.

Chapter 18

Elijah and Jerry had been traveling all night but to Elijah it seemed like days. When they had pulled into the nearest gas station. The sign read "NO SERVICE FOR COLOREDS" They continued their on hopes and prayers. Soon the men came across a gas station that sat just outside of the Mississippi state lines that did service blacks but there were no rest room facilities. Jerry looked over at Elijah shaking his head about the road trip he willingly joined.

"Elijah, you must have really gotten bit by the love bug, no way no one woman ever gonna have me driving cross state lines looking for her."

"She put a hex on you or something man?" Elijah laughed.

"One day cuz you will know what it feels like to be in love and I will be there to remind you of this day, today."

"You will be waiting a long time cuz."

Both men continued there small talk as they covered more road heading for Louisiana.

"I should wire Joshua and let him know everything is okay I'm sure he is back home wondering how we're faring." Jerry begin to laugh.

"Yeah I seen it in his eyes to, boy did he want to jump in this here truck and go with us like the old days."

Elijah shook his head.

"Cuz don't you believe that, he's right where he wants to be, believe me." The two men continued to laugh and talk as they journey brought them closer and closer to there destination. Elijah had deeper thoughts though, thoughts of Gilda. What would posses her to do what she did. He could not help feeling angry even with time he had on the road it still was not enough for him to get over what she'd done. He had given her his whole self and it appeared that had not been enough. Now he would make sure she was safe and would leave her to live her life as she had always wanted to, without him. Elijah decided to make plans of his own, once he returned to Culloden.. He made up his mind he would move out west to start a new life. He was still young man and had enough in him to re-build his life over again.

After a few more hours of riding the men finally arrived in New Orleans. The city was much larger than they expected. There were more cars than the two had seen at one time, they covered the streets and they blew there horns continuously in the streets. There was entertainment practically on every corner. Jerry was amazed. "Now this here place is a place I can hang around." Elijah shook his head.

"Yeah, but first we need to find a place to lay our head and get in touch with Joshua it will be dark soon."

"From the looks of it I don't think it's a safe place for strangers after dark."

Elijah looked across the street and seen a few black men standing on the corner conversing, singing, and laughing amongst themselves. The two of them walked over to introduce themselves. A couple of the men were tap dancing while the other two were playing a tune on the harmonica. People dropped coins in a large bucket that sat in front of the small ensemble as they walked by. When Elijah and Jerry approached them, one of the gentleman paused.

What's happening fellas, what can we do for you."

"Well we're looking for a place to bed down for the night."

"Any place around here?"

"Yeah."

The gentleman looked over Elijah and Jerry.

"You two ain't from round here are you?"

Elijah and looked down at his clothing and then at Jerry's."

"From the looks of it I guess we aren't."

All the men begin to laugh.

"Hey guys I like this cat, he catches on quick."

"Well, if you looking for a little pleasure, you diffiently come to the right place."

"We're here on business not pleasure this trip." Jerry interrupted.

"Although if time permits pleasure is absolutely an option for me."

The men begin to laugh. The tall lean one with his top hat and blue jean overalls appeared to be the leader of pack.

"If you looking for some entertainment we have just whatcha need here in New Orleans, brothels and speak easy's you name it, from the smallest places to the largest places."

"Yes suh, depending of course what your pockets can handle."

"Yep we got it all, you just name your chase and I will tell you the place."

The Gentleman took off his hat and extended it to Elijah. "Yes suh, umm for a small fee that is."

Elijah went in his pocket and obliged the man's request. "If you looking for just a cot and a squat there are a couple places just outside the city"

"Whatever you two cats decide to do, better make it quick because this ain't no place you wanna be hanging out around after dark being a stranger in town, know what I mean?" The four entertainers directed the two men to a bed and breakfast just outside of town. It was a classy modern place ran by two spinsters by the name of Lara and her sister Betty. The two women welcomed Elijah and Jerry with open arms. After an hour or two of conversation the two men retired to their quarters. Elijah still had the temperament of a tiger. "Elijah, we are not going to get anything accomplished with you all bald up."

"We'll try asking about that place tomorrow, even ask around see if anyone seen her."

"She's gotta be here somewhere." Jerry looked down at his clothes and then at Elijah's.

"In these?"

Elijah did the same.

" Your right Jerry, If we're going out we best be looking for us some decent clothes, can't be walking around in this fancy city of New Orleans"

Both agreed, it was time to blend in with the hustle and bustle of the Gulf's diamond in the rough.

The following morning Jerry and Elijah left the house and headed back towards the city. The streets were not as crowded as the evening before. They noticed a gentleman tap dancing on a large piece of wood who was entertaining the folk on the corner. Jerry stopped and watched the man shuffle and slide his feet back and forth across the large platform.

"Those are some nice moves you got there young man." As he continued to slide across the platform with ease he nodded his head smiling. Elijah tossed him some coins in his large bucket and the gentleman stopped.

"Thank you sir, much obliged to ya."

"You two cats ain't from around here."

"No we're not, from back east."

"Gotta a question or two for ya hoping you can help us."

The gentleman looked up at Elijah.

"Yeah cat what can I do for ya?"

He took his hat off for a tip.

" I dropped you a bit of coin in the basket."

"Yes sir you did and that was for the dance, but what you bout to ask is for information and that cost a tad bit mo, you see."

Elijah laughed aloud.

"Man, you good at what you do."

He then tossed him more coins in his hat.

Jerry also reached down in his pocket and did the same.

"Me and my cuz here are looking for a place we can by some nice clothes."

"Where y'all going?"

"Going out on the town tonight."

"Awww you fella's wanna clean up?"

"I know just the place just right on up this street to that there corner were the tall street light stands and make a left."

"They take good care of ya, tell em Scuffie sent cha, yes suh they will take good care of ya."

Elijah noticed that they were near the train station he looked around curiously. "Eh Scuffie one more thing."

"Yeah what is it big easy."

"I'm looking for a woman, short stature, thick in the hips small frame though, umm kinda short curly hair, dark brown, pretty face, and smile."

"She probably come through here from the train station over ther a few days ago, here name is Gilda."

"You seen her?"

The gentleman tipped his hat again with a smile.

"The birdie doesn't speak unless he gets a treat." Jerry looked at Elijah and dug into his pocket again and pulled out another silver dollar.

"Man you show better have some good news for me and my cuz today."

"Yes! I seen that young gal, pretty as a Georgia peach she was."

"Where did she go?"

"She went out to Red Velvet."

"What's the Red Velvet?" Scuffie looked at the two of then and grinned.

"You best be getting over to Sula's Place right away, cause you gone need some fine clothes to wear out there, ummhmm that there place is where the gentlemen with the real notes go."

Elijah's was relieved that she had made it safe thus far; he then pulled out the piece of paper given to him by Julia.

"Is this here the place you speaking about?"

"Yep that's the place, and it's a big ole place you can't miss it."

"Live entertainment, ladies and lots of good quality booze."

Both men went to Sula's Place as the oldtimer had directed and spent the majority of the day getting fitted and shopping to prepare for the night ahead. Elijah promised himself before arriving that once he found Gilda and knew that she was safe he would move on with his life without her. Even though his love for her was a constant unrest in his soul, Elijah he did not want her to be any where she didn't want to be including with him.

The Gentleman left out a little after seven that evening. Since they were already residing outside of town, the distance from the spinster's place to their destination was not that far. As Elijah and Jerry got closer to their destination they were able to see the night sky lit up like the county fair back home. As they continued to ride closer to the house they could hear the music much more clearly. The gentleman pulled up to the Mansion and to their surprise even the wealthy had still invested in horse driven coaches. There where men standing outside of the house conversing with cigars in their hands some with top hats and some without. All of the men were clothed in the finest fabrics and shoes. The Scuffie was right and thanks to him Elijah and Jerry had been taken good care of. The two had paid a pretty penny for the extravagant apparel they had on tonight. Elijah looked eagerly for a place to park as most of the people had looked at them in an odd fashion pulling up in a pickup truck. One of the valets stopped them and informed them that all workers had to report to the back of the house. Elijah was not offended as he modestly pulled out two silver dollars and put them in the hand of the young boy. He looked up, smiled and opened the door for Elijah. It was obvious they were looking just as good if not better than their counterparts in the elegant attire as the women gazed in delight at the newcomers.

"Young man, do you know a young lady by the name of Gilda?" You mean Miss Gillie, sure I do they usually hang out around back near the water in the evening time you can probably find her out that way."

"Saaay who are you anyway?"

"Miss Gillie ain't looking for no gentlemen."

"I'm a long time friend just visiting." Jerry and Elijah followed the cement road that led around to the back of the estate. The gentleman, just like Gilda before them had admired the lights and the décor of the grounds. They noticed this as well, but tonight the benches along the walkway occupied with men the ladies were entertaining as their guest for the night. Elijah and Jerry soon begin to catch the eye of many of the ladies as they strolled in like new money. Jerry was dressed in black trousers a white shirt and a black and silver silk vest of the finest French fabrics. He had taken his braid down and his hair fell at his shoulders under the tall top hat he insisted on purchasing. Elijah was dressed in a pair of black trousers, a white silk shirt with silver cufflinks and a silk hand woven grey vest. Both men's feet were covered with black fine leather shoes imported from Italy.

It was not long before news got around as the women began whispering amongst themselves about the two handsome newcomers.

They begin walking up to them both introducing themselves and requesting their presence either in the parlor or out back along the pathway to the river. Soon Sophie came over to the gentleman as they stood outside not far from the entrance to the Kitchen.

"Well what do we have hear?"

"Aren't you two easy on the eyes?"

She walked around the two of them observing them and admiring their strong young physiques and unique features. Sophie then stopped in front of Elijah.

"Especially you, what's your name sweetie?"

She had on a white chiffon negligee with a red lace brassiere and a pair of white linen petticoats. Elijah leaned up against the lamp pole with his arms folded looking down at Sophie.

"Elijah's the name and this here is Jerry."

Jerry then tipped his hat.

"Pleasure meeting you ma'am."

Sophie let out a small grin.

"Oh baby you don't have to be so formal here."

"Come on in the house, so we can sit and talk a spell get to know each other sweetie, you come too Jerry."

"I'm sure you will have no problem finding someone to talk to with your handsome self."

Pulling at both Jerry and Elijah by the hand, Sophie led them up the front stairs into the house. Once inside the two men looked around with curiosity, they had seen nothing like this back at home. There were beautiful young women moving around to and fro of all shades and all sizes. Jerry looked in astonishment as the ladies served drinks in their undergarments and garter belts, while the music decorated the back drop. Sophie finally settled the gentleman in a corner of the Blue room. While she thought she finally had them all to herself, Elijah was keeping an eye out for Gilda. Annoyed with the inattention of Elijah, she finally tapped him on the shoulder

"Sweetie you looking for somebody?" Elijah not even looking her way replied. "No." He didn't want to draw attention to Gilda not until he at least found out what was going on. Sophie finally gave up on Elijah and moved her attention to Jerry, who was still watching the entertainment that had been presented to him upon entry into the house. The evening continued, and finally after a couple of hours Gilda came strolling pass the large parlor. She was not dressed like the other women, but wore a Blue sleeveless knee high dress. Elijah spotted her and swiftly jumped from his seat as he followed her through the crowded hallway that led to the kitchen. Jerry jumped up and followed. Sophie thinking about the lost of a possible john for the evening grabbed at Jerry's arm.

"Baby where you going?"

Jerry tipped his hat and disappeared into the crowd. Elijah finally he reached the kitchen area. There were people enjoying a meal at several of the tables located in the corner of the room near the back entrance. He looked over at a large table with several chairs around it and noticed Gilda standing next to an elderly lady while she stirred a pot on the large coal stove.

"Gilda."

She turned around to see Elijah standing before her.

"Elijah, what on earth!"

She ran up and jumped into his arms.

"What are you doing here?"

Soon Jerry came up behind Elijah. Astonished by the events Ms. Roberta looked on in awe. After Elijah put Gilda down, she straightened out her garments and gave him a big smile.

"Uhh Ms. Roberta this is Elijah and this is his cousin Jerry."

"Please to meet you fellas."

"Please excuse us Ms. Roberta."

Gilda quickly led the gentlemen outside the kitchen door into the back courtyard. They took a stroll down the walkway until they made it to the edge of the dock. Elijah couldn't hold it any longer.

"Gilda, what has gotten into your head, leaving and not telling anyone where you were going?"

"Elijah, shush."

"Don't you dare raise your voice at me."

"I am not your child."

Elijah had missed the passionate spirit of the woman he loved so dearly.

It was one of the many reason that he loved her, she was not afraid to stand up to him.

"Well did you come down here and find what you were looking for?" She through her hands up in frustration

"Not yet, nobody seems to know anything, not even Dot."

"I was starting to get a little discouraged about the whole thing."

"As far as everyone down her is concerned Fisher is dead."

"I just don't understand it, the radio everything, it just doesn't make any sense to me Elijah."

Gilda then turned around after hearing Dot call her name. Dot walked toward them and Jerry looked up and to his surprise had seen the most beautiful women he ever laid eyes on.

"Gillie, what's going on?" Dot looked around at the gentleman.

"Everything alright?"

"Yes, I'm fine."

"Dot you remember Elijah, and that is his cousin Jerry."

"Of course Elijah, I remember seeing out at Fisher's."

She then turned and pointed to Jerry.

"But you, you I've never seen before."

Jerry took her hand.

"The pleasure is all mines."

"How about we take a little walk then sweetie?"

Enticed by the offer Jerry accepted.

"I'll be back in a bit."

Elijah nodded his head and put his attention back on Gilda.

Finally they were alone and Elijah wanted her to explain to him why she ran off and left before they were to be married. Gilda sat with him while looking out into the stars over the river. "Gilda, what is the real reason that you left."

"I know about the Fisher thing and the radio."

"But Gillie, was that enough to have you pack your bags and come all this way looking for a man that evidently doesn't wanna be found?"

"What do you mean he didn't want to be found?"

Elijah finally gave in.

"I spoke with Fisher."

"You what?"

"When Elijah?"

"Two days before we found Ted."

"I wanted to tell you but, I had made me promise not to say a word about it until I had you all safe out of Culloden."

"You packing up and leaving town was not apart of the plan."

Gilda could not believe what she was hearing. All this time Elijah had known and had not said a word.

"Did Joshua know too?"

"Not at first, just me."

"I received a wire from Missouri and it said that he was pushing out west toward Texas."

"But why Elijah?"

"Why didn't he want me to know?"

"He didn't want to put you or any of us in danger Gillie."

"I'm not saying it wasn't him Gillie, but it's not likely."

"If your intuition is correct, I'm sure he didn't expect for you to make such a foolish decision to come to Louisiana alone."

"So is he dead, or is he alive Elijah?"

"Right now, I don't know Gilda, I just don't know."

"Well what about the men that came and got him, who where they?" Elijah scratched he head, but continued.

"He spoke very little about that, but from my understanding Dot would be able to fill you in with the rest."

"Dot?"

Gilda could not believe what she was hearing, it appeared everyone knew what was going on except her. She was angry that Elijah did not inform her sooner, but more angry at Fisher for keeping this from her.

"Later on, after we found Ted, I did speak to Joshua and we were going to leave Culloden. All of us together, but after we were married."

"So now my Ki'Somma can you tell me why you really left me before our wedding day?"

Gilda looked up into his eyes which gave off a magnetism that pierced the very depths of her soul. This man was so loving and so kind, and so very patient.

"Elijah, I love you with all my heart."

Gilda teary eyed continued.

"You deserve a family and I can't give you that and I wouldn't be able to live with myself knowing that I as unable to make you happy."

Elijah slowly put his fingers softly over her lips.

"Gilda, none of that matter's to me, I love you."

"The most important thing to me in this world is you." He held her in his arms and began softly caressing her. Gilda could not believe the change of events. She knew that she was a complicated soul to deal with and she was grateful that the lord had sent her a strong man who understood.

"I love you so very much Elijah and nothing I mean nothing will ever change that.

"But Fisher, he needs our help, I know it."

"He is alive Elijah, I know it."

"What do you want to do?"

"First, I want to have a word with Dot."

. Elijah agreed and later that evening he and Jerry returned to the boarding house while Gilda and Dot retired to Dot's quarters. When they got there Martha was entertaining in the main Parlor, so the women went into Dot's quarters. It was after midnight and Gilda could still here the piano playing downstairs. She walked out onto the porch and looked out over the river and closed her eyes as she felt the breeze gently caress her face. When she returned inside she interrupted Dot who was busy preparing for her date tomorrow afternoon.

"Dot I spoke with Elijah tonight and he told me everything." Dot, never looking up continued rambling through her huge walk-in closet.

"I know all about Fisher Dot, why didn't you tell me?" Dot walked over and pressed the button on the wall, when the gentleman appeared she requested a bottle of wine and asked Gilda if she wanted something for herself Gilda nodded her head yes. Dot then began to pace the floor as she lit her cigarette.

"Gilda, it was a real touchy situation and I promised him that I would not say anything to anybody not even you."

"It was not that he didn't trust you Gillie, he was more concerned about your safety than anything."

"He knows how you are, and thought it would be better to leave you out of what was going on."

"He said he couldn't live with himself if something ever happened to you because of him."

Gilda continued to listen; she wanted to hear everything before she said a word. She also wanted to make sure if Dot knew about the gold or not.

"Me and Martha were over at Fisher's one night when Paulie's men returned from Detroit to collect for Paulie, they tossed Fisher around really bad."

"They told him that he'd better get used to the new situation or else he would not live to enjoy what he had already acquired."

"Me and Martha were in the dressing room and heard everything, it was awful."

"They talked about just letting the lynch mob come down and have their way with the both of them, Fisher and Ted because his money was no more good as far as the sheriff was concerned."

"Ted and a couple other guys I never seen before came in and knocked the men around pretty bad."

"They ran them out of town in the night with their tail between there legs." Dot continued to pace the floor she grabbed her cigarette case and lit another cigarette as she continued describing everything that she could remember.

"Afterwards he came and told me and Martha to pack our bags and leave. He made arrangements for us to come here, so here we are."

"I didn't know what was going on; we did as he said Gilda."

"At that point I was scared and feared for my life."

"Everything that I had worked for was tied up in that place, what was I suppose to do?"

"I depended on Fisher me, Martha, and Jeanine did."

"Maybe more than we should have."

He did come down about two or three weeks later. He was with a group of Mexican fellas

"They picked us all up here and took us deep into the water country."

"When I seen him, he looked as though everything was fine."

"He paid us all more than our share and he disappeared."

"Fisher is a generous man Gilda."

Gilda smiled she knew that to be true about Fisher.

"He then said that we couldn't go with him that we would have to find our own way."

"I asked him where he was going and he told me it was best I didn't know." Gilda could see the resentment in Dot's face as she continued to take long drags of her cigarette.

"Gillie, did you know Jeanine and Fisher had been seeing each other all that time?"

"Aw what the hell, none of it matters anymore."

Gilda could see that Dot was jealous that Fisher had fell in love with Jeanine, but she said nothing. Dot poured herself a glass of wine swirled it in the glass and took a sip.

"You know Gillie, I'm happy now."

"Me and Martha have met some very interesting people down here in New Orleans."

"Now I call the Red Velvet home."

"Dot, what ever happened to Jeanine?"

"Well Fisher asked Jeanine to stay with him and I haven't seen either of them since then."

"Then you Gillie, show up out of no where."

Dot was frustrated and she put here cigarette out in the ash tray and went out into the Parlor. Martha and her friend had retired to her room. Dot sat on the couch.
Gilda grabbed the bottle and a glass then joined her. After hearing the unfolding of events she felt she needed a drink and poured herself a glass of the wine.

"Well Dot, I am relieved to know that he is alive and okay, that much I can say."

"But Ted?"

She paused a moment as tears filled her eyes.

"He's dead; they lynched him only days after Fisher left."

"He never got out of Colluden Dot."

"What!"

Dot sat up in the couch.

"Oh my god Gillie, I didn't know."

Gilda continued.

"Elijah and Joshua had to cut him down from a tree."

"They say he gave them a pretty good fight from what I hear, but there were just too many of them."

Gilda shook her head.

"That Sheriff Bradford always feared him since we were kids."

Dot held her composure only briefly and began to cry. Life sure was cruel she thought. After several drinks and a lot of crying Dot retired to her bed for the night. Gilda lay on the parlor couch thinking about what the future held for her and Elijah.

Even after the long talk and bottle of wine she shared with Dot, Gilda managed to get up early. She had not been in the night life for awhile and therefore was not able to sleep into the late hours of the afternoon like Dot and Martha so effortlessly had.

After relaxing in a nice hot bath Gilda returned to the room and out of her garments she pulled out a beautiful orange sleeveless dress and grabbed a pair of dots numerous satin house slippers.

The slippers were not like the shoes that she was use to wearing at home so she enjoyed choosing among the enormous collection. As Gilda made her way downstairs she could hear the band coming in and preparing to set up for the late afternoon rush. The ladies usually started there socializing around four because this was when most of the wealthy New Orleans businessmen completed their work day.

There was something going on everyday at the Red Velvet and there was never a dull moment. The empty House looked strange to Gilda in the early morning because she was use to the parlors being filled to capacity with both entertainers and guest alike. When Gilda entered the kitchen, she noticed that Ms. Roberta wasn't alone this morning. Two young women who resided in the house were waiting for breakfast at the kitchen table. Usually the women would have their breakfast late in the afternoon and would request it be brought to their personal parlor. Today Gilda was surprise to see them up early and giving Ms. Roberta a fit. Neither was fully dressed as they sat at the long kitchen table in their pantaloons and corsets.

"Well good morning Gillie."

"Good morning Ms. Roberta, what you got smelling so good this morning?"

Gilda went over to the pot, and as usual with all the girls Ms. Roberta popped her hand with her spoon. "Ouch!"

"Breakfast is on the table chile, that there is Lunch, seafood gumbo and rice."

Gilda sniffed in the air, ummm it sho smells good." Ms. Roberta grinned at Gilda

"You'd better come get yourself a helping early before the rush because it goes fast yes suh they love my Gumbo."

Gilda sat down to have her breakfast. Many of the young women didn't have much of a conversation for her since she had come to the house. The girls had finished their breakfast and were having a cigarette and sipping their coffee. As Gilda received her plate from Ms. Roberta, one of the women spoke to the other.

"I wonder how it is that some women get to live and eat here without working for their share."

Gilda looked up from here plate just as she was about to speak there was a deep voice that spoke through the kitchen screen door.

"There is no reason for anyone to stay anywhere and not pay their fair share, now is there?"

Gilda smiled, but did not turn around. The voice was quite familiar, it was the same voice that gave her chills in the early morning back in Culloden and even here down in the Bayou it gave her that same warm feeling inside. The two young ladies quickly turned their attention to the tall dark handsome man. They both looked on in envy as he grabbed Gilda up and gave her a kiss that only a true lover could. He then turned to the two women.

"Ever get that in the morning?"

Furious, they both got up and left the kitchen. Ms. Roberta laughed out loud.

"Oh I know what it is to have a young love yes suh, ain't no feeling like it."

"The longer you hold on the stronger it gets, I'm telling you something I know."

"Me and my Randall Lee, we were together since we were thirteen years old until he left here."

Gilda and Elijah both smiled at the wise women. After Gilda finished her meal both she and Elijah gave their goodbyes to Ms. Roberta and headed down the walkway to the boat docks. As they walked Gilda looked up at this handsome tall frame of a man. Even as teenagers he seemed to tower over her and the girls in town would be green with envy watching their close companionship. When they reached the boat dock Elijah stepped onto the large rocks and made his way safely down closer to the water. He then reached up for Gilda and sat her on a rock in between his legs. As Gilda rested her arms on both of Elijah's thighs, he put his arms around her and began kissing compassionately along her neck.

"How long do you plan to stay around here my Ki'Somma?"

"I don't know, I kinda like being away for a while."

"I mean not here exactly, but just away from Culloden."

"I been there all my life, the change of pace has been good."

"Will you come stay with me and we can talk more about it?"

Gilda looked around

"Elijah, how'd you get here anyway?"

"Where's the pickup truck." Elijah turned around back toward the house, "Who said anything about a pick-up." Gilda turned around she searched and to her surprise there was no pick-up truck.

What Gilda did see was a black shiny convertible, she smiled and pointed.

"Elijah, is that your Automobile?"

"Yes ma'am."

"We all couldn't travel in that pick-up truck so I thought I might get us something a little more comfortable to ride in."

"Elijah, what did you do with your truck?"

"Oh it's back at the boarding house."

"Where'd you get the car?"

"Oh the ladies that I'm staying with gave it to me."

Quickly Gilda turned her attention to Elijah.

"Ladies, What ladies might I asked?"

Elijah noticing the slight jealousy that Gilda displayed played along.

"Well, me and Jerry we're staying with two very lovely ladies close to town.

They have a nice bed and breakfast and have been quite hospitable I might add."

"They had that car sitting out back, says they never use it so I told them I would take it off of their hands for a bit."

Gilda put her hands on her hips.

"Well will I be meeting these lady friends of yours?"

"Yeah, of course they are back at the house with Jerry."

Gilda returned to Dot's parlor and left her a message.

When she returned Elijah had the car door open for her and Gilda slid in. She looked around both the interior and exterior of the car.

After the two reached the Bed and Breakfast Gilda got out and began her inspection.

"This is a beautiful place your lady friends have."

Elijah not saying a word nodded as he escorted her up to the front porch. Outside there was a swing chair just like the one Julia had back home. The house was white washed and the front porch was so wide it extended around to both sides of the house. There were pots of beautiful flowers of all kinds lining the banister of the front porch, all which gave off a peaceful atmosphere of home Gilda thought. Elijah opened the door and Gilda walked in. There was a vestibule that had another door with beautiful stained glass window panes. Gilda turned around to Elijah and he nodded his head for Gilda to go on in. The house was huge. There was a beautiful staircase that led to the upper level of the home. To her right, Gilda noticed the library and she could easily see the bookcases reached the top of the ceiling and filled with all kinds of books. The front room was fairly large, with beautiful plants in large porcelain pots near the window and beautiful linen white furniture. There was a large mirror above the fireplace and many photographs on the mantle.

Gilda covered her mouth in surprise as she noticed a picture of Fredrick Douglas standing with another tall distinguished gentleman.

Gilda soon heard the sounds of a gramophone coming from the back of the house. She made no comments, not until she relieved her unspoken jealousy of Elijah bedding down in this very beautiful house.

Elijah led her down a hall way and the closer they got the louder was Jerry's voice as well as two others. Gilda stood astonished as she saw two beautiful white haired women both sitting at the table with Jerry. They all had playing cards in their hands and there was money spread all across the table. Jerry looked up, as if relieved to be interrupted from his continuous unsuccessful bluffing game.

"Well good morning cousin, you got out of here awfully early this morning, we missed you."

Elijah shook his head. Betty the eldest of the two ladies not wanting Jerry to be distracted spoke up.

"You'd better watch the table son, I'd hate for you to loose all of your money!" Both the ladies began to chuckle. The other who appeared much more reserved and patient set her eyes directly on Gilda.

"Well look a here, is this the angel you spoke so much about, she is a little thing.

"Morning sweetie my name is Lara."

"Good morning, please to meet you I'm Gilda, Gilda Harris."

"Well Gilda it's a pleasure, you play poker?"

"No ma'am."

Gilda turned and looked up at Elijah and he gave here a huge grin. He had gotten her back and she knew it, Gilda responded to him also with a smile and returned her attention back to the two ladies. She imagined that they must've had some stories to tell the way they studied those cards. Both women sat at the table with Jerry with the look of true gamblers.

"Sit down, sit down chile."

Betty demanded.

"You hungry?"

"I got some homemade biscuits over yonder and some fried chicken and gravy."

"Jerry he den just bout ate everything up."

"Elijah dear, you ate?"

"No Miss B."

"Well go on now, fix you and your lady friend something to eat, don't mind us now."

Gilda any other time would have turned down a second helping of breakfast but today was an exception.

Lara hit the table with her hand.

"Betty cut the cards."

"One low in the hole last card deal'em son!"

The ladies continued there game with Jerry.

Jerry looked up at Elijah like a helpless child hoping to be saved.

"Elijah don't leave me with them man, they're vicious." Elijah shook his head and laughed as he reached in the cabinet for two plates.

"You on your own man."

Betty enjoyed the whipping that she and her sister were giving Jerry.

"What's wrong Jerry you afraid of these old ladies?"

Gilda began to laugh as she and Elijah made their way up the back staircase to his room.

Once inside Gilda looked around the simple, but spacious room. It had a large bed and a small indoor bathroom there was a sink with running water, the large tub however sat near the fire place. Elijah turned the radio on and offered Gilda a seat at the small table and chair set out on the balcony.

"This home is huge Elijah, and this room, my goodness is so cozy!"

Elijah held on to the promise he'd made to himself. He would not be the one to bring up marriage again. However, he would use this opportunity to help Gilda make the obvious decision to spend the rest of her life with him.

"Elijah it's so quiet and peaceful out here and the flowers, they're so beautiful"

"Yes believe it or not, I have become quite attached to this place these last couple of days.

"I woke up this morning to the sunrise over their and it was most beautiful one that I have seen yet."

"Elijah how's Joshua and Julia?"

"That's what I wanted to talk to you about; I received a wire from Joshua this morning."

"He said Paulie was back in town, and Sheriff Bradford been snooping around the house asking questions about you and Fisher."

"I told him pack what he could carry and at night fall drive into Macon catch the train from there and bring Julia and the kids here."

"Elijah what about the gold?" Elijah took a long pause.

"It's gone."

"What do you mean it's gone?"

"Joshua said he went back to the site in the woods and all the gold was gone."

"They're bringing the money we stashed at the house."

"Elijah, that's a lot of money, how are they going to get it on the train without being noticed?"

"Joshua is very intuitive he will figure a way I promise you."

"Miss Gillie, after I received that wire I realized, I do believe our dear friend Fisher is very much alive and he is moving around here like a ghost."

"Why won't he show his face then?"

"He probably has a lot of business he needs to straighten out and he can't do it running for his life."

"That's probably why he left you that message on the radio, apparently you know him better than most and he you."

"He knew you would come looking for him I guess." Elijah laughed as he continued to eat his meal.

"That Fisher is full of surprises; he played us all like a piano, including Dot."

"He probably did show up back in Culloden for his stash and he knew Paulie probably would be waiting for him."

"But what he wanted was for you not to be there."

"Think about it Gillie."

"If Paulie and his gang had any idea that he was floating around they will come looking for him and this time they may have come after you."

Gilda listened attentively to the love of her life, but she had done her own investigating and eagerly wanted to share it with Elijah.

"Well I spoke with Dot last night about everything, I just feel so betrayed by Fisher."

"We've been through so much together."

"Gillie, don't feel betrayed, but feel protected."

"Any of those men could have easily come after you, they all knew how close you and Fisher were."

Gilda knew Elijah could be right.

"Now, my Ki'Somma it's time to relax, everything will come together I promise you."

"There is no use of either one of us pondering our head about this situation."

"When the time is right Fisher will surface, but until then we wait for Joshua and Julia."

Gilda looked up at Elijah and gave him an affirmative nod. He then reached over and kissed her on the forehead.

"You are so beautiful."

Gilda got up and went over to him and gently kissed him in return. Elijah picked her up and took her over to the large feather bed. The breeze from the early afternoon air came swiftly through the double doors of the patio. It was a cool breeze and Gilda closed her eyes as he gently laid her down. Elijah softly began caressing her breast as he played continuously with her nipples until they hardened to attention. Every touch was a command preparing her for the readiness of his wonton pleasure. Slowly he began unbuttoning her dress and gently placed his lips upon hers. He softly kissed and caressed every inch of her fullness. Gilda laid her head deep into the pillows that were piled at the top of the huge bed and slowly moved her hand around his back responding to his sensual touch. She moaned with erotic pleasure as he took both hands and gently explored the fullness of her hips. He moved his strong hands up and down, exploring and pressing them firmly shaping the body that he so desired and longed to call his own. Elijah continued his exploration of the woman he loved so dearly. Gilda responded loyally as she opened her legs giving herself completely and fully to him. Her passion arose deep inside the depths of her being as she awaited the true love of her life. She laid patiently watching him remove his clothing and soon Elijah returned to her side continuing to caress and suckle each and every part of her body. Gently he put his hand in between her thighs and with every soft touch she longed for him. He slowly moved on top of her and allowed his manhood to search for her core. Gilda moaned with pleasure as he moved inside of her with soft thrust until finally, she felt him inside of her deeper. They moved at a rhythmic pace slowly in there own world savoring the love they had for one another. Elijah gave her all of himself fully and Gilda accepted him as he plunged into the warmth of her sweet nectar. She moaned with pleasure and he continued to give her strong thrust until they reached the peak of ecstasy. Elijah then softly kissed the love of his life and laid down next to her.

"Ki'Somma, you know there are no more words left for us."

"You and I have been through it all, practically living the life of a married man and woman."

"The only difference is that we do not have the blessings or a home that we can call ours." Gilda listened, she knew he was right and she did not want to interrupt his thoughts.

"You are the air I breathe."

"I have been waiting for you to make the decision, the proper decision to be my wife."

"I can't wait any longer, you will marry me and that is final!"

Gilda smiled because she knew he was right. She had been very hard to deal with and unable to make up her mind on her own. Gilda looked deep into his eyes with all the passion that she had for him. She know longer had the option to be a free woman not if she was going to spend the rest of her life with Elijah.

"Elijah you are right sweet heart and you have been so very patient with me." I must admit I have been acting like a spoiled child and I apologize for leaving before our Wedding day."

"I will never leave your side again Elijah, I promise." Gilda then leaned over and gently began kissing him. Elijah pulled her atop him and together they travel into ecstasy once more.

Chapter 19

Julia and Joshua arrived with the children a week later. Elijah went to meet them at the train station and once they returned back to the house Gilda was standing on the porch with Ms Betty and Ms. Lara. As the car pulled up Julia hung her head out the window waving at Gilda.
Gilda could not believe her eyes.
"Chile look at yourself, I told you would drop that weight."
She grabbed the baby and gave Josie a great big kiss.
"Auntie so happy to see ya." Jerry came out of the house with Dot, who was spending more time over to the sister's house with Jerry and less time at the Red Velvet. Joshua, after helping Elijah with the large trunks went and gave Gilda a big hug.
"Hey, Gillie." Gilda hugged him back
"Hey yourself, how you Joshua?"
"I'm good; you gave this man quite the scare you know."
"I heard, but I apologized and he's quite alright now."
Elijah escorted his family to the house.
"Come on in here Josh, I want you to meet two of my favorite ladies." With all of the commotion, the spinsters had made their way to the front porch.
"Miss Betty, Miss Lara, this here is my brother Joshua, his wife Julia and there two children Josephine and Joshua Jr."
As usual Betty spoke first.
"Well hello there Julia and Josephine"
Josie spoke up.
"My friends call me Josie, Miss Betty"
"Well now since I am your friend you can call me "B" all my friends do."

"Goodness gracious all these handsome men round here."

"We haven't had such easy looking in a long while I tell you."

Lara interrupted.

"You ladies have to excuse Betty she is overwhelmed with the excitement of all this company."

She then escorted them into the kitchen.

"Y'all must be starving from that long train ride."

"I got some dinner in the stove."

"Help yourself; the plates are in the cabinet."

"I'm not hungry Ms. B."

Betty extended her hand to Josie.

"Then come on with me doll, you play cards?"

Jerry looked at Betty and shook his head as she and Lara escorted the little girl into the dining room. After they finished eating the others sat on the porch and the topic of discussion was Fisher.

"Well brother give it to me, how's everything back home?"

"Not so good man, that Lil Paulie fellow he and his cronies going around to the ole time bootleggers shaking em down and asking questions about Fisher and Gillie here."

"We closed up Gillie's house and ours. Julia took all the keys over to Miss Ann's.

"Miss Ann answered the door with her shotgun in her hand."

Elijah smiled.

"That sure is a tough little ole lady."

"The sheriff, he had been hanging around quite often."
"He finally got up the nerve and start asking questions inquiring about you and Gilda."

"He said he hadn't seen you two for a spell."

"It's some shady things going on down there in Culloden Elijah."

"One of Sherriff Bradford's cronies swore he seen Fisher in town late one night, but the good thing is most didn't believe him even the sheriff, because this man he stay drunk all the time."

"But, that still did not stop him from contacting that Paulie fella."

"They were all over the hillside searching for Fisher."

Gilda then looked over at Joshua.

"Joshua you think he was there?"

"Well Gillie, I do because nobody knew about that spot except for us and Fisher."

"It's no coincidence that when I went to get the sac it was gone."

Joshua was careful not to mention anything about Fisher's money or his family's fortune that he and Julia used to pad the bottom of their trunks.

"I'm going to tell you though; where ever he may be I hope he stay there because it ain't safe for him in Culloden."

"We had to leave like we were on the Underground Railroad."

"Mr. Payton drove us over to Macon to catch the train out this way."

Gilda shook her head as she listened to Joshua. Things had gotten really bad, she then thought about Miss Ann and the burden that they left her to deal with.

"I hope Miss Ann will be okay."

"Oh Miss Ann, Gillie she fine we told her were you were and she told me to tell you to write just as soon as you can." Gilda nodded here head then looked up at Elijah for some type of response to what Joshua was saying, but Elijah was too busy curious about what Dot was thinking.

"Eh Dot what's your take on all of this."

Dot hunched her shoulders and looked over at Gilda and Elijah."

"Who me?"

"I think Fisher is running from something and if that's the case ya'll know things gonna get worse before they get better"

Everyone nodded in agreement.

Dot stepped off of the porch.

"Pretty soon they may be coming down this way, think about it, ain't no telling who followed the two of you."

"Paulie is a treacherous man and I seen the type of people he deals with back at Fisher's Place and they're heartless I tell ya."

"They will walk right up on you and before you know it."

"Dot!"

Gilda called out.

"We do not need that type of talk right now."

"What we need is a plan of action just in case they do come down this way."

"First Joshua we need to get you, Julia and the children settled in."

"Tomorrow we will talk more."

All nodded in agreement.

Later that evening Gilda could feel herself getting sick again, it had been the second time this week she could not hold her food down. She went into the bathroom and kneeled over the toilet and began releasing the evening's dinner. Julia went to the door and knocked hard.

"Gillie, you alright?"

Gilda could not speak, she continued relieving herself. Julia opened up the door and pulled a towel off of the railing and ran some cold water on it. She then laid it gently on the back of Gilda's neck. After Gilda finished she stood up and went to the sink to rinse her mouth. Julia stood back watching her friend. "Gilda, how long have you been feeling like this?"

" Oh a couple of weeks or so."

"Have you missed your monthly Gillie?"

"No, but I haven't been feeling well lately."
"When are you due?"
"Should be this week sometime."
"Gilda, I think you may be pregnant."
"Pregnant?"
Gilda looked at her friend confused.
"Yes pregnant, you do have the symptoms."
"But Julia, I can't get pregnant."
"What gave you that idea?
"Well I never have before."
"All this time me and Elijah have been together not once have we conceived a child."
"Well Gillie, have you ever thought that it may not have been time for you to conceive a child."
"I mean after all you were too busy to sit down, let alone have a baby."
"These days you are a little more settled and the body knows, trust me."

Gilda made Julia promise not to tell Elijah or even Joshua, she had to think this thing out herself, all the while she thought that she could not have a child now down her in Louisiana she had conceived. Life was sure strange she thought.

Right away Gilda believed somehow maybe this is the place that she needed to be. Since she had arrived she felt a since of calm in her spirit. Outside of the events surrounding Fisher, Louisiana had become a dream come true to Gilda.

The next morning after breakfast, Elijah sat in the parlor with Jerry and Joshua.

"We have to make some preparations in case those clowns come down this way I am glad that you Julia and the kids were able to get out of there safe."

"Joshua not to the fault of you, but we have been thinking about what Dot said."

"We have to assume that they followed you and Julia here."

"Today we will take a trip into town and pick up some shells."

"The sisters have four or five shotguns down in the cellar, they are old but they are workable."

"What I want to do is keep this thing between us; we go into town do a little snooping around talk to some of the entertainers drop some names and see what comes out of it." All the men agreed.

Meanwhile the ladies were in the kitchen. Gilda, Julia and the sisters where sitting down at the kitchen table shelling peas for dinner while Josie spent her time chasing the cat around the house. Julia just as Gilda spent a lot of time admiring the home of the sisters

"You two ladies have a lovely home."

"Why thank you sweetie, it was our fathers along with all this land."

"You know, after a while we began selling it off to some of the black folk down in these parts."

"Yeah, me and Lara here thought we would help them get out of that old sharecropping and get into business for themselves."

"Old Jim Crow made it hard for black folks around these parts."

"Yep and some even went off to live in the swamps remember Betty."

"Yes I do, made a home there so they would not have to deal with the tyranny of these white folks down here."

"It seemed as though white folks was trying to send them back into slavery all over again, didn't Lara."

"Umhmm and that upset papa."

"You know what he did, he told them they could work the land and in a years time it would belong to them."

"That was along time ago, most of the folks even was able to send they children off to college."

"A lot of them that grew up with my father have passed on there were twelve families total on all this land."

"Now you know them same children of those folks who toiled that land will not even come down to check on it, just pay the taxes and mail out Christmas cards to me and Lara every year." Lara then interrupted.

"Their children and their families are all living up North now."

"Graduated school and became doctors and lawyers, isn't that something?"

"How can you just forget about where you come from or how your parents worked so hard to put you in such a good place in life?"

"It just breaks my heart every time I think about it."

"I tell you the worst thing that they could have done was move up there, this here is where our roots are this here is home I tell you."

"Papa was a good man you know."

"We don't even use most of this here land but we see to it that it's kept up."

"We use just enough for us to plant our summer garden."

"But all that out there is rich soil just waiting."

Later that afternoon Gilda received some exciting news from Dot. She rushed to wake Elijah from his nap.

"Elijah get up, get up."

He jumped up defensively.

"Is everything okay?"

"Yeah every thing is fine."

"I just heard from Dot that Bessie Smith is coming to New Orleans."

Elijah fell back into the large pillows. He always found it hard to become angry with Gilda. Her pretty smile had brightened the past few days of his life and he was getting use to the getting up with her by his side every morning.

"She will be here this Saturday at the Locus, where ever that is at." Elijah scratched his head.

"Well it must be in town."

"I'm sure a club with the name Locus will not be hard to find."

"Can we go Elijah?"

She climbed on top of Elijah's chest and began kissing him all over his face. Elijah grabbed hold of here and pulled her closer as he softly suckled her lips.

"Is that a good enough answer for you?"

"Why yes Mr. Mason it is and we should tell Julia and Joshua."

"I know she would love to see her too, I just know it."

That evening at dinner Gilda was excited to share the news. Elijah asked the sisters where the Locus was. They confirmed that it was not in town.

"Who told you about the Locus?" Gilda responded excitedly as she scooped a pile of potatoes into her plate.

"Dot did."

"Chile the Locus, hey that sure ain't in town."

Betty smiled as she sat the gravy on the table.

"You are talking about going into the backwoods of the Bayou baby girl."

"It's deep in the swamps child."

"The Locus, you ain't gonna get that kinda blues in them big city fancy places, no suh."

"When you take that journey to the Locus you going back in time; deep into the soul of black folks."

"White folks, they ain't heard the such I tell ya."

"Ain't that right Lara?"

"Yes ma'am she right about that, and the few that take that journey, well let's just say their lives be changed forever."

"Betty, remember Robert Jefferies, he took the trip."

"He was a young handsome white fella and he show knew how to play the piano too."

"His father was some very wealthy fella from Massachusetts."

"Some how he talked a few of the musicians from New Orleans to take him to the Locus."

"It changed his life forever when he met our friend Justine Miller."

"She was one of the singers at the time."

"That boy came back and gave up everything to marry Justine Miller and can you believe they traveled around the world as a duet and ain't been back since."

"Me and Lara get a Christmas card from England every year still."

"You will come outta there a different person."

"Let me tell you, it ain't just the music that gets you."

"The atmosphere is tranquil, spiritual; you know what I'm saying?"

"See back in there it's another world in a world where people living it and breathing it everyday."

"Living what Miss Betty?"

"The spirit of the blues of course."

"Its there you can find that very thing that will cleanse the soul."

"It's a way to life you see."

"You go to the Locus, you will truly be taking a journey."

"Oh yes, Betty here is right about all of that stuff, but it show is a lot of fun too."

"When it get's dark up in them parts it's pitch black."

"Me and Betty used to carry us an oil lamp on our journey's in there and a revolver on our first journey."

"Lara here she had a love back in them parts, Ole Clyde Perkins, remember him Lara."

Lara shook her head with a blushing smile.

"How could I forget dear Clyde?"

Betty continued.

"Anyway, that man, could he ever play the blues, he would pull out that harmonica on the way back through them dark swamps and it was pitch black I tell you."

"Nobody ever bothered us, because he blew that harmonica with all his heart and soul, he was apart of the Locus ya know."

Julia interrupted.

"How do you get there?"

"Oh it's only one way to get to the Locus, you must go by boat ."

All looked as if they were having second thoughts, but Lara attempted to ease the tension.

"Y'all don't mind Betty, in a lot of ways she is right, but the people are friendly and godly folk"

"It will be just fine."

"Most folk just stay til morning, where they can see their way out of there."

Betty slapped her thigh and laughed as she reminisced.

"I show do miss those good times."

Gilda looked over at Julia at Joshua.

"What about it guys, you wanna go with us?"

"Naw, I think we will pass on that."

"You all go on have a good time."

"We gonna hang around the house with the children." Gilda was so excited, but then felt a little guilty because she hadn't thought about the children.

Betty interrupted.

"Oh you don't have to worry about those children, me and Lara here will watch them."

"We haven't had any little people around in a long time, it will do us some good, wont it Lara?"

"I think it will Betty."

"Now you young folks go ahead and plan your Saturday night and leave those children to us you hear."

Julia smiled.

"You are so very kind, but we didn't come here to be a burden on you."

Then Gilda spoke up while pointing at Joshua and Julia.

"Ladies, these two here you just wasting your time with

them, so just let it be they ain't separating from them children."

Julia turned from the stove and threw her towel at Gilda, "Oh Gillie you just be quiet chile."

"Julia, you know I ain't lying." Julia shook her head and continued fixing Josephine's plate. Gilda smiled.

Well what about you Jerry, will you join us?"

"Are you kidding me?"

"I wouldn't miss this for the world Gillie."

That night Dot returned to the house and provided Gilda with the details for their journey. Betsy Smith would be performing at the Locus Saturday night only.

That evening the ladies discussed what they were going to wear. Dot wanted to take Gilda to the city so that she could pick up something nice for Saturday Night.

Gilda was very excited, in all her years she never thought she would see her favorite blues artist perform or even make it back out of Colluden. Life was looking up she thought to herself.

The following morning Gilda got out of bed and left Elijah to sleep in. She overheard him with Joshua and Jerry on the porch discussing the issues surrounding Fisher before she turned in. Gilda figured she would get the details once she and Dot returned from the city. After freshening up, she went downstairs to the kitchen. Julia was at the stove helping Ms. Lara and Josephine was at the table with Jerry and Joshua. Joshua was holding the baby and feeding him his bottle.

"Good morning auntie Gillie."

" Morning suga."

Julia turned from the stove and gave both Josephine and Jerry a full plate of eggs, grits, fried catfish and biscuits.

"Gillie, you want some breakfast, chile Miss Lara den gave me a new recipe for deep-frying catfish, here taste it."

Miss Gilda's Blues

Gilda with a look of nausea on her face looked at the fish and then at Julia.

"No thanks, I ain't really hungry right now."

"Miss Lara you got some hot tea over there?"

"Yes chile."

Ms. Lara was looking at Gilda in an awkward fashion. " Gillie, honey, you know peppermint tea with a twist of lemon is good for you first thing in the morning when you don't have much of an appetite."

"Thank you Miss Lara, I'll have some then"

Gilda sat down to the table, and not soon after Dot knocked on the back kitchen door.

"Dot that you, come on in."

"Good morning ya'll, ummm smells good in here."

Dot was wearing a fitted off the shoulder yellow Chiffon dress with satin lining that came just above her knees. She also had on a pair of yellow high heel shoes and a large white hat with a beautiful yellow flower in the front.

Dot went for the pot and Miss Lara popped her hand with the large soup spoon.

"Girl I know you been raised better than that."

"If you hungry I can fix you a plate."

Dot snatched her hand back grabbing the top of it with the other and rolled her eyes at Miss Lara.
She then walked over to Jerry, took his fork out of his hand, dug into his plate of grits and put it into her mouth.

"No thanks ma'am."
Miss Lara shook her head in disgrace and handed Gilda her tea. Josephine, knowing the look on her mother's face finished her breakfast and joined Miss Betty and her father in the library.

"Gillie honey, are you all ready to hit the street?"

"My car is out back, or I should say my friend's car."
Gilda looked out of the kitchen window and seen a shinny white convertible. Jerry looked over at Dot and shook his

head while he cleaned his plate in the sink. She didn't care one way or the other.

"Oh sweetie don't mind that there, that belongs to Santa Claus is all."
By this time Miss Lara was fed up with the conversation and left the kitchen with Jerry to join the others.

Dot was eager to show the girls the latest in fashion downtown; she could hardly sleep the night before. There was one thing that she enjoyed and that was shopping for clothes. Dot had grown up a poor child in Louisiana, but once she was introduced to the life she had back at Fisher's Place she lived fearlessly, and vowed never to be poor in her life again no matter the cost.

"Girls what are you waiting for, we have places to go people to see."

Julia took off her waist apron and began styling her hair in the mirror on the side of the pantry.

"Wait a minute Dot, some of us do have other responsibilities."

Gilda got up as well.

"Let's do this."

The girls hit the highway and after about thirty minutes of riding they finally made it downtown. The city was vibrant as ever. It was Friday afternoon and on Friday's many of the bed and breakfast establishments in the Latin Quarters were preparing for their weekend guest. These guests usually consisted of wealthy French and English seamen that came by boat to the gulf coast. The streets were filled with dozens of bars, restaurants and also clothing boutiques. While Julia and Gilda were gazing around at all the opportunities to indulge in being beautiful, Dot waved at Gilda.

"Gillie, you two come over here."

"I want you to meet someone."
Gilda and Julia walked over toward Dot. She was standing in between two men with her arms locked underneath theirs.

"Ladies I would like you to meet two very dear friends of mine to my left is Mr. Pierre Lacrosse and to my right Mr. Wolfgang Perry."

Both men were of African and French decent. Pierre was a tall very handsome man with a frail physique and Wolfgang appeared to be much larger in stature, in a lot of ways he reminded Gilda of her dear friend Ted. It was obvious that both gentlemen were quite well off.

Gilda always had an eye for fine linens, and she knew that each were very expensively dressed. Gilda spoke first as she extended her hand.

"It's a pleasure meeting you both."

Wolfgang without hesitation took it and gently kissed it. "The pleasure is all mind my petite."

Gilda stepped back next to Julia.

Seeing the incorrigible demeanor of the gentlemen, Julia stood were she was and just waved.

"Hi ya'll."

The two men nodded in unison. Dot then continued talking to the two gentlemen.

"What are you two doing in the city; I haven't seen you two in months?"

It was obvious that Dot was very much attracted to Pierre and she made no attempts to hide it as she walked up to him and gently kissed him on the lips.

"I hope I will be seeing you sometime during your visit." Pierre not backing down from the obvious foreplay, grabbed Dot's hand and whispered in her ear, she begin to chuckle.

"Well I see that you have not changed your strips much Mr. Lacrosse."

Wolfgang interrupted.

"Where are you lovely ladies off to Dottie?"

"We're are out shopping for something fabulous to wear." "We're going to the Locus, Betsy Smith is performing tonight."

"Ahh"

Wolfgang moaned.

"The Locus, it has been sometime since I made that trip."

"It is truly unfortunate that we will not be able to join you ladies tonight only because we have much business to attend to."

He then looked over at Gilda.

"Maybe another time perhaps?"

Gilda gave him a polite smile and then turned to Dot.

"I think we should continue our shopping, you know that we haven't much time before the boat leaves."

Julia stood without a word; she had her eyes on a dress in the window of a boutique across the street. Joshua had given her enough money to buy herself and Josie something really nice and she was awfully anxious to get started. Dot turned her attention back to the fella's.

"Yes we really must be going, but we will meet again soon."

"Good day gentlemen."

The gentlemen parted and the ladies continued there stroll in the shopping district. After a long day of shopping and a big New Orleans lunch, Dot dropped the girls off back at the house.

"I'll be back this evening around six, to pick you guys up." The ladies said their goodbyes and Dot sped off onto the road.

Chapter 20

Later that evening Gilda removed from the cabinet the homemade oils of honeysuckle she'd made and begin putting it on the most sensual parts of her body. Tonight was her turn to be incorrigible.

Gilda looked over the beautiful, yet sensual black embroided evening dress covered in black shimmering beads and thought she had done quite well on her shopping trip with the girls. She also purchased a soft headpiece with beads as well, which matched perfectly. Her shoes were a black satin exposing her toes with a strap that wrapped around and tied just above her ankles. Gilda looked in the mirror and noticed she resembled the beautifully adorned Queens of Africa.

Elijah was sitting out on the porch playing his harmonica; the sounds echoed into the room and drew Gilda to him. She stood in the doorway and watched as he played a tune that reminded her of her childhood. Elijah was dressed as immaculate as the gentlemen she had met in town yesterday. He wore a pair of black slacks a crisp white shirt with a black silk tie, a silk burgundy vest on top and a pair of soft black leather boots. He also wore silver cuff links with a black eagle engraved in each one. Elijah looked around toward Gilda, immediately he stopped playing his tune and waved her to come to him. Gilda sat in his lap and he observed her from head to toe.

"My darling Ki'Somma, how beautiful you look this evening."

The smell of sweet honeysuckle on her body enticed him to take her right there. Elijah then placed Gilda's hand over his chest.

"You are overwhelming for my heart Ki'Somma."

"Feel that, that's what you do to me."

Gilda gently kissed his lips.

"I love you Elijah."
Suddenly there was a knock on the bedroom door.
"Hey guys Dots here?"
Elijah frustrated from the interruption shouted out.
"Be out in a minute."

When Gilda went downstairs the ladies spent their time complimenting each other. Julia and Miss Lara joined in as well, while the men took a drink with Miss Betty at the dining room table. Elijah was surprised Dot was alone.

"Are you gonna drive us Dot?"

"Oh just to the dock sweetie."

"No cars allowed and you guys better get a change of clothes for morning to."

"I got a friend that lives out there we can stay at his place."

Gilda returned to her room and quickly got her and Elijah an overnight bag and Jerry did the same. Finally all made it to the porch with Joshua and the sisters. To Gilda this trip was beginning to seem awfully strange. Even though the sisters had told her, this was how you traveled to the Locus; things just did not sit right with her. Gilda had encouraged Joshua to talk to Elijah about her feelings. Elijah had the upmost respect for her concern and as a result to be safe he took one of the old revolvers that the sisters had down in the cellar. Shortly afterward they all rode off into the sunset.

After reaching the river's edge, there was a gentleman with a long narrow row boat waiting for them. Dot jumped out of the car. "Come on guys, Martha will come by and get the car later."

"Gillie, come on."

They all stepped down into the boat. It was a small wooden boat, but Gilda was thankful they had padded the benches. Elijah inquired about the weight to the controller, but he encouraged him that it could hold all of them. Slowly he pushed off and they began their journey. Never in a mllion years had Gilda thought she would be floating down the bayou with Elijah. Life was strange she thought. Gilda also thought about the advice that Julia had given her, about being still and seeing what would come to you. She knew that she was carrying Elijah's child for sure. She was now two months late for her monthly. Gilda's thoughts were interrupted by the scenery as they floated deeper into the Bayou.

The waterway became a lot narrower the further they went. Other boats begin to join in the journey from other waterways. People were dressed in their finest in these lantern lit boats as they all traveled following one another down the narrow river path. There were people sitting along the river banks fishing. There were houses along the waterway most made of wood and there was smoke coming out of the Chimney's. Gilda thought maybe the women were inside preparing dinner. The children were still playing outside skipping rocks by bon fire. Dot pointed to the rear of the boat.

"You guys see that?"

Gilda turned around and to her amazement the waterway was now a convoy of boats just like theirs, as far as she could see.

"Gillie, this is the crowd that Bessie brings out when she comes."

The boat's begin docking at the many long wooden docks that lined the water way. Some where waving to others as they paddled along.

As they continued their journey Gilda began to appreciate the beauty of the swamp. It had beautiful trees that hung solemnly along the waterway, she had been to the woods back home in Georgia along the river bank, but this place had a more mystical atmosphere. Jerry had become restless with the boat ride and begin to nag the navigator until finally he pulled up to an old run down dock.

"You people be careful you hear, you have to go one at a time."

"That old dock will not be able to carry the weight of all of yah."

Elijah lifted Gilda up and he encouraged her to walk on to solid ground. She looked further up the road and noticed a group of people going into a large two level wood frame building. She heard the sounds of a saxophone and piano in the night air. Gilda began snapping her fingers and as the others unloaded off the boat she danced, anxiously waiting to move in closer. They all finally made it to the infamous Locus and like the sisters said the atmosphere was overwhelming. It was a wide open space it had no windows or doors. There were people sitting at tables along the sides of the large wooden banister frames off of the waterway. As they walked further inside there were people dancing, laughing and singing. Gilda had recognized the distinguishing looking faces of some of the men from the Red Velvet. Dot went right into action greeting and hugging people and Jerry began putting on his charm as well. He began working the room searching for his love for the night. Gilda couldn't understand the relationship they shared. Elijah gave a tug and pulled Gilda close to him around the waste.

"Let's go over there."

Elijah grabbed Gilda by the hand and led her through the crowd of people. There were both young and old here enjoying the good old sounds of the blues. As Gilda moved further to the back she looked in what appeared to be a small kitchen. Further to the left was a small bar with about ten wooden stools all had been filled. Above the bar on the second level was a gentleman sitting with his feet hanging down over the bar holding a shotgun. He appeared to be the watchman, as he observed intensely who came in and out. Gilda noticed every once in a while they would pass him some food or a soda. She could smell the seasonings of a dish that she had grown to love while down in Louisiana.

"*Ahh seafood gumbo.*"

Finally Gilda and Elijah found a space just outside of the frame of the building. There was a ramp that led to another deck were chairs and tables. The wooden banister was lined with lanterns to help guide them to their destination. Once they were comfortably seated, Gilda looked out onto the waterway and noticed that people were still coming to enjoy tonight's entertainment. Elijah interrupted her thoughts.

"Did I tell you how beautiful you look this evening?"
Gilda gave him a blushing smile.

"Well Mr. Mason I believe you have, but I never grow tired of hearing it."

"Well I had to make sure I tell you, because I'm looking around her and it appears that all eyes are on you my Ki'Somma"

A young woman came over to the table to take their order. She did not hesitate to boldly approach Elijah.

"Well hello there handsome, is there something I can get for you and your date."
With her attention totally at Elijah, Gilda politely cleared her throat.

"Excuse us, umm, what it your name?"
"Beulah."
"Well is it Ms. or Mrs.?"
"Well its Mrs. I'm the owner of this place and that there is my Husband."
She pointed at the bar.
"That's Jessee Lee Jr. son of the founder Jessee Lee Sr."
"That's with two E's."
"I could not help but noticing such a beautiful couple."
"I love looking at handsome men of course."
Gilda couldn't believe what she was hearing and gave the woman a look of disbelief. However, before she could respond Elijah defused the situation by placing an order from the menu.

"Well, I think I would like to try some of that Gumbo, smells good and afterward you can bring me a shot of your best."

"Okay."

She then looked over at Gilda.

"What about you darling?"

"Do you have wine?"

"Show do, made it myself."

" I'll have a glass and a bowl of gumbo as well."

When Beulah walked off Gilda turned to Elijah.

"The nerve of that woman, as if I wasn't even sitting here."

Elijah laughed out loud and quickly reminded Gilda of his feelings about her working at Fisher's Place and why he never came there while she worked. Gilda smiled, now she knew why Elijah felt the way he did.

The four of them had a great time. Bessie Smith came on and performed and even sat down for a cocktail with Elijah and Gilda. Gilda had finally had the opportunity to meet her favorite Blues singer and get her autograph.

They sang and danced until the early hours of the morning. The gentleman that brought them up the river was no longer at the dock, but had taken their bags as Dot had instructed him to the cottage. The cottage was not far from the Lotus and they where all able to walk the short distance. Gilda was exhausted and wanted nothing more but to lay down. It was a fairly large two story cottage deep in a wooded area. Gilda looked the place over. "

"This is awfully nice place Dot."

"Whose is it?"

"Oh just a friend of mine."

"You should get to meet him before old Carson comes back with the boat."

"Hey ya'll there's no running water but there is a water pump and outhouse outback."

"There is a tub in the back room and another upstairs you guys can use to bathe in."

Gilda walked around the modest cabin, There was a kitchen area with a large wood burning stove next to a cold box and a small pantry area near the back door. There was a fire place with a large untorched log inside and a beautiful large black bear rug in front on the wooden floor. Candles lined the wax covered mantle along with empty liquor bottles. There was a large wooden table in the middle of the floor and five chairs shoved underneath. Gilda soon found a radio, but when she turned it on she received a poor reception. Dot warned her as she fumbled with the knobs.

"Chile back in these here swamps, they don't listen to no radio music, they make there own."

Jerry stretched out on the couch in front of the fire place and before anyone could realize it he was sound asleep. Before long everyone found a space in the house to rest. After a few hours Gilda had awaken. She and Elijah had retired in the room on the second floor. Gilda looked over and Elijah was still sounding asleep. She noticed he had filled the tub and she was grateful. She then grabbed her bag and freshened up. Gilda could hear familiar voices downstairs and she slowly climbed down the wooden ladder, when she got there she could not believe her eyes, Jerry and Dot where sitting at the table having coffee with Fisher.

"Oh my god!" Gilda yelled out.

"Fisher!"

Fisher was using a cane as he slowly sat down at the table. There were two other men with him, each wearing a bandana covering the lower part of their faces. They were bidding Fisher farewell and departed without a greeting or introduction.

"Fisher oh my god, look at you."

She then looked over at Dot.

"I guess this is the house owner."

Dot smiled and handed her a cup of coffee

Fisher was dressed in a large brimmed cowhide hat and a red bandana tied to his neck. He wore moccasin boots on his feet and a jacket to match made out of pure buffalo skin. He spoke slowly to Gilda.

"I didn't want to wake you, I figured you would be up soon enough."

Fisher opened his arms and gave Gilda a big hug.

"Sir you know you have a lot of explaining to do."

"I thought you were dead."

"Did they tell you about Big Ted?"

Fisher nodded mournfully.

"Yeah, Dot just informed me."

"What is going on Fisher?"

"Where have you been?"

"I have been worried sick wondering if you were dead or alive."

"Well my sweet Gillie, It's been a long road."

"I've been around staying here and there for the past year."

"I did come back home and that damn Hightower saw me and my fella's."

"Man thought I was in for it for sure." He then started to laugh.

"The old fool was too drunk to even see straight." Gilda continued her questions.

"What happened?"

"Where'd you go Fisher?"

"Well the men who came to get me they were not friends of Paulie's, they were friends of mine."

"Remember when I told you about Joey and there was another guy who ran with us sometimes, Franco?"

"Yes!"

"Well he sent those guys to come and get me."
The intent was to make it seem as though Paulie set it up so the sheriff wouldn't had contacted Paulie before we finished the job at the Place, but I waited too late"

Fisher paused for a moment to think about his dear friend. He'd made every attempt to make sure Ted would get out safe. Fisher hadn't realized that Paulie and his posse were so close.

"I knew after the meeting I had with them the day you stopped by my place, I needed to make a move soon."

"I spent all night counting all that money I had hidden in the walls, me and Ted buried the gold"

"Most of the gold that I had acquired had been buried for a while and the rest was safe in Mexico."

"I had just recently added the money because Paulie had me coming out of so much dough, paying him more than fifty percent."

"I was just glad I had listened to you Gillie and Big Paulie before he died."

"Now the only thing that is left for him to do is kill me and I'm not about to let that happen."

"There was no way that Paulie was gonna allow me to continue to run my business in peace."

"Everybody knows that his days are numbered for the bootlegging business and he wanted all or nothing and willing to kill me for it too."

"Now he don't care bout the money, he wants the gold All stood and listen attentively to Fisher. Dot hadn't known as much, especially about gold, but Gilda didn't stop asking questions she wanted to know everything.

"Fisher, where did you go once you left?"

"I was so worried about you and the note that you left with the money I did not know what to think."

By this time Elijah had finally climbed down from the second level. He and Fisher embraced and gave each other a slap on the back.

"I told Gillie that you knew how to deal with those city slickers from up North." Gilda encouraged Dot to join her on the porch for another cup of coffee while the men folk talked among themselves.

"Everything alright man?" Fisher nodded his head.
"I'm fine as cat hair man."
Both men started laughing. Elijah sat down and joined the huddle and after Fisher brought Elijah up to date on the situation, a plan was in order. The gentlemen went outside and Fisher continued his conversation while the women went inside and prepared to leave. Fisher began to question Elijah and Jerry about Dot.
"How often has Dot been around you and your folks man?"
"Ever since we come down here from Culloden I believe she kind of sweet on Jerry."
Fisher gave Elijah and Jerry a serious look.
"I don't trust her man."
"Jeanine said that she was acting strange before I came back to get her."
"She told me Dot was entertaining Lil Paulie quite often."
"I know she got that habit she gotta support, but she giving me a real eerie feeling."
Elijah was not surprised. Fisher continued.
"If my intuition is correct, Paulie is possibly on his way to Louisiana, he won't stop until he gets me and the gold!"
Elijah spoke in a low tone of voice.
"Well Joshua dug up what was left of the money and brought it with him and Julia down here."
Fisher was relieved.
"I need you fella's to be on your guard once you get back to that house."
Fisher gave Elijah instructions to where he would be. Elijah took it all in.
"That's near the border of Mexico man?"
"Yes, the rest of the gold is there safe with friends."
"I will send a boat out every evening until sunrise for the next five days off that river bank."

"I don't know how many Paulie may have with him, and far as I know them cats are probably looking for Gillie as well."

Fisher didn't want to mention that to Elijah, but he knew if his suspicions were correct about Dot it was highly possible that Paulie and his posse were headed their way. Fisher went into his pocket and pulled out a map.

"You see this it's a map from the train station to the river bank and it's about a days trip."

"Somebody is gonna have to meet us there."

"This has gone on long enough."

Fisher began rolling the map and then gave it to Elijah. Elijah reached for it, but Fisher held on to it .

"You know, once I loved her man, but I had to let it go because her heart belonged to you."

Elijah nodded his head.

"Elijah you have yourself a good genuine woman who will do anything for you man, I just want you to remember that."

The two men hugged and Jerry patted them both on the shoulder

"Fella's, Fella's, we will get through this just wait and see and then we can live a wonderful rich and happy life."

Soon after Dot and Gilda returned to let them know the boat had arrived. Fisher gave his farewells to his dear friends and they began their journey back into the woody swamp land of Louisiana. Jerry knew now that his affiliation with Dot had been just another one of her scams. Now knowing the betrayal, Jerry would play along until everything was finished.

When they returned to the rendezvous Martha was waiting for them at the dock when they arrived. The ride back to the house was silent until Dot suddenly addressed Elijah.

"So what did ole Po Fisher put in your ear?"

"He tell you were the gold is?" Dot pulled the gun out of the glove compartment and turned around facing Elijah, Jerry and Gilda in the back seat. Gillie's eyes widened with shock. Dot continued to focus her attention back on Elijah.

"Hand it over Elijah darling, I know you packing." Elijah did not say a word.

"I mean it, I know Miss Gillie here don't wanna see your brains all scattered across that lovely back seat."

"Now hand it over!"

Elijah went down in the back of his pants and pulled out the small revolver and gave it to Dot.

"Now that all of that is settled, we are going to take a little trip back to that house Paulie and his men should be there now."

Elijah became furious as he thought about the sisters and his family." Jerry gave Dot a piercing stare.

. "Oh honey, you surprised at little old Dot."

"Do not be angry sweetheart; I always liked my money way more than I liked my men."

"Now Paulie that is a smart man he picked up on that real early and you know what he used it to his advantage."

"Unlike Fisher, he was so naïve."

"I could smell he was vulnerable the first day I met him."

Gilda spoke up, she was furious. "You are nothing but a piece of trash Dot, how could I have ever."

"You'd just better shut your mouth girl or that baby of yours will never see the light of day."

Elijah turned and looked at Gilda. That was all he needed now he had not only her to worry about but also their unborn child. Dot looked over at Elijah.

"You sure are mighty quiet big man." Elijah turned his attention back to Dot.

"Well what is there to talk about you're the one holding the gun."

"Oh he's Handsome and funny."

Elijah irritably responded.

"Dot what is it that you want?"

"If its money I will give you all you need, because you my lady have gotten yourself in a very dangerous situation that I'm sure you will soon regret."

Jerry spoke out in frustration.

"She ain't no lady she is a whore the both of them." Martha laughed aloud.

"Well you didn't feel that way when you were rubbing up against the both of us now did you."

"So you know what that makes you, It makes you a whoremonger you self righteous pathetic fool."

When they reached the house there were two black Ford's parked out front. There was a man in a grey suit on the porch and another leaned up against the car smoking a cigarette. Elijah was thinking of a way that he could get his other gun out of his bag, but from the looks of the situation that would not be enough for them, he needed to come up with a better plan fast. As Martha pulled up closer to the house she blew the horn and soon after Paulie stepped out on the porch.

"My, my, my what do we have here?"

"It is truly a surprise to see the likes of you down here in Bayou country."

Elijah gave him no conversation, but simply asked him one question.

"Where are the sisters and my family Paulie?"

"They're in the house and if you wanna make some trouble it will be on your conscious, I promise you boy."

Paulie stepped aside and with the wave of his hand invited them in. Gilda went in first and Elijah and Jerry followed. Everyone was sitting in the front parlor. Josie jumped out of her seat and ran over to Gilda.

"Auntie Gillie these men are mean, and they hurt daddy."

Julia had Joshua lying on the couch, wiping his face and head with a cool wash cloth, he had been beat up pretty bad.

Betty was holding the baby and was sitting in the chair by the window she appeared more angry than scarred.

"You back, and it's a good thing these hoodlums came through here like they owned the place."

"They got a lot of nerve pushing us around."

"I may be an old woman but I don't need to tolerate this type of crap." Lara was sitting in the adjacent room at the dining room table with her hands folded, looking out of the large paned window that faced the land out back. She summoned Elijah to her and softly whispered to him.

"Elijah son, I don't know what the hell is going on here but somebody sure as hell better tell me."

"I may be old, but I'm no fool."

"Neither one of us."

"Nothing motivates folks to do such evil things but money I tell you, money."

Paulie stepped into the room.

"You are so very right old lady." Paulie spoke up with a calm even tone. He was very sure of himself and all that he had planned. Three other men walked out of the kitchen holding sandwiches.

"Hey Paulie, we gone let em have it now."

Paulie looked over at Penske as if he had been a thorn in his side for quite awhile.

"Penske, why would you say such things we have no reason to bring harm to these good folks."

He then turned his attention back to Gilda

"All I want is what belongs to me." Gilda spoke out in a hateful tone.

"What is that may I ask?"

"The gold of course!"

The two sisters looked at each other and then to Gilda. "Gold?"

"Oh sir, you must be mistaken we don't have any gold around here."

"She's lying!" Dot spoke out.

Miss Gilda's Blues

"We were with Po Fisher in the swamp."

"I'm sure he told them where it was and I bet he will be coming too."

"These two had a long discussion with him before we left."

Paulie turned his attention to Elijah.

"Okay big man I know we are two men who take life very seriously."

"Neither of us likes to play games unless it's a gentleman's game of poker of course."

"What did Po Fisher say?" Elijah gave Paulie a cold look of discontent.

"Man, we are nothing alike and Fisher did not speak of any gold, we discussed him possibly finding away to get him out of Louisiana without running into you and your posse."

"My My so you are a tough guy, you know what I do to tough guys Elijah."

"He's lying Paulie, Fisher is coming here I know it and he will have the gold."

Elijah looked over at Dot as if he wanted to kill her.

"She doesn't know what she's talking about."

Paulie responded.

" I hope she doesn't, because I would hate for your family to watch me do you like I did that big stud Ted."

"By the way you should make plans to be staying on here that's if you live."

"I just recently left Culloden and the nice house on that land of yours has been burned to the ground and you Gilda what a waste of such a beautiful home." Elijah leaped out at Paulie, but to no avail his gunmen grabbed hold of him. Then Paulie gave him two swift punches to the stomach. Paulie begin to speak with a very impatient tone,

"You all are making this much harder than it has to be people."

"I need to know where the gold is and I need to know now." Everyone looked on in a quiet shock as Paulie's men let Elijah fall to the ground. Gilda rushed to his side and looked up at Paulie.

"You will pay for this I promise you that." She then turned to Dot.

"And as for you, you snake I will deal with you myself when the time is right."

Dot snapped back.

"Oh shut up silly woman, you may not have that long to live."

Dot then rolled her eyes as she gave a swift push of the screen door and walked out. Paulie stepped over Elijah and Gilda and followed behind her. Once on the porch, Paulie summoned the men to his attention. Gilda looked on, but could not hear what was being said. She moved slowly to the side of the door and listened near the screen. Pauli was leaving his posse behind to hold hostages and wait for Fisher's arrival. Lil Paulie would return in two days time. It appeared he had more pressing business in Chicago that he needed to deal with. He also informed his men if they valued their lives to do nothing until he returned. Gilda slid away from the door and back into the family room. She told everything that she had heard.

Dot went over to Paulie after hearing his instructions to his gang,

"What about me, will you take me with you?"

Paulie grabbed Dot by the chin and gave her kiss.

"Not this time brown sugar, but I have a little package for you in the car."

"Why don't you go and get it, it will make you feel really good."

Dot didn't hesitate and slid into the car, grabbed her package and she and Martha left.

Paulie got inside the car and pointed at two of the men in his posse to take charge. Rocko stood well over six feet tall he was very slim and had a patch over his right eye. Penske was short in stature but had numerous battle scares and cuts in his face. Julia pulled the curtain slightly open while Gilda talked with the others. She shook her head at the events that were taking place outside. Julia then looked down at little Joshua sound asleep with no clue about the turn of events in their lives. Julia also thought about her home and how they had stripped away everything that they had worked so hard for.

All of her belongings, all of her photos and memories, burned to the ground. Tears began to roll down her face as she looked at the men with a heart of stone. They had gotten to Julia and she had thoughts of revenge burning through her like lightening. Julia then looked over at Gilda, who could see the frustration in her dear friends eyes.

"Julia just breathe chile, breathe, It's in these times our true faith in the lord is tested."

The two sisters nodded there head in agreement. As they continued to whisper to one another Betty shared stories of adventures they had of their own.

"Chile I can recall a time that we were in a big ruckus in Oklahoma."

"Our cousin Nettie had settled there in 1872 and we were just going to visit."

"Rumor was the men folk were plentiful down that way."

"Chile them white folks did not want us around there no sir."

"They were hanging folk."

"The women too."

"I tell you we've had some rough times chile, so don't go getting all tensed up about this here stuff."

"We gonna make it through you'll see."

Gilda thought to herself as she held on to Josie, there was no way on Gods green earth these men were going to succeed in destroying their future especially her unborn child's. Elijah was on the other side of the room with Jerry.

Gilda knew they had a plan already in place before leaving Fisher.

"*How could Paulie be so dumb?*"

She thought to herself. Fisher had him pegged right he was not smart at all. Elijah knew they had to get to Fisher because he had people in place to help. He knew he would have to risk his life to do it. The other gun that the sister had given him was still in his carpet bag. He hoped that Paulie and his men had not gone snooping around the house and came across any of the other guns that the sisters kept in the cellar. He needed to get the two sisters alone. Now Penske was in the house and stood at the parlor door. Jerry looked him over and noticed he had a gun harness around his shoulder and he held the tommy gun with one hand on the barrel pointed straight up in the air. Jerry got up and walked over to the man.

"What do you want?" He snapped.

"Sir, if you do not mind the women don't need to be down here."

"This is having an unnecessary effect on the children."

The man looked over at Josie, she was shaking madly.

"Please sir would you allow the women to go upstairs."

"It's us that you should really be worried about."

The man looked over at Elijah and Joshua then tipped his hat at them and laughed.

"I don't have to worry about none of you."

"Capeche?"

Rocko walked into the house, leaving two others outside. His demeanor was cold much more ruthless than Paulie. Elijah could understand why Paulie left him behind to oversee with the situation. He had a scar from ear to ear under his neck as if someone had attempted to slash his throat. His hands were burned as if they had also been set on fire. Meanwhile Gilda thought to herself. *"Things can't end like this."*

Someone has to go meet up with Fisher. Gilda knew deep down if anything happened to anyone she would never forgive herself. After all she was the reason why they had come to Louisiana in the first place. However, Elijah reminded her that if they wouldn't have left they may have eventually had a more terrible fate back in Culloden. Elijah agreed with Gilda, someone would have to take the risk to get word to Fisher.

Gilda spoke out relentlessly, "May we have our bags before we go upstairs sir." Penske looked over at Elijah and Jerry

"You two, go out and get them bags."

Elijah got up, still filling uncomfortable from the blows he had taken from Paulie, and he and Jerry went outside and brought the bags into the house. The women followed them up the stairs into Elijah's room. Once inside, Elijah stood at the door checking to see if anyone was coming down the hall. Gilda, Julia and Josephine along with the two sisters watched him carefully.

"Okay ladies, this is gonna be quick and to the point."

Elijah pulled a map out of his pants pocket and gave it to Gilda.

"Fisher gave this to me to guide us to Texas near the Texas and Mexico meet."

"I told you Betty, didn't I tell you."

"Shush will you Lara." Betty snapped.

Gilda thought.

"Me and Julia will have to go."

Julia looked at Elijah, he knew what she was thinking.

"Julia, we will lose our lives before anything happens to Josie or the baby you here?"

He went into his carpet bag and dug until he pulled out the revolver. Elijah then looked over at the sisters.

"Okay between you two ladies who is the best shooter."

Without hesitation Betty raised her hand.

"I am."

"Okay Betty, I am giving you the gun that is because you will have a better chance than me with it."

"They would expect me and check me often to see if I'm carrying."

Okay, we don't have much time, later tonight when Paulie's men start taking turns during the night watch you and Julia will leave in the pick up."

"When the coast is clear me and Jerry I will push it out to the road." Paulie will be back in a few of days, so we have to act quickly."

"When you get to Fisher, you tell him where we are and what has happened. Tell him we need help right away."

Both women nodded.

Josie began to cry.

"Mommy don't leave us." Julia grabbed her daughter and held on tightly.

"Sweetie, everything is going to be okay you here."

"I'm just taking a little trip sweetheart, mama will be back before you know it." Julia continued to talk to Josie.

"But the secret is, the bad men downstairs can not know that mommy is leaving okay." Josie nodded her head.

"Daddy, Uncle Elijah, cousin Jerry and the sisters will be here with you."

"Be a big girl for mommy okay and look after your brother."

Josie nodded her head again. Suddenly they heard the sound of footsteps. Betty took the revolver and she stuffed it down in her bosom. Elijah knew with Joshua injured he and Jerry wouldn't have a chance with the four men all carrying Tommy guns grew closer and closer until finally Penske pushed the door wide open with his finger on the trigger.

"Okay fella, the ladies don't need you up here keeping them company get downstairs with the others."

Elijah slowly walked passed Penske and promised himself when the opportunity presented itself he would put the hood in his place. Penske stood up straight and escorted him back downstairs. After they left the ladies began silently whispering to one another.

Gilda handed the map to Betty.

"Girls, Me and Lara know these parts well."

"We will give you the quickest route to get to the train station, once you get there these directions look pretty simple."

Lara looked over the map impressed.

"It appears this fella Fisher knows his way around these here parts." Betty responded

"Lara maybe so, but I believe he had some help because these are some old Spanish-American war trails."

Gilda confirmed their assumptions by explaining there where two hispanic gentleman with Fisher at the cottage near the Lotus.

Betty sand Lara continued to point along the coast of the gulf.

"Here, we have some good friends over near Brownsville Texas they could help you on your journey."

"That will be a long exhausting trip, not much time for stopping much with the time and all."

"Sam and Sherell Porter, they own a shrimp boat just outside of here."

Betty pointed again on the map.

"You just tell them that we sent you and they will make sure you get to your destination."

The girls nodded in confirmation.

"You will also need something else."

Lara stuck her head outside of the room to see if the coast was clear then she went down the hall to her bedroom. When she returned she had a white cotton pillow case wrapped up in her hand once she unwrapped it both Gilda and Julia looked on in surprise, inside was a tiny nickel plated six shooter.

"This will be a little insurance just in case you two have problems along the way." She twirled the the trigger with her finger and pointed the handle toward Gilda.

"Here take it now."

Gilda was bewildered.

Lara smiled.

"It's a long story."

"I use to be in love with a cowboy during the 1880's goldrush."

"I'll tell you all about it when you return."

"Here let me."

Lara took the gun.

"It's best to stash it there." Lara showed Gilda how to hide the little revolver. She placed it in the side of Gilda's brassiere. "There that should hold it the elastic will keep it in place." Lara tugged on it to double check.

"Julia, what is the matter sweetie?"

"Miss Lara, I ain't ever left my children before."

Okay we gonna work out something, but in the meantime me and Lara gonna go on downstairs, these hoods don't stop nothing it's time to make some supper."

Lara turned on the radio and the sound of the delta blues swept the room. Julia sat back in the couch and tended to her children.

After dinner the women returned up stairs Gilda began packing, they would have to travel light. Gilda turned to Miss Betty,

"Do you think we can make it."

"I hope so, that's just twenty miles outside of Brownsville Texas. I want you girls to stop at Sam Porter's house so he can make sure you get the rest of the way."

Gilda leaned up against the doorway and silently blamed Fisher for all the mishaps. She had warned him about the men from up north. His ambition had led him down a very dangerous path and had taken all of them with him. Gilda knew that she would have to speak to the men about the journey. Someone else would have to go with her and it had to be one of them. Gilda went to the bottom of the stairs that led into the kitchen and whispered to the sisters who were seeing after dinner. Gilda knew her friend far to well and she also knew emotionally Julia could not make the trip. After confiding in the sisters and Julia they came up with a plan that could be dangerous, but worth the risk. Lara was known for her medicinal herbs and she thought this would be a good time to give the hoodlums a sedative sleep that would give them enough time them to get a word to Fisher.

"Oh ya'll don't have to worry about my potion, it works."

"They'll fall asleep like a newborn baby and when they wake up, won't have a clue about nothing."

Betty begin to laugh.

"That's true, she know what she talking about, only thing is the length ot time isn't guaranteed."

Gilda looked over at Lara.

"Will it give us enough time to get the truck onto the road?"

"I don't see why not, but we gotta make it quick though."

"Their waiting for dinner so I will serve them first."

"It don't take much you know."

The sister got word to Elijah and Jerry and went into action as planned.

After dinner Elijah mananged to meet with Gilda and the sisters in the kitchen.

"Elijah, Julia will be no good, you know that."

"She has the baby and Josie let alone Joshua to worry about."

"I think it would be better if we let her stay and see after Joshua while you and me go."

"I think they will be fine after all Jerry and the sisters are here."

"Those hoods, they can't make a decision pass their nose without instructions from Paulie."

"By the time they figure it out we will be long gone."

"They won't do anything until Paulie returns and hopefully with Godspeed we will be back before then."

"What do you think Elijah?"

"I think we will leave as soon as possible."

Gilda pulled the map out of her skirt pocket and handed it to Elijah. She then hugged and kissed him and returned upstairs with the news.

Later that night Elijah and Gilda prepared for their journey. However before leaving Gilda quietly left her room to go speak with Betty. She was starled when she ran upon Penske who was standing in the dark hallway.

She thought by now Lara's potion would have worked, but it appeared it was taking a bit more time to reach Penske.

"My you are up late this evening uh Gilda is it?"

Gilda could smell the whiskey on his breathe and knew it would be a short time before he joined the others.
She stood stiff as she looked down at his gun.

"I have to go to the ladies room."

"Yeah! well, I got my eye on you."

"When the boss get's back and i'm hoping he comes real soon."

"I'm going to persuade him to allow me to string that man of yours up on that tree out there and then I will take you for myself."

He took his hand and he began to rub the back side of it across her face. Gilda was praying with each second that Elijah did not walk up those stairs so she kept real quiet. The incident alone would send him into a rage and possibly create a situation that would end in disaster.

"Excuse me sir."

Gilda went along side of the man and retired to the backroom. Once she was behind the door, she locked it tight.

She held an ear to the door and listened to the heavy boots walking across the squeaky wood floor. There she stood a minute wondering when this tragedy would end. Finally the footsteps faded down the main staircase. Gilda looked down and realized that she had been holding her stomach all along.

"*Dear God, I'm having a baby.*"

Gilda went over to the full length mirror and took a long look at herself and for the first time in her life, Gilda had finally seen beyond the blues she carried for so very long. What she saw was a beautiful young women deserving of unconditional love. She began to wonder what her mother and grandmother would think about having a grandchild. Tears slowly filled her eyes and she softly wept to herself. Of all the times that she had been sad this one moment on this particular night seemed to have healed all of that. It had brought her a peace she had never felt before, a peace so deep in a place that she believed could never be touched again. Now, she would fight to keep that peace even if it meant going up against Paulie and his hoods. Gilda knew with her faith in God and Elijah by her side nothing was impossible. Elijah had never stopped loving her and patiently he waited while she was searching for something that was always with her all the while. She wiped her eyes and began to laugh at herself softly in the mirror.

"*Was it all just that simple?*"

"*Oh what a fool I've been.*"

Suddenly, her thoughts were interrupted by a knock on the door and it was Betty and Julia.

"Gilda you alright honey?"

"Yes Ma'am."

She straightened herself and then slowly opened the door.

"I heard everything, that no good hoodlum."

Betty was furious.

"He has a lot of nerve."

She then gave Gilda a comforting hug.

"I was just on my way to see you Miss Betty."
"Where is Elijah?"
"He's gone to push the truck to the back road."
"You guys are a little over 400 miles away from Brownsville Texas and we are hoping by the time those idiots realize your gone you all would have made it to your destination and preparing for your return."

Gilda nodded in agreement.

Julia gave Gilda a long hug

"Julia don't worry, the plan is solid and we have the good lord on our side right?"

Julia nodded in confirmation.

"Right, you watch yourself you here?"

Gilda smiled

"I will."

Betty peeked outside the door for a sign from her sister.

"Lara is downstairs waiting for you now Gillie."

She hugged Gilda tightly.

"Dear child, I'm praying for y'all every step of the way." She then grabbed her by the hand.

"C'mon Gillie you gotta get outta here, Eljah is waiting" Gilda reached for the carpet bag she had packed for her and Elijah and followed Betty.

She gave Betty another hug and told her to tell everyone she and Elijah would return with help as soon as they could. Betty then escorted Gilda down the back steps that led into the kitchen. She was careful before she would allow Gilda to come any further down the staircase. Betty stopped and continued on into the large hallway that led to the front of the house and as she expected, Penske appeared from out of the darkness.

"What are you doing up so late old woman."

Betty put her hand on her chest as if frightened by his reappearance. It seemed as though he hadn't had dinner like the others.

"I was feeling a bit restless and thought I would take a walk on the back porch dear."

Penske looked her over and then went into the back of the house to the kitchen. Lara slowly moved into the large walk in pantry and softly closed the door.

Gilda stood quietly at the top of the stairwell.

"Dear Lord please do not let him come up these stairs if he do I swear I will kill him."

He went through the ice box and then through the cabinets where he found a box of crackers and returned to the front of the house. Betty stood stiff as a board as she watched him walk pass her and then let out a long quiet sigh. She waited until the coast was clear and signaled to Gilda

"Go now get outta here chile." Lara was waiting for her at the back door and gave her a bag of food and a canister of water for their journey. She then hugged Gilda tightly and whispered.

"Ya'll hurry back now."

Lara and Betty watched out the window until Gilda disappeared into the darkness of the night.

Gilda moved swiftly and managed to find her way to the truck. Elijah was there with a small butane lighter he had picked up in the house looking over the map.

"What took you so long?"

"I ran into some problems back at the house."

"Elijah, we have to make sure we get back soon I feel real uneasy about that Penske character, he really scares me."

Elijah started the truck and they drove off .

Chapter 21

Near Brownsville, Texas

When Gilda woke up it was daylight and the car was parked. She could hear the loud cries of seagulls as they swarmed relentlessly around the fishing boats that were docked along the pier. The weather was warm and she pulled her handkerchief out of her dress pocket while looking around for Elijah, but there was no sign of him. Gilda begin to smile when she saw Elijah and another gentleman in the distance. She hopped out the truck and waited patiently as they walked in her direction.

"Gillie I want you to meet Mr. Porter"

"Mr. Porter this is Gillie."

"Please to meet you Gillie."

"You can call me Sam ain't no use of us being so formal and all."

"Is there anything I can get you, the house is just right over that hill."

Well, I would like to freshen up a bit if you don't mind we are in a bit of a rush."

"I know about all that Elijah here explained everything you are only about 20 miles just outside of Brownsville"

"Miss Gillie, you need to rest, you have some serious business ahead of you now."

Elijah nodded his head.

"He's right we have to meet that boat."

"In the mean time, I really do need to give this truck a thorough check before we continue."

"It has done more traveling than it has done in a while."

"Yeah that way the two of you can get a little rest and freshen up."

"Sherell got some good ole Lobster Jambalaya and grits cooking too, it's my favorite."

"You gonna love Sherell she the best cook in these parts I tell you."

****

Just before lunch Sherell had been a big help to Gilda. Even though she was relieved to get a nice hot bath and a nap Gilda had gotten sick again. Sherell questioned Gilda about her condition and Gilda confirmed her pregnancy. However, when she asked Gilda if her and Elijah were married, to her surprise Gilda replied no. It was now a quiet mission for Mrs. Sherell to get Elijah and Gilda hitched.

Mrs. Sherell's goal was to help them realize they had already started a family and since she was in the family business her quest begin at lunch.

"Elijah and Gillie you two make such a wonderful couple are you to planning to marry?"

Elijah looked over at Gilda.

"Well my Ki'Somma are you gonna answer the question or should I."

He then looked over at Mrs. Porter.

"This here woman I have been trying to marry for the past seven years and I have loved her since we were in our teens."

"Gilda, you mean to tell me this here man has been chasing you down to marry you and you haven't accepted?"

"Look at him the most handsome young man that I den seen in a long time and he has passionate eyes too."

"I know about passionate eyes."

"Look at my Sam he has em too!"

Sherell smiled.

"Do you want to marry him Gilda?"

"I can see that he loves you the way he looks at you like the sun rise and set on ya."

Gilda began to blush.

"If I could marry him right now Mrs. Sherell I would."

"Oh would you?"

"What about you Elijah?"

"I told ya I been waiting a long time Mrs. Sherell."

"Well let's do this right now and I'll draw up the papers." They both looked over at Sam, who was still eating his breakfast Sam began to explain. "Well my baby here was a traveling preacher; she den married lots a folk, especially during the migration to Kansas."

"Come on now, y'all come on in here, ain't no use of going on another day like this."

Gilda and Elijah got up and followed the couple.

"Come on through here."

They finally led them into a small room made of cherry wood. There was a book case full of books and a small desk with a lantern on it and a picture of Sam and Sherell on the wall in their younger years.

"You see that picture that was when me and Sherell were in our prime, time sure will get away from ya."

"That was taken after the last time I took a journey with Betty and Lara."

"After I met Sam I just settled down."

"You two please have a seat."

Sherell pulled out the papers and began filling them out. "We can mail these into Baton Rouge and you should get your license in no time"

"I'll have them mailed to Betty and Lara's and you can get them later."

"Come on now Sam you will be the witness."

Sherell had Elijah and Gilda stand together and after about five minutes of wedding rituals they were pronounced them man and wife. With all the excitement Elijah hollered Gilda's name at the top of his voice. He picked her up and swung her around and afterward gave her the most passionate kiss he had ever laid on her lips. When he was through Gilda stood there with her eyes closed and a big smile came over her face she screamed his name back and again they kissed passionately. Sherell and Sam looked on with admiration.

"Young love, what a beautiful thing."

Later that afternoon while the men were preparing the truck for there departure Gilda and Sherell sat in the kitchen with sweet potato pie and vanilla ice-cream. Gilda had insisted that Mrs. Sherell bring the radio into the kitchen so that she would be able to listen to the sweet sound of the blues.

"Mrs. Sherell I really want to thank you for what you did this afternoon, for so long I was lost in what direction that I wanted to go in my life."

"My best friend Julia is at the house with the sisters would tell me; Gilda just be still, peace be still she would say."

"At the time I could not understand what she meant by that."

"But now I think I do, I think I really do."

"Yes Gillie, we all have our time when we have that transformation in our life."

"We have a few of them in our lifetime, if we paying attention."

"Some we don't want to see that age creeping up for one." She then began to laugh.

"But besides that life is so beautiful, it's what you make it you know."

"I just helped the two of you do something that the both of you wanted to do but just didn't know how."

"Now its business as usual, but now you're Mrs. Mason."

"That sounds good right."

Gilda begin to smile.

"That baby you carrying will light both of your lives up." Sherell then questioned Gilda about the Sisters.

"So how are them gals Betty and Lara?"

"That pair is something; we use to be the terrible threesome back in our day."

"Chile we had some fun fun fun when we were younger women and we would travel back and forth from California to Texas to Mexico and back again."

"I tell you them was the days, Betty was the hustler she made sure we ate."

"Lara was the gun slinger she made sure them hustlers stayed off our back and I was the doctor I kept us all well and lord knows I prayed enough for all of us too."

". I'll have to get together with them old hens one day I haven't talked with them in over ten years."

"No bad blood just living that's all, we send Christmas cards though."

Not long after both Elijah and Sam came into the house.

"The trucks already to go, so we best be getting on up the road."

Elijah turned around to Sam. "

"Well Mr. Porter thanks for everything, here's a little something for your trouble."

Elijah reached in his pocket and pulled out a handkerchief and in it he'd wrapped several gold coins. Mr. Porter looked inside and patted him on the shoulder.

"Thanks Elijah, you're a good man."

. He then turned back at Sherell; he gave her a big hug.

"I want you to know that I owe you my life for giving this woman to me, I will never forget you for that."

"You two are very special people, very special."

Mrs. Sherell was so elated by the compliment she began to cry and Gilda seeing her cry, begin to cry as well. Sam shook his head.

"Elijah look what you den done you know how emotional the women folk get, now get on outta here."

Sam shook Elijah's hand and they both walked out the house. Gilda followed, but stopped and turned around to face Mrs. Sherell.

"Thank-you"

She gave her a big hug.

"I am expecting to be seeing you soon and I'm not gonna let year past by without seeing the sisters."

"Godspeed my dear girl, I will be praying for all of you."

"Thank you Mrs. Sherell and I will see again really soon, I promise."

****

Elijah felt blessed that they had not run into any problems with the law on their journey. He looked over at Gilda as she slept soundly. Realistically, he didn't know how this situation would end, but he did know that he would die to protect his family. Before long Elijah had come up on a sign that read

"Brownsville Bayou" it was now evening and the sun was beginning to set.

"Are we there yet Elijah?"

"Yes we are."

She leaned over and gave him a kiss.

"Why couldn't we just do it Elijah?"

"It doesn't matter now it is done and I'm the happiest man in the world for it."

They pulled up along the river and got out the car at the location described on the map. The two of them sat at the edge of the bank until in the distance they could see a long canoe boat carrying two people. Elijah held his gun close to his side inconspicuously. Gilda knew they must have been sent by Fisher, but still was cautious.

"Elijah, they're heading right for us."

Once the canoe made it closer to the river bank Gilda right away recognized the gentleman wearing the red bandanas.

Elijah and Gilda stood up and waited as they waved their hands to them. As the boat touched the rivers edge the conversation continued the gentlemen greeted them

"¡ Buenos Dias!" Gilda smiled.

"Hello."

"Ahh you must be Gillie that means good evening in Spanish."

"I'm Honcho and this is Poncho."

Poncho then gave Elijah a hand shake.

"You must be Elijah, heard a lot about you."

"Really, I hope it's good."

"Absolutely."

"We need to speak with Fisher, things are bad back in Louisiana, and we gotta get back."

Gilda looked at the two men they were identical twins and were quite handsome as well. Honcho could sense the state of urgency in them both.

"Fisher is just on the other side of the bayou, please get in."

Elijah stepped into the boat and then stuck his hand out and pulled Gilda in and they sat down and took the journey. Gilda was anxious to see Fisher and tell him about all of the confusion that had taken place and even about Dot who had sold him out to a drug addiction.

After awhile they arrived at a small dock on the banks of Mexico. There were several other men at the campsite and they all had guns that rested in their holsters. Poncho pulled the boat to the dock and quickly wrapped the rope around the wooden pole to hold it still. The houses along the shore were small but modest. Gilda looked around as Elijah helped her out of the boat. There were women socializing while hanging clothes and cooking at the campfires. There were also children playing tag, while others were taking turns swinging on an old tire off the shore. Honcho and Poncho greeted the residence in Spanish as they walked passed. Gilda and Elijah followed them as they continued up a narrow dirt road. They approached a tall pickett fence. Poncho lifted the latch and there on the porch with his shot gun was Fisher. He got up with his cane in his hand to greet his dear friends.

"My goodness Gilda how are you, Elijah."

He grabbed them both.

"I've been expecting you guys."

Elijah nodded.

"You were right about Dot and thanks to her Pauli's on to you."

"Come on let's go into the house."

Poncho and Honcho followed and for the next hour Gilda and Elijah explained everything to Fisher. Fisher was very upset at the turn of events. Paulie has put to many people close to him in danger and he knew that it was time to put his long awaited plan into action.

"We will end this once and for all."

He looked over to Honcho and Poncho.

"Did you warn the others?"

"Yes just before we arrived at the bank, the bird will land tonight brother." Fisher then continued.

"Penske is a thinker, by now he has contacted Paulie and he is probably on his way back to Louisiana with company."

"The good thing is Penske and the others won't do anything until he arrives, so that gives us some time."

Poncho shook his head.

"Fisher, we need to go further up the river and get the rest of the crew-those scoundrels would enjoy a little excitement."

Honcho clapped his hands.

"Yes, finally some action, it's been a longtime."

"Eh Elijah you mind navigating the third canoe, we will need it for the return."

"No I don't mind."

Elijah then looked over at his friend and then his wife.

"Take care of here Fisher, she's carrying my baby and she is my wife now."

Elijah kissed his wife and followed Honcho and Poncho out of the door. Fisher looked over at Gilda.

"Congratulations you two finally did it, what happened?"

"Oh it's a long story."

"Just know all roads were always leading here."

Gilda and Fisher spent those few hours together talking about old times and the juke joint. Gilda could see that he had missed the dream that he had finally fulfilled. They laughed and cried over big Ted. Fisher had missed him dearly. They had been through a lot together and just knowing he died fulfilling a request of him just tore him up inside.

"Gilda I am praying for better days."

"Me too Fisher, me too!"

Later that evening there was a knock on the door. Fisher walked over to the door and released the latch. To Gilda's surprise when the door opened there were three more men with Elijah, Honcho and Poncho. Fisher invited them in.

"Miss Gilda meet the Brown brothers."

The tallest and the most handsome of the men stepped into the room first; he walked over to Gilda and then looked over at Elijah.

"Elijah you didn't tell me that you were married to a beautiful Nubian Queen."

Gilda blushed at the compliment. Diaz took Gilda's hand and gently kissed it as he introduced himself.

"My name is Diaz the clever one; it is pleasure to serve you."

Gilda blushed.

"Pleased to meet you as well."

Diaz continued.

"Hermanas, please give me the pleasure of introducing you to the Brown brothers."

As the men stood towering over her, Gilda was amazed at the strong African-Mexican lineage that stood before her.

"That is Cortez, the swift one."

Cortez bowed to Gilda and she returned the gesture.

"You've already met Honcho and Poncho the twins."

"Our sling shot and bow and arrow experts."

They also bowed as well and Gilda returned the gesture once more.

And last but not least, Quervo the youngest and most mischievous of us all."

"Please to meet you all."

Gilda then turned to Fisher.

"My, my Fisher what a little secret you've been keeping."

"Oh these old bums." Fisher laughed.

"Me, Joey and these fellas ran a whole lot of Tequila through this trail up from Mexico to the States."

"We made a lot of money."

"These here are my brothers and I couldn't have my life in the hands of a better group of renegades."

Diaz walked over.

"Oh it gets better Miss Gillie, your husband, I know him from way back."

Gilda looked over at Elijah as the two exchanged a brotherly hand shake.

"It is truly destiny that we have come together once more in this life time my brother."

Diaz began to explain.

"We moved to Mexico from South Carolina."

"Elijah's mom and my mom were dear friends back home, so we also became friends."

"My father was forced to flee a few years later for murder, just like Elijah and Joshua."

"His brother was shot and killed in a misunderstanding with a white man in town."

"Afterwards, my momma feared for his life talked him into going to her old country were he would be safe, hence Mexico."

Diaz continued.

"We were maybe seven or eight years old when we lost contact."

"None of these fella's were even born all except Cortez and I."

"Father was hesitant at first going to a new country, but later on he realized that it was a lot easier than running for his life and living under Jim Crow."

"He came across some property in Mexico and continued to farm and as you can see the family has grown." Gilda looked in awe.

"Wow, how did you two recognize one another?"

"That was a very long time ago?"

Diaz looked at Elijah.

"Should I tell her or should you?"

Elijah looked over at Gilda and turned his hand face up.

"You see this scare, it is the scare of lightening carved from grandpa Black Eagle's hunting blade."

"When we were young boys me and Diaz got a hold to some of my father's homemade white lightening and decided to become blood brothers."

Diaz laughed.

"Yeah and our mothers nearly killed us, the doc had to give us fifty stitches each too, we were wild."

"But we have plenty time to discuss all of that."

Fisher agreed.

"Yeah Elijah is right, from my understanding we have work to do and there are people back in Louisiana that are depending on us." Gilda interrupted.

"Are you guys hungry, you really need to eat something first, we have a long night ahead of us."

While they were away Gilda had whipped up some soup with some vegetables that Fisher had in the pantry, she also made some lemonade and warmed some leftover biscuits.

"My My Miss Gillie, you have been busy."

Cortez was the first to dive in.

The others soon swarmed over the large pot and each grabbed himself a helping. When they where finished Gilda cleaned the table and they continued. Elijah and Diaz joined Cortez at the table. Quervo, Poncho and Honcho stood behind them as they all followed the map Elijah had drawn from memory of the area.

"How far is that from the river bank?"

"Oh I'd say about four miles or so."

Diaz then pointed toward Fisher, Gilda and Elijah.

"Me, Quervo and Cortez will drive you guys to Elijah's truck and then trail you from there."

"Honcho and Poncho will use their usual transportation by boat along the Gulf's coast."

"We will need to leave here as soon as possible." Honcho spoke up.

"We'll take the shortcut through the swamps and will surface right here."

He pointed to the place on the map.

Elijah looked over at his wife; he could see the look of concern on her face.

"Ki'Somma, everything will be fine, the plan will work."

"I would never let anyone or anything hurt you or the family."

Diaz continued.

"Elijah once you guys get to the rendezvous we will go from there."

"More than likely my brothers will arrive soon after and then we can begin to take our positions.

Gilda with all the commotion soon felt herself growing overwhelmed and retired for rest.

Chapter 22

After much discussion about the events to occur Fisher continued to share more with his friends.

"Elijah, these brothers here are the reason why I am still breathing today."

"I'm sure there are a lot of questions both you and Gillie may have."

"Man, I got plenty."

"Fisher did you go back for the gold?"

Fisher laughed.

"Of course I did, I worked hard for that fortune, risked my life too."

"Good."

Elijah was relieved.

"Joshua was concerned after he'd gone back to the site."

"He thought someone had found it."

"He and Julia brought the money with them."

"There's no going back to Culloden, you do understand that."

Fisher looked over at Elijah and laughed.

"Yeah, who knows that better than me Elijah?"

"There is absolutely a noose with all our names on it, especially mine."

The Brown brothers looked on with concern, but Fisher got up from the table, shaking his head and made his way to the door.

"The end is near."

He thought to himself.

Elijah addressed the group.

"If we leave now we should get back to Louisiana by daybreak."

Diaz spoke up.

"Elijah, how many men do you think they have on watch?" Well when me and Gilda left their were three and that's not including Paulie. Fisher looked over at both Elijah and Diaz.

"Lil Paulie is a coward, trust me more men will come."

"I'm expecting to meet with some family members of our friend Paulie once we get back to Louisiana. Trust me, they're waiting to hear from me."

Fisher shook his head.

"I don't want the shed of anymore innocent blood."
Later that night under a foggy full moon and the loud cries of swamp crickets the gang headed back to Louisiana.
As the pick up truck made its way down the dirt road Gilda sat in between both the two men that had impacted her life.
She thought of Julia and the children and prayed for the safety of everyone they had left in the house. She thought about the memories she had of her grandmother and mother. They had given her so much in so little time.

Gilda had used the Blues to capture her thoughts, her feelings, and her very existence. It had saved her life as she struggled with faith, hope and love. At one time she thought she had lost it all, but now she knew life was truly worth fighting for. All these things she thought about as the desire for peace continued to fuel her dreams for a new beginning. She knew that after all, time had been a friend to her as she closed her eyes and drifted off to sleep.

Elijah continued to drive all night with Diaz and Quervo following close by. They finally arrived a few miles from the house. They stopped off the road near the edge of the gulf. A few hours later the remaining Brown brothers made their way along the river edge. Fisher bent down slowly as he struggled to sit under the tree.

"First I want everyone to know this, Lil Paulie wants me."

"He knows someone is coming, he just doesn't know who."

Fisher knew that someone had to be the bait for his plan to work.

"If Elijah went back it's a good chance he would kill him and everyone else."

Elijah could not bare the thought of sending Gilda. He looked at Fisher.

"No!!!"

"Well what do you suggest Elijah?"

"If you go in they will kill you on the spot at least with Gilda she will have a better chance and anyway everybody knows that Paulie has been soft on her a long time."

Diaz spoke.

"Honcho and Poncho will escort Gillie to the house." He then looked over at Elijah.

"They will protect her with their life."

Elijah looked over at his friend, he knew it to be true, but was still hesitant. Diaz spoke again.

"Besides I owe you one man and I promise once we get in I will save this Paulie bum just for you."

Gilda stepped in.

"Elijah it is the right thing to do."

"I will be fine."

"I will go in with Honcho and Poncho and walk the rest of the way."

I would have to look run down like I've been in a struggle."

"I will tell them that Elijah was killed by a lynch mob and I got away."

"I will threaten him with Fisher coming; he doesn't know I know anything about the Gold." Gilda then smiled.

"He will fall for it, I know he will."

"Paulie wants that gold more than anything and he will stop at nothing to get it."

"Somebody has got to do it, and besides they will never suspect that we have gotten so much done in so little time."

"God has been with us this far, he won't leave us."

"Look at me; I'm not a threat as far as they are concerned." She then looked into Elijah eyes again.

"I will be fine."

Fisher nodded his head in confirmation.

"Okay Gillie, but we say when, Elijah I still need a ride into town can you take me?"

Cortez jumped in the back bed of the pick up.

"I'll join you two."

"We will meet you guys back here in a few."

Diaz, Honcho and Poncho took the remaining food and supplies from Elijah's truck and Quervo started to set up camp.

Chapter 23

New Orleans, Louisiana

When Elijah, Fisher and Cortez arrived into town the streets were full of the hustle and bustle of the early morning. Fisher instructed Elijah into the alleyway just off of Yellowstone Avenue. As he drove through slowly, Elijah noticed a tall black gentleman standing at the dead end of alley. He had on a long overcoat and his hands rested inside the pockets. As the truck moved in a little closer Fisher instructed Elijah to slow down. He instructed Elijah to the left which lead into another alleyway. There stood a group of men whose garments reminded him of the Wild West. They wore long dusters, large brim cowhide hats and boots with metal spurs. Each also carried guns in holsters around their waste. In front of the building were several beautiful stallions. Cortez jumped out of the truck and greeted the men.

Elijah looked around as they continued to slowly move through the narrow alleyway. There were men sitting at a table cleaning their guns and looking over bullets, while others were highly attentive to a poker game that looked as though it had been going on all night.

They rode past the crowd of men until Fisher instructed Elijah to pull on the opposite side of the alleyway. On the other side was a large wood framed door. Fisher got out of the truck grabbed his cane and knocked twice. The door opened wide and Fisher was greeted by a short lean gentlemen.

"Elijah this here is Ginny the giant."

"Ginny this is Elijah."

The men shook hands and Ginny escorted them into the building. Ginny turned the key to another door and once opened, there were two more men inside standing at the bar with tommy guns hanging over their shoulders. Behind the bar to Elijah's surprise stood Jeanine. Once she recognized Elijah she came from behind the bar. She gave Fisher a big hug and kiss then looked to Elijah.

"Good morning Elijah, how is Gillie?" Attempting not to be confused with the recent disappearing and reappearing acts of Jeanine lately Elijah responded.

"She's fine."

"Elijah, I'm so sorry for what has happened, everything."

"Come, come, over here please and sit down both of you."

"You must be starving."

"Fisher you look so weak darling have you been eating and taking your medicine."

Fisher through his hand up as if irritated with the questions. After making the men comfortable Jeanine sat down.

"I didn't know that Dot was working with Paulie, she had been informing him about Fishers business all the while."

"I barely got out with my life thanks to Fisher."

"I never thought she would stoop so low." Elijah responded.

"Its alright, the main thing now is making them pay for all they have done."

Fisher shook his head in agreement. Moments later Jeanine left the men and two more gentlemen entered the room. They both appeared to be happy to see Fisher as he struggled to get up.

"Please my friend stay seated"

Fisher, nodded in compliance.

"Elijah I like you to meet Franco Tonelli and this is his brother Roberto."

"They're cousins of Paulie and Joey, all the way from Sicily."

"They're very disturbed about the events that have taken place in the last few years."

"They are here to straighten out some of their own family business, if you know what I mean."

Both extended their hand to Elijah and he obliged them both with a strong hand shake.

Franco spoke.

"We will sit and talk business."

Ginny approached the table.

"You need anything else Franco?"

"No thanks, we're are fine."

Franco turned his attention back to Elijah.

"Ginny here is our explosive expert."

Ginny this job will be light, your work is done my friend go hang out with that lady friend of yours."

Ginny tipped his hat at the gentleman and bid them all farewell. Franco turned his attention back to Fisher.

"Hey, how are you man?"

"You hungry?"

Before he could answer Jeanine came out the tall wooden swing doors from the kitchen. On the four wheeled metal foot tray she had two large platters of crawfish, three bowls of butter, and a large bowl of red beans and rice with hush puppies.

"I'll have Hank bring you guys some plates and silverware and now I will leave you guys to your business."

Fisher must eat something and he won't eat if you guys don't eat with him."

Fisher looked over at Jeanine and shook his head he knew she meant well and loved him very much. Therefore, he grabbed a crawfish and broke it open with his malnourished hands. Afterwards the rest of the men joined him. Elijah had no appetite he wanted to get straight to business. Fisher dipped the crawfish into the bowl of butter he looked over to Franco.

"Roberto, put the fellas up on what we have found out." As Franco scooped up a helping of red beans and rice, Roberto began.

"I had Ginny ride down by the house to deliver a telegram, I got friends at the Post office you know."

"He said that Paulie had returned and there were seven armed men."

"They didn't let him inside the house or near the porch."

"He did say he could see a little girl with two elderly women and one young woman with a baby looking through the front window."

"They didn't appear to be in any type of danger at the time."

"There was another woman on the porch with Paulie." Elijah figured it must had been Dot. He didn't want to think the worst of the situation so he allowed Roberto to continue.

"Understand this, we've been doing some investigating of our own in Chicago."

"It appears that Paulie has pissed off a lot of people, messed up a lot of money, know what I mean?"

"They say he's created a lot of bad blood."

"His thirst for power has become a disease to the family."

"Even a dog knows he shouldn't defecate were he sleeps, you know what I mean?"

"So, me and my brother here have made an executive decision to straighten things out."

"I'm sure it would be to your advantage as well Fisher."

Fisher gave him a grin.

"How sweet is revenge, he killed Joey man, his own brother, what's the plan?"

Franco continued.

"Well Fisher, he has two men with him and they work for me and we tend to end this once and for all."

"Paulie is interfering with progress."

Elijah continued to listen and it appeared to him that everything was working out for the better every minute. Franco spent about an hour or so explaining the damage that Paulie had done in both Detroit and Chicago.

"He has been mis-managing everything he touches and he is more interested in power than profit."

"He is nothing like his father."

"He's a time bomb who doesn't value such things as loyalty and respect."

Fisher nodded in agreement.

"He killed Joey, and my best friend big Ted." Fisher hit his fist on the table

"I want him to get what he has coming to him." Franco nodded his head.

"Oh he will my friend, he will."

"Franco I have a gift for you guys at the house near the Locus, you know the place."

"I left you a little something in the cellar, a gift from me." Fisher reached in his pocket and tossed the key to Franco.

"I appreciate what you are doing my friend."

"Gracias, it has been a pleasure doing business with you."

"Big Paulie always spoke very highly of you Fisher."

"You have no idea how well he respected your loyalty to himas well as the family all those years."

Fisher stood up at the table.

"We will move tonight."

"The others are waiting at the swamp for back up." Elijah pulled out a small map and handed it to Franco.

"Your people will need to know how the grounds are set up."

Franco stood up.

"I will go prepare my men and I'll see you guys at the swamp by dusk."

Chapter 24

New Orleans, Louisiana

Gilda sat under the willow tree along the bank waiting patiently for Fisher and Elijah to return. Poncho offered her a cool drink.

"You look like you might need this."

"Thank you."

"Gilda, go inside, it is much cooler away from the sun."

She gave the twin a tiring smile and did as instructed. She had to admit it did feel a lot cooler and without a second thought laid on the colorful handmade blanket that Honcho placed inside.

Gilda fixed her mind on everybody at the house. She also thought about Dot. Gilda promised herself she would do her in once they returned. Dot had committed the ultimate betrayal and would have to pay for such a deception. After all Fisher had done for them, she had not appreciated any of it. How could she turn on him for the likes of Paulie and his gang of thugs? Before she knew it she was sound asleep.

Fisher and Elijah arrived at the meeting point about two hours later. Poncho went to the road to meet them and had them pull the truck deep into the woods not far from the camp. Elijah went into the tent to greet Gilda, while Fisher, went over the plan with the brothers.

Elijah watched Gilda as she slept soundly; he imagined what their child would look like and if it was a boy or a girl. He also knew that after this he would take her as far away from danger as he possible could without looking back. They would start a new life. He gently took his hand and glided along the side of Gilda's face; she woke up seeing her husband and smiled.

"So, you're back, did you bring something to eat?"

"Yes my Ki'Somma."

Elijah took out a bag full of turkey sandwiches and fried potatoes that Jeanine had made for her.

"Oh one more thing I have a surprise for you." Elijah shouted out of the tent.

"You can come on in now." Gilda's eyes widened as she watched Jeanine stoop down inside.

"Jeanine, oh my goodness, it's really you." The ladies hugged then begin to cry and laugh at the same time. Elijah, after seeing the ladies in all their excitement slowly slipped out of the tent and joined the other men.

After his discussion with the others, Fisher joined Gilda and Jeanine in the tent. He prepared Gilda for her part of the plan while Elijah and Diaz peeked in from outside.

"Fisher, I'll be fine."

"We've gone over this a hundred times already."

Elijah, Diaz and Jeanine looked on in silence.

"You guys what's the matter?"

"I'll be fine."

Gilda scooted to the entrance and crawled out of the tent and held Elijah's hand tight as she stood to her feet.

"This time tomorrow we will be one step closer to a little peace and joy."

Elijah responded with a short grin and Gilda placed her hand on his cheek.

"Don't worry Elijah everything will work out fine."

"The good lord brought us this far, I know he won't leave us now."

Fisher coughing struggled out of the tent and Jeanine helped him to his feet. He looked up to the sky the sun was finally going down. Franco and his crew will be arriving shortly.

Gilda kissed Elijah and hopped in the truck with Honcho and Poncho while Elijah and Diaz followed behind. The house was down the hill so there was no way for them to be seen. Honcho spoke to Gilda.

"You will not be able to return to us, I'm sure they will attempt to back track your steps."

Elijah got out of the truck behind them and then assisted Gilda. He then gave her a tight hug and long kiss. Gilda grabbed him back not wanting to let go, but knowing that this had to end once and for all. They spoke no words; each knew how the other felt.

Gilda picked up mud from the ground and rubbed it all over her face, in her hair and her clothes. She took off her shoes and threw them back in the truck bed then borrowed Diaz's knife to rip tears in her dress. Once she finished she waited for approval from them. Diaz spoke

"She looks like she's been through a ruckus, a real wretched alright."

"Why thank you." Gilda gladly took the compliment said her goodbyes and began her journey through the trees. After reaching the open field, it was not long before she could see the large white house, there was a light on in the kitchen, as the sun began to surrender the day to the full moon.

"Dear lord I know you with me, I need you now more than ever."

"I'm carrying my child dear lord protect us and all who are involved in the ending of this chaos amen."

Once Gilda got up close to the house she could see a little more, Julia was out on the back porch with the baby and Ms. Betty was coming out the back door. Gilda saw two of the men standing on the side of the house with their guns hanging on their shoulders not seeing Josie, Gilda was startled by her scream.

"Auntie Gillie, Auntie Gillie."

Everyone's attention turned to Gilda and Pauli's men ran out toward her. Gilda began limping as if she had been in a fight for her life as she fell to the ground. Dot came out the back door and seeing Gilda smirked.

"Humph, serves her right, she shouldn't have ran."

As they brought Gilda closer to the house she got a good look at Dot. To Gilda she looked a mess. Dot rolled her eyes at Gilda and took a long drag off her cigarette.

"Where's that man of yours?"

Gilda continued to lay there in a lifeless state. Paulie instructed the men to take her into the dining room of the house. Everyone was standing around here.

"Give her some air!"

Miss Lara yelled.

"She can hardly catch her breath as it is."

Once inside Gilda began to cough continuously she coughed and coughed until they were convinced that she was really near her death

"Where is Elijah?"

Paulie asked coldly. "

Where is he?"

He grabbed his switchblade out of his pocket flipped it open and put up to Gilda's neck. Unable to speak Gilda shook her head as tears ran down her eyes.

"I don't know."

"There was a lynch mob and they ran the truck down about 10 miles outside of Louisiana it was pitched black, I was so scarred, I could not see a thing."

"Ohhh it happened so fast." Gilda began crying even more.

"Elijah ran into a tree and I saw him lying slumped over."

"I seen them coming, so I Jumped out and I started running for my life into the woods."

"I didn't look back."

"Oh Miss. Lara, If they would have caught me, who knows what they would have done."

"Oh Elijah, my dear Elijah."

Gilda was crying for the life of her unborn child, Big Ted, her mother and her grandmother, but most of all she was crying for all the pain that had been built up inside.

"Umph, I don't believe her."

Dot shouted.

"I know she's seen Fisher, tell them haven't you miss goodie two shoes."

Dot grabbed at Gilda and Julia gave her crying baby to Betty and took her by the neck and tossed her down.

"Oh you don't want to do that."

Dot looked up at Paulie for help as she struggled to get up from the floor, but all his attention was on Gilda.

"Gillie?"

Paulie spoke in a calm low-toned voice.

"Have you seen Fisher girl?"

Dot shouted again.

"Yeah she seen him and he will be here too, I bet you that."

Paulie looked over at Dot.

"Shut up, you are beginning to really irritate me girl close your mouth or I will have it closed for you permanently."

Dot scrambled to her feet in dismay and stomped outside the house. Paulie walked up on Gilda again, this time he grabbed her and took her outside on the front porch and dragged her down the stairs. Gilda was screaming and the Sisters as well as Julia ran out crying behind her. Josphine ran ahead of them all, but Julia grabbed her up and sent her into the house. Josie stood watching in the screen door as the commotion continued. Paulie pulled a gun from behind his waist, the barrow shining like a silver dollar in the high moonlight. Julia hesitantly began to approach Paulie, but Gilda shook her head to ward her off. Paulie grabbed Gilda and put his arm around her neck and kissed her on the cheek.

"You know I always wanted to do that girl, but you were always so uppidity."

Gilda didn't want to do anything to provoke him any further. She knew that he had been drinking because she could smell it on his breath. All she could think about was protecting her baby. Josephinee watched only briefly from the front door, she soon thought about her father and went to the kitchen. Inside the large pantry Joshua and Jerry lay gagged and tied at both the legs and arms. They were wrestling desperately to get out of the ties that Paulie's men put them in after hearing Gilda's voice.

Josie opened the door and ran over to her father's side. She untied the knot that held the handkerchief around his mouth.

"Gillie's back daddy, but not Uncle Elijah."

"Josie, listen hear, can you untie daddy?"

"I will try daddy." Julia begin tugging on the ropes, but they would not give.

"Hurry baby."

Joshua encouraged his brave daughter. Jerry was moaning intensely.

"Josie go over and take the handkerchief from Uncle Jerry's mouth." Soon as she pulled it out Jerry instructed her to a knife that lay on top of the counter.

"Take that knife to your daddy sweetheart."

Josie followed instructions and handed the knife to her father.

"Josie, daddy needs you to go back into the kitchen before anyone notices that you are gone and close the door behind you."

You're my very brave soldier, now go."

Josie closed the pantry door while silently crying and went back to the front of the house. No one but Betty had noticed that she had left. When she returned her eyes grew wide as she saw Paulie with a gun held to Gilda's head. Julia turned and seen her in the doorway. Julia then waved to Betty and Lara on the porch and they took both Josie and the baby inside the house. Once Lara realized all of Pauli's men were outside she shut the door. Betty headed toward the pantry to finally check on Joshua and Jerry while Lara attended to the children.

Even as helpless as she felt, Julia would give her life for her friend. Deep down she knew Gilda would do the same for her. Gilda did not say a word, but continued to listen to Paulie squabble about the old times at the Juke joint, while a couple of his men stood by. Elijah, Diaz and his brothers where in clear range. Elijah could see what was taking place from afar and was grateful, because for some odd reason the moon had shined more brightly than ever tonight. He was anxious to go in, but Diaz held him back.

"If he was gonna kill her he would have done it when she arrived, we must wait for a sign from the others and stick with the plan."

Meanwhile, Paulie continued to talk while gently caressing the side of Gilda's face.

"You know Gillie, you was so different compared to the other girls."

Still Gilda said nothing as she felt disgusted from his touch. L'il Paulie then began to curse Elijah to both Julia and Gilda.

"If I as much hear or even see any sign of Fisher or that damned Elijah, I will let you both watch me torture them and then I will kill you both."

Gilda's stomach began to turn, but she managed to keep her composure. The fact that Paulie had the gun lying up against her neck was serious and the thought of Elijah or Fisher hanging from a tree made her feel even worse. Paulie spent the next few minutes tormenting Gilda while his men stood by and watched.

Inside the house Jerry and Joshua finally untied themselves and were greeted by Betty at the pantry door.

"Oh my god, they have Gillie out front, Paulie has a gun"

Joshua grabbed Betty by the shoulders and looked her intensely in the eye.

"Where is Julia?"

"She's out there too; she didn't want to leave Gillie."

She waved us into the house with the children and I locked the door."

Suddenly they heard a noise coming from the cellar, so Jerry and Joshua informed Betty to backup. Joshua grabbed a vase and Jerry pulled out his slingshot and they stood on opposite sides of the cellar door. The door opened slowly and it was Elijah.

"Elijah?"

Jerry reached down to help Elijah with the shotguns and Elijah lifted himself out of the cellar. Behind Elijah were Diaz, Quervo, and Fisher. Jerry and Joshua helped Fisher as his weak body struggled to make it to the top. They each grabbed a gun while the sister's took Fisher into the front room. Elijah looked out of the curtain window and saw the girls out front. Paulie's men were standing around as they watched Paulie pull and tug at Gilda. Dot stood at the bottom of the porch with two more of his men. Now, Julia was also being held under gunpoint by another one of Paulie's men. Elijah was on his way to the front door with rifle in hand, but Jerry stopped him.

"Elijah you know I'm not a gunman." He then took his sling shot out of his jacket.

"I'm better in the trees." Elijah nodded his head.

"Jerry you, Joshua follow Quervo the back way and stay down

"We'll meet you in the front."

Elijah and Diaz carefully made their way to the front door. Cuervo, Jerry and Joshua went out the back door and quietly laid up against the house. Joshua and Cuervo gave cover as he directed Jerry toward Honcho and Poncho in the woods. Outside Gilda could see both Lara and Betty looking out of the living room window. She then gave her attention back to Paulie. Gilda watched Paulie as the sweat ran down his face. Suddenly Penske shouted to Paulie

"Paulie come up here quick."

Paulie straightened his drunken posture and made his way to the side of the house. Dot was at it again fighting with one of the men. Paulie summoned the short fat gunman to keep an eye on Gillie. Before Gilda knew it the man fell to the ground. She looked out into the field and seen no one. The remaining men pulled their guns out of their holsters and begin looking around for a target, but found none. Paulie dragged Dot back to the front followed by the others to see what the commotion was about.

"What the hell is going on around here?"

From the woods a swift arrow landed in the back of another one of Paulie's men. He tossed Dot to the ground and grabbed for Gilda. The smell of the liquor on his breath continued to make her nauseous. There were no bullets so she knew it had to be the brothers. This time it was Jerry's turn; he pulled back his sling and before anyone could blink two more of Pauli's men were down. Cortez gave out a loud whistle and Gilda could not believe her eyes as four men on horseback came out of the woods. Elijah and Diaz pushed through the front door, one of Paulie's men attempted to shoot, but Elijah and Diaz were faster and he fell to the ground. Paulie, looking at both Elijah and Diaz quickly loosed Gilda, dropped his gun on the ground and slowly lifted his hands straight in the air.

The Posse was loud and quite aggressive waving their guns and firing shots in the air. Gilda quickly moved away from Paulie and she and Julia grabbed one another with an embrace of relief. Through out the commotion Dot had made her way back to the other side of the house attempting to make her escape. Joshua seen her and led her back to the front of the house at gun point. Elijah instructed all that were still standing to drop to their knees and put their hands behind their back. Soon after three shiny black automobiles were spotted coming up the road with a large ice truck. Honcho and Poncho, along with Jerry had also made their way to the house from the wooded area and they were joined by Cortez. Fisher came out while the two sisters stayed inside with Josie and the baby. He stepped down off the porch with his cane to meet his friend. Jeanine got out of the car, followed by Franco. He greeted all four horsemen and tossed them each a satchel. They nodded and rode off just as swiftly as they had come. Franco then walked over to his cousin.

"Well well, what do we have here?"

Paulie began speaking in his father's native tongue to his cousin.

"No Paulie, I will not let you dishonor my cousin nor my uncles blood with secrets; you will speak in the tongue you have used for your destruction, capeche!"

Franco continued.

"You have made a lot of people back home very unhappy Paulie."

"Please Franco, I can explain."

Fisher didn't say a word he only shook his head at the final defeat of L'il Paulie.

"You will, but not now my cousin."

Franco snapped his finger and Paulie along with his posse voluntarily made their way into the back seats of the cars. Franco instructed the others to put the remaining bodies in the truck. Franco looked over at Gillie who was being held up by Elijah in his arm.

"Are you the little lady that has caused all this commotion?"

Gilda nodded her head with relief, but was too exhausted to even respond.

"Well my lady, you will not have to worry about any of these characters again, I promise you."

Jeanine pointed over toward Dot.

"What about her?"

Franco looked over at Gilda and Jeanine.

"She's not my problem; I have kept my end of the bargain just as Fisher."

"Everyone in your family is safe now."

Franco walked up to Fisher and gave him a hug.

"You're a good man Fisher now you can start a life of your own, no more running capeche?"

Fisher began to laugh.

"Yes suh that sounds real good, no more running."

The men said their goodbyes and Franco and his men disappeared into the night.

Meanwhile, Dot laid on the front lawn in dismay and she couldn't even lift her head as running mascara covered her eyes.

"I am so ashamed!"

She cried out to everyone, but Jeanine showed no remorse for her.

"Just look at you, you look a mess Dot."

"How dare you want sympathy from these people?" Gilda spoke.

"Jeanine please."

"She's sick and she needs help."

"Yeah, she's sick alright."

"Gillie you can't help her, she's evil."

Gilda went to grab for Dot, and she got up.

"I'm so very sorry Gilda, please forgive me, I didn't mean any of it."

"It's the drugs that got me acting this way."

She then looked over at Fisher.

"Fisher, please forgive me."

Dot held her head down and Fisher walked over to her in an attempt to hug her. Dot swiftly pulled a small gun from her chest and fired it at Fisher. Quervo, then took his gun and shot Dot in the chest. Gilda screamed as Dot fell to her knees with her eyes still wide open as her face hit the ground. Gilda, Jeanine and Julia ran over to Fisher, as he lay in a pool of blood.

"Fisher, no, no Fisher, It can't end this way."

"Not this way."

Gilda turned to Elijah.

"Elijah please, please help him."

Miss Betty came out of the house she grabbed hold of Elijah's shoulder, she had seen this kind of a wound many times before. The bullet had punctured his lung and she knew it would not be long before he would leave them. Gilda sat with Fisher's head in her lap, her eyes filled with tears. Julia sat next to her holding his hand close to her heart. Jeanine looked on in shock as Jerry held her. Fisher began to speak

"I wanna thank you, thank you so much for loving me all my life."

"You two were my first look at love outside my mama you know."

Fisher forced himself to continue talking as blood begin to spill slowly from the side of his mouth.

Gilda whispered.

"Fisher, please don't talk, you will only make it worse."

"Gillie, you helped me fight off my blues."

"Everything I have the gold and the money I want you all to share it take it, it's enough to go around you know." Fisher tried to laugh.

"I want you to take it, for the children, for the children."

"You take care of Elijah too; he's a good man, a real good man."

Gilda continued to slowly rock him in her arms.

"No Fisher, you stop that nonsense, you gone be fine, just fine."

Fisher looked over to Julia on her knees as tears ran down her face.

"My dearest Julia, we had some good ole times didn't we lil sis?"

Julia nodded her head laughing and crying at the same time as she reminisced on their childhood.

"Yes we did ole' man, yes we did."

Not long after that moment Po Fisher left this world. They buried him right on Miss Lara and Miss Betty's land.

Gilda sat at the front of his tombstone were she had planted a beautiful yellow tea rose bush.

"Fisher I'm going away for awhile."

"Me and Elijah, we're going down to Mexico with the twins for a spell."

"I wanna see how living is down there."

"Diaz told us there ain't no segregation, lynching, or Klu Klux Klan around them parts."

"I think I would like that."

"You know how I was always talking about a little peace of mind."

"Joshua and Julia, they gonna hang around here with Miss Lara and Miss Betty for a spell."

"They told Joshua he can build as much as he want to on the land, since ain't no one else making any use of it."

"Joshua say he gonna start a little town and name it Fisher's Grove, ain't that something, your own town named after ya."

"Josie promised me she will come by from time to time to check on you and bring you some fresh flowers on your birthday and every holiday, but don't you worry I will be back to see you."

"I don't plan on staying away from you to long."

"Until we see each other again rest in peace my dearest Fisher."

About The Author

Adrienne is a native of Detroit Michigan. She holds a Bachelors degree in Business from Wayne State University and a Masters of Occupational Therapy from Eastern Michigan University.

She grew up with a love for all types of music including Blues and Jazz. She was introduced to the literary world at a young age thanks to her mother and also enjoys writing poetry and motion pictures. History has always been an intriguing subject for her. The oral history of her family has contributed heavily to her imagination and desire to write.

Adrienne is a wife and a mother of a son Jereme. She is also an advocate for community outreach and a member of Sigma Gamma Rho Sorority Inc. She enjoys traveling to the Caribbean and spending the majority of her time with family and friends. She is currently planning her next adventure and residing in Miami, Florida.

www.ingramcontent.com/pod-product-compliance
Ingram Content Group UK Ltd.
Pitfield, Milton Keynes, MK11 3LW, UK
UKHW041415180426
11947UKWH00007B/154